BF

Judy Baker

Mainstream Romance

Sweet Cravings Publishing
www.sweetcravingspublishing.com

A Sweet Cravings Publishing Book
Mainstream Romance

Better She Die
Copyright © 2013 Judy Baker
Print ISBN: 978-1-61885-866-5

First E-book Publication: May 2013
First Print Publication: August 2013

Cover design by Dawné Dominique
Edited by Sue Toth
Proofread by Courtney Karmiller
All cover art and logo copyright © 2013 by Secret Cravings
Publishing

PUBLISHER
Sweet Cravings Publishing
www.sweetcravingspublishing.com

DEDICATION

To Brett, my husband − If I could write a book for the reasons why my life is fuller, warmer, and brighter, it would be because of Brett, and so I'll say the greatest three words…I love you. You always brighten my day. *Judy*

Judy Baker

BETTER SHE DIE
Judy Baker
Copyright © 2013

Chapter One

1858 US Texas Territory

Clare Rose Coulson Montgomery strolled along the boardwalk with a contented sparkle in her eyes. The morning breeze and blue sky made for a perfect day. Her gaze followed a tumbleweed rolling along the dusty main street of Silver Sage Creek, Texas. She raised her left hand and touched her thumb to the slim silver band on her ring finger. She could almost see her reflection on the shiny metal. She was married now. A woman.

Deep in thought and daydreaming, she failed to notice the man stepping from the cafe door until the collision sent her bonnet sliding down her forehead. His hands splayed wide, snug against her ribs on either side of her body, which seemed more like a caress than a polite attempt to keep her from losing her balance.

"Oh, my heavenly days…uh…sir, do watch your step," ordered Clare Rose. She paused, shifted her bonnet back in place, and then shot an annoyed glare into a charming grin on the sun-browned face of the man she knew to be a Ranger. It only took seconds for her to take in his entire being. He didn't look like any Ranger in her mind, more like some lonesome desperado. His thick, sunlit mustache hovered over a perfectly formed mouth, showing off unusually white teeth. A dusty, black cowboy hat covered light, flaxen curls escaping from beneath it to linger along the nape of his neck.

When she lifted her eyes, her sight locked on his left cheek. Embedded in a slight growth of whiskers was a deep, half-moon scar. She frowned.

Looking up, she connected to crystal blue eyes sinking into hers. The man's penetrating look dropped to her lips, and then traveled down her throat to her bosom. His intense stare jarred her awareness. She had the uncanny sensation of being undressed.

Butterflies tickled the walls of her stomach, shooting a hot flash down to the core between her legs. Breathlessly, she forced her feet to back away. She blinked. There was something excitingly wicked about the way he touched her with his eyes.

When his arms dropped from her sides, he tipped his Stetson hat and with a slow, deep, soothing drawl, he said, "Ma'am."

Not until he stepped past her did he release his gaze. Unable to move, she stood there, conscious of his black boots echoing on the boardwalk before finally disappearing into the Texas Rangers' administration office.

Huh, of all the...how rude. She had detected amusement in his expression, rather than regret for bumping into her. Appalled at her reactions to not only the Ranger's rough good looks, but also his touch, she swallowed hard and sucked in a deep breath to calm the rapid beating inside her chest. How absurd. Time seemed to have stopped for a brief moment while in contact with him. What was wrong with her? She was married.

Her jaw tightened. The funny little quiver inside her abdomen was a puzzle. Why did he have an effect on her body in such a way? The experience stirred her emotions. Why? He wasn't even handsome like her husband.

Jonathan was taller, slim, and clean-shaven. While this man was...was roughly a half-foot, or so, taller than her five foot five height, he was more square and thick, and yet, she was certain, a definite, solid wall of muscles, especially, the hard chest she had bumped into.

A hand flew up to touch her heated cheek.

"Mornin', Mrs. Montgomery."

Clare jerked. She nodded at the woman passing by. "Good morning, Mrs. Waterford."

For a moment, she had forgotten her married name. Suddenly mindful of many other townspeople strolling along the boardwalk greeting her with smiles, comments, and men tipping their hats toward her, Clare squared her shoulders and replied with a slight nod. Goodness, what was she thinking? She hurried and spread her lips into a bright smile to conceal the strange fascination with a man other than her husband.

A loud squeal drew her gaze ahead. "Clare Rose, where have you been?"

Clare giggled at her two dearest friends approaching her with opened arms.

"Sally…Betsy, it's so good to see you." Her tone matched her friends' delight while returning their warm hugs.

"We've missed you, dear. Look." Sally bubbled, thrusting the Silver Sage weekly gazette into her hand. "Look what we've been reading."

"You're the talk of the town, naturally. They wrote about your exquisite wedding, and oh, Clare Rose, I still can't get over how beautiful you looked all dressed in white with your long, red hair streaming down your back."

Clare nodded. "Yes, I did make a striking bride, didn't I?" she declared, and glanced over the newspaper, dated July 2, 1858. Her eyes connected with the headline, *Jonathan Montgomery Weds Clare Rose Coulson.* Quickly, she skimmed the article asking whether the new bride, Mrs. Clare Rose Montgomery, could possibly be the next governor's wife of Texas. Her mouth dropped.

"Jonathan's running for governor?" Her widened eyes scurried from the article to her friends. "He never said."

"You didn't know?" Betsy bit her lower lip and glanced at Sally.

Clare shook her head. She frowned and read a few more lines in the article. "My husband is running for Governor of Texas…against Sam Houston?" She looked up at her friends.

Sally shrugged. "Just think, Mrs. Montgomery, you may well be living in a fine house with Negro servants or even a…ah," she darted a questioning probe toward Betsy, "What did we hear Ruby call her freed slave the other day?"

Betsy puckered her lips and thought for a moment. "Oh…Ruby, the saloon woman. She was in the mercantile talking to your ma the other day, Clare Rose." Betsy gritted her teeth and lowered her voice, and said, "That woman called her Negro girl a yellow winch."

"Right. Anyway, Clare Rose, when you're in the governor's mansion and have one or several of those Negro servants, don't forget your best friends." Sally tilted her head and fluttered her eyelashes.

Clare giggled. "How could I, you would never allow such. Besides, you know the two of you will be my first guests to come for tea in my fine house."

She looked down at the newspaper in her hands. "Can I keep this? It appears my husband and I have some serious conversing to do about his future endeavors of becoming Texas' next governor."

"Sure," Sally nodded. She raised a shoulder. "All seems fitting to me. After all, Jonathan is now married to the granddaughter of the founder of Silver Sage Creek. Why shouldn't he be governor? Texas is a big territory, why not spread his wings? Why mayor when you can be governor?" She giggled and reached for Clare's left hand and rubbed the silver wedding band.

"Never mind, that's all men's doings anyway. Now, Clare Rose, you have to tell us everything." She glanced at Betsy and twitched her head toward Clare.

"Oh, right." Betsy fixed her eyes on Clare Rose's ring and purposely arched her brows. "We want details," she whispered. "After all, we're two eighteen-year-old women on the verge of being called spinsters."

Betsy lowered her head and rolled her eyes toward Sally. "Pa called me a spinster the other day when I didn't accept Jesse Meek's invitation to the dance."

"And...why didn't you?" Sally's suspicious tone shot back at Betsy.

Betsy shrugged, lifted her nose into the air, and said, "Let's not talk about me." Her dark eyes darted to Clare. "Clare Rose, you must tell us everything...you know...your wedding night. Tell us what it felt like, so, if we ever get a chance to have our own..."

Several horses rode past, sending a plume of dust swirling around them. Clare coughed and waved her hand in front of her face while blinking her eyes.

Sally coughed and, like Clare, waved her hand to clear the dust swirling around them. She nudged Betsy and shot her narrowed eyes at her. "It's *the* Ranger isn't it?" Sally's accusing tone drew their attention to the riders drawing their horses to a halt near the Ranger's office.

The girls and the entire townsfolk recognized and appreciated the Rangers for protecting the frontier from hostile Indians. Marauding savages continued to plunder, murder, and exterminate families settling in the outskirts of the towns. Clare Rose had heard horrible stories while growing up, but such things never worried her since her parents, the Rangers, and now, her husband protected her.

Clare glanced up at the tall, skinny rider on the chestnut horse. He tipped his hat at all three of them, and then fixed his eyes on Betsy. She noticed her friend lock eyes with the man. "What's going on, Betsy? Sally?" Clare darted her gaze back and forth to each one.

Betsy gave her an I-don't-know-what-you're-talking-about look, and then turned her brown eyes back to the Ranger. "Really, Clare Rose, you have to agree the Rangers are handsome, and can you imagine what an exciting life they live?"

Clare watched the girls turn their shy smiles toward the men sitting patiently upon their horses, evidently waiting for someone. Her gaze swung to the three Rangers. They hadn't bothered to dismount. She noticed that the man with the oversized, white cowboy hat continued to stare at Betsy while holding the reins of a huge, black stallion. The big horse stomped the dust, waiting for his rider. Clare speculated about the rider.

She glanced at her friend and witnessed her face turning a deep shade of pink. *Oh my.* "Betsy..." Her low, bemused tone drew both girls' gazes to her. "Is there something going on? Why haven't I heard? Who is he?"

"Betsy..." Sally nudged her with a restrained grin.

"Oh fiddlesticks, in spite of what you think you witnessed, it's nothing, really."

"Oh lardy, Betsy."

Sally's uncompromising tone caused Clare to study Betsy a little closer. "What happened?"

Betsy's gaze danced around looking for an excuse to change the subject.

"Betsy—"

"Oh, fiddlesticks. Sally caught Wade McCoy kissing me."

"My lardy, I'd say you were doing a little more than kissing. I watched. Your lips weren't closed. You opened your mouth, Betsy." Sally squared her shoulder, daring Betsy to deny her words.

"Oh lardy days, Sally, shush." Betsy glanced around.

"Who's Wade McCoy?" Clare intervened, pulling her brows together. "And why haven't I heard about any of this?"

Betsy swung her head toward the Ranger with eyes only for her.

He tipped his large hat at them, grinned at Betsy, and then winked.

She turned a brighter pink.

Clare reached out and put her hand on her friend's arm. "Betsy, is this true?"

Observing Betsy's deliberate nod, Clare, genuinely surprised, covered her mouth, giggled, and then laughed out loud. From the girls' expression, neither one understood what she thought was funny.

"I'm sorry. This just seems a little humorous, since I'm the one married. Jonathan and I never kissed. I mean, not until our wedding day."

Clare flicked her hand toward Betsy. "And here you are kissing in some passageway or someplace, with a Ranger you probably don't even know very well."

Betsy quietly released a nervous laugh and dipped her head. "We've talked *some*."

"Some?" Clare heard her high-pitched voice. She shot the Rangers an accusing glance, and then forced her voice lower. "How long has this been going on?"

Betsy, unable to hide her pleasure, blushed. "A couple of months."

Her mouth dropped. "Why didn't I know about this?"

"Oh please, Clare Rose, we never had a moment to talk once you and Jonathan started making wedding plans."

Betsy shot a quick, nervous glance toward the Ranger who evidently had captured her heart. Looking back, she pleaded, "I have to ask you not to mention this to Pa. If he knew, he'd have my hide."

Taken aback by Betsy's confession, Clare nodded her promise.

"Clare Rose." Sally wrinkled up her nose. "We're serious. My goodness, this is the first time we've seen you since you've been married. What have you been doing this past week?"

Betsy giggled, seemingly conscious of her implications.

Clare's mouth flew open. Her hand slapped against her chest, she cleared her throat, and mumbled, "Why don't you two come with me to the mercantile and we'll talk."

"Oh no." Betsy shook her head several times and frowned. "We can't talk there. What if your ma heard us?"

Clare's head drew back. "Why? Why can't Ma hear what we have to talk about?"

"Because," Sally emphasized, "we want to know about you-know-what."

"What   "

"You know…" Sally leaned in with Betsy's head closing in on the two. She whispered, "What's it like?"

Clare stepped back and wrung her hands together. "We shouldn't talk about—"

"Why?" Betsy's large, innocent, brown eyes bore into hers.

"Because…" Clare paused and glanced around to make sure that no one was close enough to hear their conversation. The Rangers were still waiting, but not near enough to hear. The one with the dingy Stetson was still eyeing Betsy.

Sally glanced over both shoulders; like Clare, she wanted to make sure some old busybody wasn't standing nearby. "Clare Rose." She stepped closer and lowered her voice. "You're our best friend and we've always told each other our secrets. This is no different. After all, you'll expect some kind of detailed description when *the* night happens for us."

Betsy's head bobbed, then leaned near her ear and, in an intimate whisper, asked, "What does a man look like without his clothes? We want the particulates."

Clare pulled back. Her brain scrambled for an answer. She needed time to think. "Well...why don't we have tea at Molly's Café? First, I have to see Ma at the mercantile, and then I'll meet you there. I won't be able to stay long. Jonathan will expect me to meet him at McGregory's soon."

The two girls, bubbling with anticipation, hugged her and took one last glance at the Rangers before hurrying on toward Molly's. There they'd wait patiently to hear firsthand knowledge of something they could only speculate about...a man's naked body.

Clare headed toward the mercantile while chewing on her bottom lip. What could she tell the girls? A small croaking sound escaped her throat. Her wedding night wasn't what she had expected and certainly not what her mother had instructed her on lovemaking.

There was nothing romantic about having a relationship with a man. What did the Reverend call it? An almighty, sanctified act. The intimate act hurt...well, not now, but the first time...unsettling...and...painful. Afterward, she didn't have to even think about what he was doing. She'd gotten pretty good at making mental lists for the next day's chores during his continuous pumping inside her.

She thanked the Lord above the *deed* didn't last very long. Huh, the so-called almighty, sanctified *deed* was selfish, done solely for pleasure on the man's part and procreation on the woman's. If it wasn't for women having to have babies, well, women probably could get along just fine without men. One day, she'd tell the girls about her own opinion regarding matters of the *act*. But, not yet.

Clare glanced across the main road. Ruby, the proprietor of the Silver Sage Saloon, stood outside the swinging double doors with one of her customers.

Ruby laughed and fanned her face with a bright red fan. Her yellow and black lacy dress revealed much with its extremely low bodice, giving the cowboy a perfect view. Even from where Clare stood, she could see the bulge of Ruby's large bosoms bounce up and down.

Why did a soiled dove enjoy a man poking her all the time? Not just one man, but men. She'd never understand, nor would she ever enjoy such a revolting act. If it wasn't for her wifely duties, she'd have no man touching her, not even her husband.

She'd have to think of something to tell the girls. Anyway, being married didn't mean she knew what a man looked like naked. She only knew what parts of his nakedness did inside of her. Jonathan went to bed wearing a nightshirt. The only part of his body she had ever seen was his chest, which only happened during the hot part of the day when he was working on the roof of their cabin, which didn't happen very often.

Clare stepped down off the porch to cross the road toward the mercantile. She hesitated at the sound of horses approaching. Shifting her gaze upward, she waited for the riders to pass before taking the last step. Three of the Rangers rode by, but the fourth slowed his horse to a prance.

The captivating Ranger who had knocked her off balance and caught her earlier, fixed his eyes upon her, tipped his dingy, black hat, and kicked his horse in the flanks to catch up with the others.

Again, tingling sensations traveled from her stomach downward. His look had traveled over her, making her feel like he'd undressed her again. Her trapped gaze watched until the rider disappeared down the road and out of town.

Clare stiffened and lifted her nose into the air. She frowned, sucked in a quick breath, and glanced at the ring on her finger. With pressed lips, she took a step, held up the hem of her dress, and then rushed to the other side of the dusty road. Hesitating in front of the mercantile store, she gazed at her reflection in the windows. Why was she blushing?

The flirting Ranger left a giddy twitter inside her body. She tilted her head and almost grinned, but instead cleared her throat and straightened her bonnet. She was a married woman for an entire week now, and already she'd had another man make eyes at her. After a quick glance down at the end of town, she stepped inside her parents' mercantile.

"Ma?" she hollered, searching behind the counter and the far end of the room.

A loud bang permeated from the back storeroom. Alarmed, she hurried in the direction of the noise. Her pa laid flat on the floor, breathing heavily. Kneeling down she touched his shoulder and tried to lift him. "Pa, what happened?"

"Clare Rose, I be fine, gotta catch my breath. Rotten old barrel rolled on my foot…tried to push it off and lost my balance."

Clare sat back on the floor and waited for her father's color to return to his face. "Maybe I should get doc."

"Na, nothing wrong with me," he mumbled, rolling to his knees. He grabbed the side of the shelf and pulled to his feet. After clearing his throat, he took a deep breath and fixed his eyes on his daughter. "You need something?"

Clare shook her head and followed him into the front store area. "Jonathan had to come into town to get some hardware."

"That boy 'bout done with your cabin?" He shook his head and frowned. "A cold winter will be upon us before you have a roof over your head, gal."

"Oh, Pa, we have a roof, just not over the second half of the house yet."

"Heavenly days, he started roofing before you got married…that boy'd rather talk politics than do a good day's work."

"Now, Pa, don't be difficult. He said it'll be done in the next couple of days. Where's Ma?"

"Took off home to fetch me something to eat. You hungry?"

"No, Jonathan and I had a bite before we rode into town."

When he picked up a lantern and took a step onto a ladder, she grabbed his arm. "Here let me help," she demanded, pulling him down. Clare lifted her skirt and raised her foot stepping up on the ladder before her father could protest. She climbed a couple of feet and reached down for the kerosene lamp he handed up to her. Without hesitating, she placed it on the shelf and looked down at him.

He shook his head. "You move faster than anyone I hired to work around here, and Otis, hell, he's a hell of a lot older than me and slower than an old mare."

She searched the store. "Where is the boy you hired last week? You shouldn't be climbing up this ladder. Not at your age, Pa."

"Whadaya mean? I'm no spring chicken, but I can do my share of work around here."

Clare smiled, climbed down, and gave him a kiss on the cheek. "That you can," she agreed. "Pa, did you know Jonathan is considering the governor's position..."

He reached out, grabbed her arm and squeezed tightly. His gaze shot around to the opened doors.

"What—" Taken aback, her brows furrowed in a questioning expression.

Shrill, Indian war cries screamed above the thundering horse hooves running quickly down the middle of town. Dust swirled around a dozen or more Apache Indians riding past the mercantile.

Clare's eyes widened. Her father pulled her behind the counter and reached for the rifle. The sound of the war party continued in the distance, heading toward the other end of town. "Pa?"

"Shush," he whispered and stepped to the opened door, listening.

Clare hurried to his side. She couldn't hear a thing. All was quiet.

"They're gone," she whispered and turned to search her father's face. The last time he'd grabbed his rifle, a band of outlaws had ridden into town. Then, he had expressed anger, but now the look on his face frightened her. Her gaze trailed out across the road toward McGregory's hardware store. Jonathan stood on the steps in front of the store with Thomas, the owner. Her breath hitched. Both had their pistols drawn, waiting for the Indians to return.

Clare brushed against her pa to step around him with full intentions of joining Jonathan, but he grabbed her arm and all but flung her back into the store. Catching her foot on the hem of her dress, she fell against the counter. Clare pushed to her feet and rubbed her arm where she was sure her pa had left a massive bruise. The second she opened her mouth to protest, she heard the rolling thunder of stampeding horses growing louder with Indians howling their war cries.

Her pa's face went white. He raised the long barreled rifle, rested the butt stock against his shoulder, and aimed.

Blood rushed to her head. "Pa."

"Get behind the counter, Clare Rose."

"But Pa—"

"Now."

Clare's eyes widened. Her pa rushed out of the store and quickly threw a hurried warning glance toward her before he slammed the doors shut behind him.

The maddening sounds of Indians whooping and hollering became a deafening roar. Covering her ears, she ran behind the counter, squatted, and peeked through the bottom corner of the window.

One after another, exploding gunshots ricocheted down the center of town. Her pa's rifle went off again, and again. A woman screamed.

Clare peeked over the counter and out the window. She watched Jonathan aim his pistol and shoot. An arrow flew through the air, barely missing him. Several savages halted their horses in front of the window blocking her view of her husband.

Her gaze swung to her father. He cocked the rifle, aimed and fired. A half-dressed Redskin fell from the horse, hitting the edge of the porch. Blood splattered on the glass. Clare covered her mouth.

Unceasingly, bare-chested, painted faced savages rode up and down the main road, shooting arrows from atop their painted horses. She couldn't see Jonathan across the way. Indians crowded between the buildings, shrieking in a manner of disjointed tongues. Gunshot after gunshot echoed throughout the town. With all the commotion between her and her husband, she couldn't see him. Cautiously, she stood and moved from behind the counter, keeping her eyes on the wild savages outside the windows, all the while searching through the madness for her husband.

Clare darted a glance in her pa's direction. An arrow swished through the air straight into her father's gut.

A woman screamed again, but this time she recognized her own voice. Without thinking, she took off, jerked opened the door and tried to reach him before he fell. Unable to keep him from falling, she struggled to drag him into the store. Once she managed to pull him inside, she dropped to cradle his head in her lap. She blinked away tears blurring her vision. An arrow piercing his stomach caused his labored breath to shake his entire body.

A pair of moccasins crept into her lowered vision. Without raising her head, she stared at the Indian's feet. Her brain froze, unable to stop the panic bubbling up inside. Slowly she lifted her gaze to the Redskin, standing not three feet from her.

She couldn't breathe.

His black, beady eyes stared into hers. Three horizontal, black, painted lines marked his face from ear to ear.

He grinned.

Outside the store, gunshot after gunshot exploded. Somewhere down the main road of town, a woman's unbroken screams struck deep into Clare's soul. Panic quivered up her spine from the bloodcurdling echoes.

The Apache stepped toward her in his silent moccasins.

Short, choppy breaths lifted her chest so rapidly, she went weak. Deliberately staring into the face of her enemy, she slowly and gently placed her father's head on the floor and scooted back toward the counter. The black, painted marks on the savage's face wrinkled from his ugly sneer.

He stepped toward her.

Clare couldn't stop her body from shaking when his nasty gleam slithered over her like she was some animal to devour.

He stretched out his hand toward her and motioned for her to come.

She shook her head. Was he crazy? She wasn't going anywhere with him.

Again, he motioned for her to come.

Again, she shook her head.

His face turned into a mass of painted anger. Before she could make her body move, he reached out, grabbed her arm, and jerked her to her feet and out the door toward his horse.

Chapter Two

Clare strained to release the scream lodged inside her throat, but nothing came from her mouth. Rapid palpitations tightened her chest doubling her over. The savage released her hand and stepped away.

Jonathan. Where was Jonathan? Straightening, she swung her head from side to side looking for…oh my God…her knees buckled, dropping her to the ground. Hot tears stung her eyes.

Sally's blonde curls sprayed over the road where she laid sprawled out with eyes wide open, lifeless. Blood covered her bosom, half her scalp ripped from her head, and her dress torn from her waist, revealing her bare body.

Clare's hand flew up to cover her mouth. Dragging herself away from the image of Sally, she aimed her gaze toward the hardware store where she set eyes on Jonathan, face down on the steps. Panic crawled up her stomach, pushing the scream from her throat.

They had killed him…her husband of only a week.

Tears swelled her eyes until her sight blurred. She squeezed her eyes shut and wadded her fists into a ball. *Clare Rose, wake up, you hear me? Wake up. This is not happening.*

A rough pair of hands took hold and hauled her to her feet. She turned and looked up into the face covered with black war paint.

A repulsive grin spread over his lips while his black eyes eagerly inspected her head of hair.

Fight, run, Clare Rose, run. But her muscles froze against the command of her brain.

He wound a rope tightly around her wrist, and then he mounted his horse.

The animal slowly took off, yanking her forward. She caught her breath. Sucking in a mouth full of dust, she coughed, running to keep up.

The horse started to gallop a little faster.

She stumbled.

The horse stopped.

Clare struggled to her knees. Squinting from the harsh midmorning sun, she glared up at the Redskin on the horse, smirking. If she didn't get to her feet, he'd drag her down the middle of town like a dead animal. She had to keep up or else…

* * * *

Her body had gone numb hours ago. The effort to keep moving was becoming greatly overwhelming. It took all the strength she had left to lift one foot in front of the other to keep the rope from pulling on her raw wrist. Her heavy feet could barely take another step. Her chest hurt, her legs wobbled, and her eyes stung from the sweat dripping down her face.

Again, she drew in a lungful of air. There didn't seem to be enough air to keep her mind alert. Her shoulders slumped from her outstretched arms and the pain from her bloody hands gripping the rope shot through her muscles and up her arm. Unable to keep her knees from buckling, she collapsed to the ground.

Her body yanked forward, causing her to hit the hard earth passing beneath her, shredding her dress and scraping her legs. Her beautiful bonnet…long gone.

Death, please, why can't you come to me? Please God, please, please…

Finally, divine blackness consumed her.

* * * *

Clare swallowed, coughed, and tried to swallow again. Her dry throat choked like a pipe full of dirt. She tried to lift her eyelids, but they were too heavy. Her tongue swept across her lower lip. A bloody taste touched her senses.

A low banter sounded nearby. Her mouth tried to form words, but nothing came out. Forcing her eyelids up, she turned toward the sound. She blinked several times to clear her blurred vision.

A band of Indians squatted near a campfire.

A tear slid from an eye down to the corner of her lips. She tasted the salty drop. When she raised her hand to touch her mouth, she flinched with pain. Dry blood covered the rope binding her raw wrists.

They had taken her from her home, her parents, and her husband. They had killed him. Pa too. She squeezed her eyes shut to the image of an arrow sticking out of his gut, and Sally…Sally…lying in the middle of town, dead.

Why did they not kill her too? What did they want with her? *God, please have them be quick and get it over with*…she wanted to die.

The sound of soft-footed moccasins came near. Clare kept her eyes closed. Her body shook. When she no longer heard any movement, she peeked through small slits. Her eyes flew open only to stare into the black-painted face of the Apache squatting next to her.

She tried to scoot back, but every muscle in her body rejected any movement.

He reached out.

A whimper escaped her lips. She turned her head away.

He grabbed a handful of hair and jerked her back to face him.

"Ow," she cried between clenched jaws.

The savage glanced at her hair and gathered her thick strands in his rough fingers. When his head swung toward the band of Indians, a long, black braid slapped her face.

"*Ekapitu piahp*," he spoke.

Whatever he said, Clare knew he was their leader from the tone of his voice.

Tightening his fist around her hair, he pulled.

"Ow."

"Uhn." He motioned.

Before she could react, he jerked her head back and flooded her mouth with water until she had a coughing fit. Finally, when she took a breath, he shoved some kind of moist substances into her mouth and poured more water down her throat. A strangled coughing fit vibrated her body until she rolled over and threw up.

Laughter rang in her ears. She straightened. Again, he forced the nasty, bitter stuff into her mouth, but this time he held his hand over her mouth.

She swallowed hard and jerked her head from his hand. Squinting at him, her jaw tightened. A galling anger rose from deep inside her, something she'd never experienced before. Lifting an eyebrow, Clare reared back and spat in his face.

The backhand came so fast she didn't see it coming. Silent blackness wrapped around her mind once more.

****

Clare's eyelids fluttered slightly. *Ahh, pain.* Her brain began to float backward to a safety net called darkness. *Ahh,* if she awoke, surely she'd find her nightmare ending.

A horse neighed.

Forcing her heavy eyelids open, she shoved the warm cover away from her face and frowned. Her gaze landed on a cold, empty fire pit in the center of…oh my God…a teepee. The savages put her inside their teepee. Warm tears slid from her eyes and down her cheeks.

Jonathan…Sally…Pa…everything happening was real. What was to become of her? Her fingers grabbed a fistful of fur from the deerskin thrown over her body. Clare quickly glanced under the weighty cover. A relieved breath pushed from her lungs. She was still clothed. Even though her lovely, green dress was torn and filthy, she was still covered.

An uncontrollable shudder caused her to pull the cover up close around her head. Her body trembled, but it wasn't from cold. She glanced toward the entrance to the teepee. A chill ran down her spine from the unpleasant, rowdy voices and laughter surrounding the teepee.

Why was this happening to her? What was to become of her?

A soft moan drew her gaze toward the far corner on the other side of the teepee. Something moved underneath the black fur hide.

Shrinking back under the cover, Clare peeked out.

Again another whimper flowed from the cover and this time an arm appeared.

Her breath hitched. Clare's brows tightened. A tattered yellow dress sleeve covered the bruised, bloody arm.

"Betsy," she whispered.

A soft cry reached out to her.

Clare threw back the protective hide and crawled toward the form. "Betsy." She reached over to uncover her face, but drew back. It couldn't be.

Then she heard an incoherent murmur.

This time, she recognized her friend's voice. Without hesitating, she lifted the hide. Her breath shot from her lungs allowing a sob to escape her throat.

"Don't," Betsy's painful tone muttered.

Misty-eyed, Clare tried to swallow the lump choking the sound in her throat.

Betsy's face appeared black and blue. She looked like someone had taken a whip to her. Her lips, swollen with dried blood, pasted the corner of her mouth shut. A large cut on the left side of her cheek oozed greenish stuff. Dark, matted hair, once beautiful, was bonded against the side of her cheek from the slimy substance.

"Oh, Betsy." Sniffling, she tried to rouse her friend. "Can you hear me? Betsy."

Swollen eyelids parted. Her blank stare looked up into Clare's eyes for a second and then closed.

Tears spilled over the corner of Clare's eyelids and down. What had they done to her dear, sweet friend? She could only imagine.

"Betsy," Clare whispered, pressing the palm of her hand gently against her friend's shoulder, she gave her a slight shake. When Betsy's eyelids lifted again, Clare stared into her dark, glassy eyes knowing she didn't comprehend her whereabouts. She appeared drugged. Clare frowned and covered her friend watching her drift off again, sending her into the safe haven of darkness.

Clare whirled to the sound of someone shoving the teepee's flap aside. She pressed her lips to trap the air inside her chest. Oh Lord, they're coming for her. She reached for a rock placed around the fire pit, but pulled back when an Indian stuck his head inside. Without looking directly into her eyes, his gaze traveled over her long hair falling down over her shoulder. He seemed ambivalent about entering. She swallowed hard, took in a long, hard breath, and returned his stare with a glare.

What the hell did he want? Clare demanded, "What?"

As if frightened, the Redskin disappeared so fast Clare almost thought it hilarious if she wasn't in such a dangerous situation. Her brows pulled together, wondering why she intimidated the Indian. She reached down, gripped a rock in her hand, and crawled toward the flap. Raising the rock above her head, in case another Indian had evil intentions, her shaking fingers reached out and pulled back the opening. Some dozen or so Apache Indians sat around a blazing fire drinking from a bottle of what appeared to be whiskey. A wooden smoking pipe made its way around the group, each Indian took a draw off the long stick.

Clare dropped her hand holding the rock and backed up to Betsy's side. She lifted the buffalo hide and crawled underneath the cover to hold her friend close. Betsy didn't move.

She glanced around the interior of the teepee that was growing darker with the late evening drawing near. For a long period of time she couldn't control her shaking body, until finally, she relaxed against Betsy's form. Eventually, sleep overcame her heavy eyelids while listening to the drunken sounds of the band outside their teepee.

Clare awoke to a dead silence.

The quietness helped clear her mind while thoughts of escape formed in her head. Had it been long enough for the band to fall into a deep stupor? If she could awaken Betsy, maybe they could find a way to escape. Without thinking any further, she crawled to the opening and peeked out of the teepee. Slowly, she studied the bodies sleeping on the ground throughout the camp, and then turned her gaze toward the horses, calculating the direction she would have to take to get to them.

Hurrying back to the bed, she whispered, "Betsy, wake up."

Clare pulled her friend to her feet and wrapped her arms around her waist. "We're leaving." She gave Betsy a firm shake and demanded, "You have to help."

For a split second, Clare noticed a glint of recognition in her eyes. "Come." Clare wrapped her arm around Betsy and headed for the opening. "If we can get to the horses, we'll have a chance to run for it."

Sucking in a deep breath, she tightened her arm around Betsy's waist and stepped out. Careful not to make any unnecessary noise, Clare moved quietly around the Indians, who appeared to have had more than enough whiskey. With a determined focus on her objective, she took one step at a time until they made their way to the horses tethered to a shrub.

Clare hung on to Betsy's limp body and held out her free hand to the nearest animal, and whispered, "Shush." She untied a rope and led the horse away from the others.

After what she hoped was a safe distance, she quickly glanced back at the enemy's camp. She could do this.

Betsy's body slouched against her. She glanced down at her friend, heaved in a breath, gave her a rough shake, and whispered, "Betsy."

No response. Clare shook her again. "Betsy, listen to me, you're going to have to stand on your own? Do you hear me?"

A twig snapped.

Clare whirled.

An Indian stood near, slanted his head to the side waiting to see what she was up to.

Her mind raced. Clare swung her gaze toward the camp. He seemed to be alone.

Turning her hard glare back to the Redskin, she returned his stare with the overwhelming desire to holler, *Boo.* From the way he was gawking at her, she was sure he'd run. However, he'd head straight to his band, putting her in worse danger.

Clare continued to bore her angry look into the savage's eyes. If she couldn't escape with Betsy, she'd do the unthinkable.

No sooner had the thought slipped into her mind, her body reacted. With a strong force, she shoved Betsy toward the hesitant

Indian, knocking him backward. With one swift movement, she mounted the horse, leaving Betsy in the clutches of the Redskin.

Without looking back, Clare whipped the rope against the horse and took off. God help her. She had just left Betsy in the hands of the enemy.

In the early dawn of the morning light, Clare turned the horse toward a canyon. She had no idea what direction to take, but the one thing she knew for sure, she had to get away and bring back help for Betsy.

The moment she breathed in a sigh of relief for successfully escaping, than two Indians rode out in front of her from out of nowhere. Before she was able to pull back on the rope, her startled horse hoisted his front legs into the air, dropping her like a dead body. She hit the hard ground, thrusting the air from her lungs.

Once a gulp of air sucked into her lungs, her eyes jerked open. While trying to breathe deeply, she looked up into the face of a savage. When he squatted down next to her, she tried to scoot back, but her shaking arms failed to hold her weight. His black angry eyes drilled into hers. God help her, she'd been captured—again.

While struggling to sit up, she didn't take her eyes off the Indian staring at her. Something was different about him. This Indian didn't wear the black war paint like the others. She trembled from his intense study of her.

He reached his hand out to touch her.

She flinched, falling back on her arms.

He hesitated, drew back, and waited.

Under his close scrutiny she pushed herself up into a sitting position. She boldly returned his gaze, aware of every muscle in her body trembling. This time, when he reached out and touched her temple, she didn't flinch, just held her ground and stared back. He gathered a handful of her hair and with gentle fingers lifted her locks. Leaning over, he took a whiff, and said, "*Ekapitu.*"

A half dozen or more Indians approached on horseback and halted in a circle around her. They stared at her like they'd never seen a white woman before. She frowned.

The one who touched her face and sniffed her hair had a calming effect over her nerves. His eyes, though black, showed a glimmer of compassion she had never seen in a savage. Clare drew in a shaky breath.

Suddenly, he stood, spoke to another, and turned toward an approaching rider.

While observing the Redskins, Clare realized they were not the same Indians that had captured her, but now, a different band had restrained her. Once again, she'd have to plot an escape.

A short, fat Indian stepped near, reached down, and pulled her to her feet. He loosely tied her hands being careful not to further harm her wounded wrists.

She glanced at several Indians talking in low, serious tones with the rider and the one who appeared to be the leader. Hurrying, but with an unruffled, controlled tone, the one in charge spoke. Her Indian boosted her onto a horse, tethered her rope to his horse, mounted, and headed out following the others. Clare grabbed the horse's mane and squeezed her legs around the animal's belly to keep from bouncing off. Riding bareback was not something she was accustomed to.

They pushed their horses harder and faster through the canyon passes. Clare sensed urgency feeling her horse's sides swell from his deep huffing snorts, pushing against her legs. Gunshot booms ricocheted off the canyon walls.

Clare jerked her head around. Exploding pistol shots roared through the air from the direction of her escape. Continuous gun blasts thundered inside her head shooting images through her brain sending a tear rolling down her cheek.

Betsy...

Chapter Three

Captain Drury Burchett leaned forward and rested an arm on the saddle horn. With his other hand, he rubbed his cheek, fingering the long, half-moon scar while searching the scene below the hill where the small band of Apaches had made camp. A dozen or so drunken warriors were sprawled out around the low, smoldering campfire, sending its lazy, grey cloud into the first light of dawn. There was only one teepee in camp. She had to be inside.

He didn't detect any movement. He lifted the corner of his mouth and nodded. Those savages were in for a big surprise. Straightening, he pulled his cowboy hat down snug on his head, glanced over at the other nine Rangers, and gave the order. "Spread out. We'll hit 'em from all sides."

"McCoy." The captain drew the Ranger's gaze toward him. "Betsy and the Coulson woman could be inside the teepee. I'll check it out. Cover my back."

McCoy nodded and with a worried frown, he turned his gaze back down the hillside toward the camp.

Captain Burchett pulled his Colt revolver from its holster, and with a dark and angry look studied the area below. He rubbed the scar running along his cheek, and then, without another word, took the leather reins, whipped his black stallion in the flank and rushed down the hillside toward the unsuspecting savages. The others followed, all drawing their .45 colts, ready to do the job the government had paid them to do, and to take back what was theirs.

Drury had one thing on his mind. They had taken Clare Rose Coulson from Silver Sage Creek, and he intended to get her back. He wasn't going to let another woman become a victim of Indian savages.

By the time the galloping horses thundered into camp, the slumbering band had aroused and appeared stupefied for only a second before the Ranger's bullets flew through the air to land in their chests, heads, and guts.

A staggering Apache stumbled from the teepee, rubbing his temple and looking confused. Drury aimed and plugged the black-painted faced Indian in the middle of his forehead. He dropped.

Drury swung from his horse, leaving the furor behind. He ran for the teepee and stepped inside, searching. Someone lay on hides in the corner. He knelt, rolled the body over and frowned. Even with all the discoloration on her face and her swollen lips, he knew she wasn't the Coulson woman, but Betsy, McCoy's woman. After skirting a quick glance around to make sure there wasn't another body, he gently gathered her into his arms and stepped from the teepee.

The exploding pistols had ceased, no longer ringing throughout the canyon. The Rangers waited on their horses, eyeing him as he stepped toward them with the woman in his arms.

Drury's gaze connected with McCoy's. He didn't have to say a word. His lifelong padre jumped from the horse and tenderly took the woman from Drury's arms.

McCoy whispered, "Is she dead?"

"I don't think so, but she looks pretty beat up."

"Those sons-of-bitches, we'll kill 'em all." McCoy gently knelt, holding her close while he waited for Drury to bring water from the saddlebag.

"Betsy," he whispered.

She moaned and opened an eyelid.

"Betsy, it's okay. I'm here. You're safe now." McCoy frowned. "Drury, she isn't responding."

Squatting, Drury reached out and moved a clump of her dark, matted hair from her face. While staring at the deep cut, the scar on his cheek twitched. He held the canteen near her mouth, and dribbled water onto her lips. He whispered, "Betsy, where's Clare Rose?"

Her glassy eyes didn't seem to focus. Drury placed his hand on McCoy's shoulder and tried to reassure his padre. "She's drugged. Peyote. Could come to her senses by the time you get back to town. Come on. I'll help you get her on the horse."

McCoy gathered her into his arms and strolled to his horse. Handing her over to Drury, he mounted and reached for her. Drury recognized the pain in his friend's eyes. Pain he understood.

Betsy's state of mine, he was afraid, had been compromised and she'd never be the same again.

Drury did a quick look around the area. Where was the Coulson woman?

"Hey, Burchett, let's get out of here before another band hits Silver Sage."

"You fellows head back. I'm gonna scout around a bit and see if I can pick up any tracks."

"You want company?" asked the youngest Ranger in the group.

"Nope."

Drury mounted the black stallion and led him in a small circle around the camp, widening his search in the vicinity until he found a single horse trail leading away from the campsite. The horse's hooves didn't sink too deep into the soft earth, which meant a lightweight rider, Clare. His keen eyes never strayed from the trail leading up the canyon. After following for a mile or so, he pulled back on the reins and studied the ground.

His heart skipped a beat. Horse tracks in the soft dirt turned his blood cold. He knew exactly what had happened. Clare had been taken. Again. There looked to be a dozen or so unshod horses, which meant another band of Indians had come upon her while she tried to escape.

Drury stared ahead and listened. All was quiet. They had ridden off, no doubt, alerted by the Rangers' attack on the other band. No telling how far they'd travel before stopping.

His eyes narrowed beneath the wide brim hat. He still had time to catch up with the Rangers heading back to Silver Sage Creek. His gaze dropped to focus on the hoof prints. Tracks vanished fast in wind and rain. Straightening, he pulled on the reins, made a clicking sound with his mouth ordering his horse to move forward toward the distant mountains, keeping his eyes on the band's tracks.

Several hours later, he pursued them through a cedar forest, making it harder for him to follow their hoof marks. When his stomach rumbled, his stallion's ears perked up. "Me too, big boy, I'm hungry too. We'll stop soon."

As the sun dropped lower into the western sky, the air sent a shiver down Drury's back. He came to a halt and dug into the saddlebag. Once he slipped into his coat, he pulled the collar up around his neck, stared ahead, and listened. Nothing, but the breeze whistling through the trees. He took in a deep breath through his nose. He sniffed again…wood burning. Once again, he breathed deeply through his nose and with narrowed eyes he stared toward the burning cedar. He swung his leg over his horse to stand solid on the ground. He took another sniff. Sure enough, cedar burning.

Drury led Big Black out of sight, tied him to a tree, and quietly turned in the direction of what he hoped to be the place where the Indians settled for the night. Campfire? It had to be. If so, maybe he'd have a chance to rescue Clare.

The stronger the smell, the lower he crouched to keep invisible from the enemy. When he laid eyes on their fire flickering in the distance through the cedar trees and underbrush, he quietly snaked his way to a hiding place within sight of their camp. He scanned the area for the Coulson woman…she hovered near the fire with a deer hide around her slumped shoulders. He waited.

* * * *

In the hour when the sky was the darkest before the dawn, Drury set eyes on Clare Rose's sleeping form, beneath the deerskin cover. She appeared to be sound asleep. He needed to awaken her without alarming the enemy.

He waited.

She stirred.

As if sensing someone near, she sat up and stared directly at him. Drury stepped slightly out into the clearing, hoping Clare recognized his presence.

She did.

He motioned to her.

Clare quickly glanced around the group slumbering near the fire pit. Then, she threw back the hide and crawled to her feet while keeping her eyes on the Indians sleeping near her. Moving ghostly, she crept toward the Ranger.

* * * *

Her upper teeth bit down on her lower lip, willing her mind to stay in control of her movements, forcing herself to tip toe away, even though she desperately wanted to run like hell. Her heart pounded against her chest like the loud Indian drums she remembered hearing when she was a small child.

When near enough to Drury, Clare couldn't stop her feet from taking off. Running, she threw her arms wide and lunged at the Ranger. The moment Drury wrapped his arms around her and pulled her close to his body, warmth spread over her like the blanket she had just deserted. Except his warmth made her feel safe. With her face buried into his neck, she clung tightly. She didn't know why he came after her, but she knew she'd be forever in his debt.

When his worried eyes glanced around the camp, she did the same. They had to make sure they had not disturbed the slumbering savages. His arm circled her waist and all but carried her into the deep covers of the forest, toward his horse.

Clare recognized his big, black horse and knew they had made it. When he dropped his arm from her body, she grabbed him around the waist and hugged the solid chest. His gentle, secure hands splayed over her back. Looking up into his face, she whispered, "You came for me."

He nodded.

"Alone," she asked, glancing around.

She hugged him again, burying her face into his chest, basking in the warms of his arms.

"Hurry," he whispered, and then turned to help her onto the horse.

She raised her arms to the saddle horn. A loud crack whipped through her ears. Her breath cut off from her lungs, shooting splinters through her veins.

Her Ranger collapsed.

A hand gently touched her arm.

She flinched and swung her head around to stare into the familiar black eyes of the short, fat Indian. She should have known he was guarding from somewhere in the dark.

Clare dropped to Drury's side. He was breathing, but out cold.

The Indian babbled, reprimanding her in his own language.

She pressed her lips against her teeth, curled her fingers into a tight fist, and stood. With glaring daggers shooting at him, she whirled and flung her fist to connect with his jaw, only to have her wrist slapped into a vice grip.

Clare's eyes widened. Swinging her head up, she connected with the black angry eyes of the one who appeared to be the leader. He held her wrist firmly and stared down at the Ranger. Alert eyes searched out toward the dark forest. He quickly gave an order, sending the Indian waddling off toward the camp.

Dragging her gaze from his, she stared at his hand gripping her wrist. He splayed his hand and released her. A frowned formed above her squinting eyes. What was he thinking? Watching his every move, her eyes widened when he pulled a knife from his belt and knelt next to the Ranger. She sucked in a short breath, swallowed hard, and watched closely. When he shoved the hat from the Ranger's head, Clare grabbed the Indian's shoulder and hollered, "No."

She gathered a fistful of buckskin and jerked, bringing his gaze upon her. "No." She shook her head. "You can't kill him."

Clare pleaded, looking him straight in the eye. Tears gathered and dropped down her cheeks. She recognized a flicker of concern in his eyes. Without blinking, she let the tears flow.

"Please."

His gaze returned to her.

"Take me with you, but let him live, please. I'll not run away…just let him live." She begged. Clare wasn't sure how he understood, but she knew he did.

The chief impatiently pushed her aside, put away his knife, reached down and pulled off the Ranger's boots and socks.

Clare swung her gaze beyond the chief. Her eyes widened. More Indians had gathered around to stare down at her. Curious Redskins eyed the stranger lying on the ground. They all wanted him dead so he couldn't cause them harm by living and returning with other Rangers to destroy their village.

The chief turned and spoke to several of the band, evidently, issuing an order. An Indian dismounted and stepped to the Ranger's horse, reached up and unbuckled the saddle strap. He slid the saddle off the stallion's back and dropped it, but left the blanket on the horse.

The chief cocked his head and studied the Ranger for a second, and then turned, swept Clare into his arms and onto the stallion.

The chubby Indian who had knocked out the Ranger, rode his horse near her, reached out his hand, and took her reins. Once his chief mounted his pinto, he led her away from the area. Clare followed her chubby Indian's gaze. His scowl probed the Ranger flat out on the ground, barefoot with blood near his head.

Clare looked down. He wasn't dead. He'd live. He had to.

* * * *

Moaning echoed inside Drury's ears. His eyelids slowly opened. Another moan.

For hell's sake, it was him. Why? Then a sharp, excruciating pain blasted through his brain. He pushed his hands against the earth to sit up, swayed sideways, and slumped back. A black, dizzy whirl engulfed him. He reached up and pressed his hand to his head. Pain permeated his skull, shooting down through his chest.

Breathing heavily, he waited until the agony subsided. He dropped his hand and stared at his wet fingers. Blood. Lying flat, he waited for his blurred visions to clear and his brain to stop spinning.

Shit, Burchett, what happened? Think.

Slowly, he rolled his head to the side to look around. A slight glow from a bright moon filtered down through the trees and over the area. Night. Last he remembered it was daylight. Where was his horse? Big Black wouldn't have left unless forced. Someone had chucked his saddle up against a tree. He closed his eyes and took in a deep breath. No horse.

Drury eased upon his elbow and squeezed his eyes to clear the muddled thoughts inside his head. The pain was tolerable now, something he'd have to ignore. Cautiously, he pulled his legs up to stand. He wavered, reached out for a tree limb, waited to catch his breath and his balance. He pulled his bandana from his neck and held it against the back of his head.

His gaze fell on his bare feet. Thick brows pulled together. Who took his boots? The Indians. Son-of-a-bitch. He'd been careless. He should have known they'd have at least one Redskin on lookout.

Stupid. You forgot your job by letting her get into your head. Shit, he was careless. For what? She's married. Or was she? Someone had said Montgomery was pretty bad off. Doc dug an arrow out of his chest, but didn't expect him to live. So, what? Even if he had rescued the woman, what made him think she'd have anything to do with him? A mere Ranger.

Nonetheless, he still remembered her arms around him when he rescued her. Even with the dirt and smudges on her face, and matted hair, she was beautiful. She had looked more like a frightened, little girl than a young, married woman. Those sons-of-bitches. Where did they take her?

Drury reached up and rubbed his scar, smearing blood over his cheek. Jerking his hand down, he bent, grabbed a large broken tree limb, and leaned on it while straining to see through the moon shadows. No body. The slight fear creeping into his veins subsided. Clare was still alive and was their captive.

Why didn't they kill him? Indians didn't have a habit of leaving their enemy behind alive. And…then taking boots. Usually scalps were the rewards for their kill, and of course, horses. Not only did they have Clare, they took his horse, too.

Drury leaned against the stick and stared into the moon-filtered forest, loud with katydids and night creatures. He limped toward the thickest area to find a good hiding place, but with enough visibility to observe any approaching enemy. He'd have a long way to go, barefooted no less, in the dark. He needed a place to hide until daylight. He couldn't take the chance that they would come back to finish the job.

Chapter Four

With each trotting movement made by the horse beneath her, Clare's temper rose, boiling her blood. She released a growl from deep inside her throat. Anger heated her neck rising up through her face. Anger at being kidnapped, anger at not succeeding in escaping, anger for being imprisoned by another band of savages, and anger for being taken further away from her life. And, if they didn't stop soon, she'd pee on the horse.

The constant jostle made her body scream out for relief. They rode at a steady pace for what seemed forever to Clare. Finally, she could take no more. If they didn't like it, they could just kill her.

"Stop," she shouted in the loudest voice she could muster. "I said, stop."

The short, fat Indian turned his head toward her and slowed his horse.

"I need to pee. I'm in pain." Shit, didn't anyone speak English? Clare pulled hard on the mane to make the horse come to a halt.

The Indian halted his horse and glowered at her.

Returning a threatened glare, Clare said, "I'll not go another step until I pee. Do you understand me?"

No, he didn't from his baffled expression. She shook her head and sucked in an exasperating breath and without another word, threw her leg over the horse and slid down.

The Redskin's eyes widened.

Clare stuck her tongue out at him and stomped toward the sagebrush several feet away, all the while listening to the little fat Indian babble his Indian language, clearly demanding her to return. With her wrists still tied and with some difficulty, she was able to lift her dress and relieve herself. Taking her time, she lifted her head and looked out across the desert land, serene in the early morning sun.

Should she run? Where were they? Where were they going? She'd never traveled so deep into Texas territory, if in fact, they were still in Texas.

Run. Her gaze swung in all directions. *Where?* She turned her gaze up at the sun toward the east. Which way to Silver Sage Creek and how far? No. If she ran into the harsh desert, without water, its beauty would become a death trap for someone like her. She'd die.

Death. There were worse things than death. Clare dropped her head, and turned to step out of the brush toward her horse, shaking her head. Considering her uncertain future ahead, she might have to choose death sooner or later.

Chubby was still chattering away, but this time to his chief. When she moved toward the horse, she reached up, grabbed its mane, and turned her gaze toward them.

"Well," her obstinate tone drew their gaze. "I cannot mount on my own."

The Indian with the long, straight, black hair and black eyes raised an eyebrow. He pulled on his horse's rein and trotted toward her.

He gracefully raised his leg over and slid down from the brown and white pinto. She could see the morning light reflect off his shiny hair, hair dark as night. With eyes fixed on her, he reached down, pulled a long bladed knife from his high-topped moccasins, and straightened.

Her eyes widened from sudden fear, jarring her intense gaze.

Before she knew it, he cut the rope from her wrists, picked her up, and swung her on the horse.

With swift movements, he turned, mounted, spoke to the one guarding her, and then rode ahead of the band without another look in her direction.

Her relieved gaze swung to the chubby Indian who held the rope to her horse. He appeared amused.

She straightened and glared back at him.

He shrugged a shoulder and took off.

Clare grabbed the horse's mane and hung on.

Even though she was somewhat anxious around these Redskins, she didn't fear this band, not yet anyway. They mostly ignored her, and the only one keeping a keen eye on her was the chubby, short Indian. The more she observed them, the more she wondered about them. Why didn't they wear black-painted faces like the other Apaches? And, why didn't they give her the impression of mean savage like those who had kidnapped her? Why did he untie her hands?

She almost believed they'd let her go, if she wanted. So far, they had not harmed her in any way and always made sure she was given water and a blanket when they made camp. Once night covered the area, they stopped to rest the horses and sleep until the few hours before dawn.

After traveling two more days, Clare was sure her bottom had grown into the horse's back. If they continued to ride much longer, she'd just die. Her slumped shoulders and numb body moved to the sway of the horse. When the horse heaved a heavy snort, she knew he was tired...so was she. Heading up a trail into a mountainous area, they weaved in and out of thick canyons of shrub oaks and Juniper trees. On the morning of the third day, Clare was never so glad to see a hidden village deep in a ravine.

Oh my heavenly days. Thank God. She so wanted to get off the damn horse.

The band snaked their way down a trail and into the Indian camp. Teepees were scattered everywhere with fire pits throughout the site and corrals filled with horses. Clare's horse halted behind the others in the village center. To her surprise, the village came alive with small children, women, braves, and old men. She couldn't get over the sounds of excitement at their arrival. God help her. She was surrounded by hundreds of Indians.

For a moment, she went unnoticed and was left sitting on her horse to watch the scene before her, utterly shocking her. Squaws and little children ran to greet the Indians dismounting from their horses in the middle of the village. She assumed they were husbands and fathers. They materialized in front of her with happy faces, laughter, giggles, and opened arms. Not so different from the way her ma greeted her pa, or how she hugged her own pa. It was a cheerful scene. She never considered Indians having a life or being happy. No white man she ever knew considered them people either.

Clare glanced down to find an ancient looking squaw's squinting eyes roaming over her hair, her clothing, and finally, her face. The deep brown face, covered with wrinkles, especially around the eyes, smiled up at her, deepening the lines. Her long hair had more white than black and hung over her shoulder in a thick braid. Her eyes, brown like her skin, reflected a kindness, seemingly to comfort some of Clare's anxiety. She didn't say a word, just stared.

An arm circled the old woman's shoulders giving her a slight hug. Clare's gaze swung to meet the black-eyed chief. He spoke to the squaw and nodded toward her, and then turned and walked away.

With a wrinkled hand gesture, she ordered Clare to dismount. Doing so, Clare lifted her taut leg over and slid from the horse. But, when trying to stand on her leg muscles, stiff and weak from the long ride, they buckled. She hit the hard ground. Clare couldn't stop the tears. She just wanted to lie down and die.

The old squaw helped her to her feet and practically carried her to a teepee. In obedience to the woman's command, Clare stumbled through the opening.

The teepee looked much like the one she and Betsy…no don't think of Betsy now…don't think of anything but surviving. Her eyes skimmed over the bedding on the side and the cold ashes in the fire pit in the middle of the teepee. Only, this teepee appeared to be a home to someone with their belongings left behind.

Clare turned expecting to find the old Indian squaw observing her, but she was alone. She hung her head, moved over to the bedding and dropped her exhausted body to the soft hides. When she closed her eyelids, a tear slid out the corner.

Warmth and security seeped into Clare's mind, while a soothing heat soaked into her rested body. She took a deep breath and lifted her eyelids.

She turned her head toward the blazing fire pit inside a teepee. Now, she remembered. She'd been dreaming she was at home, safe in the arms of her husband. She pulled her body up and sat staring into the pit. How long had she been asleep? When had they built the fire to keep her warm? A plate of food and water had been placed on a log next to the fire. They had even covered her with an animal hide for warmth. Her body must have been exhausted to sleep through all they had done for her.

Stretching the kinks out, she stood and listened. Not a sound. She had no idea what time of day it was. Curious, she stepped to the opening and pulled back the flap to peek out. The only things skulking through the dark night were a few fire pits that burned low throughout the village. Clare glanced up at the stars sparkling in the sky and figured it had to be about midnight. She squinted throughout the dark village.

Could she escape? She bit down on her bottom lip. A movement caught her attention. Several Indians guarding the entire camp and two overlooking the corralled horses swished a defeated breath from her lungs. Why couldn't they drink whiskey like those other savages?

Turning back, she crawled beneath the warm cover and let her mind replay the past several days and the terrifying turn of events her life had taken. She closed her eyes. *God, please let the Ranger live. He tried to rescue me, but I guess you didn't want him to, so please let him be able to return home safely. And Betsy, if she isn't dead, please help her because I didn't. I know I did an unforgiveable deed by leaving her, please forgive me. Betsy, forgive me.*

Clare rolled over, opened her eyelids, and stared into the blazing fire. If the Ranger had been successful in rescuing her, what kind of consequences might she have had to face at Silver Sage Creek? She'd heard horror stories of white women living through Indian attacks just to be outcasts by their own people. According to the white man's standards she was ruined—never again to be a reputable woman in the town. White women were shunned by their families because they did the unthinkable and lived. She was alive. Maybe, she'd be better off if they killed her because the life she had before could never be. Better she died.

Clare closed her eyelids over the tears and let her mind sink into a safe dream state again. The soft noise stirred her senses enough for Clare to open her eyes to sunlight streaming through the tied back flap revealing a bright view of the outdoors. The old, wrinkled squaw stepped near and placed a bundle on the bedding. Clare glanced at it and up at her.

The woman's head cocked to the side, held out her hand, and stared at her. Clare didn't move. The woman kept staring.

"What? Is it time I got up for a reason?"

The woman's eyes widened at Clare's question. She frowned and motioned for her to get up. The aged Indian squaw stood holding out her hand persistently, waiting for Clare to get up. Against her will, she crawled from beneath the cover, took the soft, wrinkled hand, and allowed the woman to lead her out the teepee.

Clare stood waiting when the old woman turned back to retrieve the bundle she had place on the bedding. She took a deep breath and raised her face to the sun. Its warmth filled her with energy she hadn't had for days.

When the squaw exited the teepee, she shoved the bundle under Clare's arm and hurried onward. Clare glanced down at what appeared to be a pair of moccasins and some kind of animal hide dress. For the first time, since kidnapped, she examined her own dress.

Her once beautiful green outfit was dirty, ripped, shredded in places, and barely hanging on her shoulders. Her bare feet no longer wore her pretty shoes—she couldn't remember when she lost them. Her hand reached up to touch her hair. Tears formed. Just over a week ago, she had been such a beautiful bride, and now she was an ugly old woman at eighteen. Her life was over. She looked up.

The squaw shot a quick glimpse over her shoulder and stopped to motion for Clare to follow.

Nothing more to do, Clare fell into step with her fast pace.

The village buzzed with Indians everywhere, doing all kinds of chores. Clare's steps slowed as she observed squaws cooking over open fires, naked children running and playing, men smoking in small groups, several young braves training with bows and arrows, and others tending to horses.

By the time Clare caught up to the old woman, she had stopped at the riverbank and stripped down to her bare bottom and was strolling into the water.

Wide-eyed, Clare glanced over each shoulder. No one seemed to bother to watch her bathe or even care. Her gaze turned back to the squaw working up a lather from the soap in her hands. Clare bit down on her bottom lip while appraising the white foam covering her brown body. She wanted to feel clean again.

What the hell, no matter how short her life, she wanted to wash the dirt away. After a quick glance around, she stepped behind a shrub and pulled the tattered dress from her body along with what remained of her underclothes.

She waded out into the cool, refreshing water and made her way toward the squaw, who ignored her and didn't seem to care whether or not she bathed. Alarmed at baring all, she sank down into the water until it lapped around her neck. Standing next to the woman, Clare became aware of the contrast in their skin. The squaw's sun-leathered skin appeared darker against the white, foamy soap spreading over her body. Clare took a deep breath through her nose, smelling the wonderful, soapy scent.

Kind, brown eyes turned on her and crinkled in the corner when she smiled. Then she held out the soap.

Clare reached for it and begrudgingly mumbled, "Thanks."

The squaw looked into her eyes.

Clare bit her lower lip. She hadn't meant to sound so bitter. Holding onto the bar, she sank down into the river to completely submerge her entire head, basking in its wonderful wetness. The warmth of the sun touched her face the moment she splashed to the surface. She smiled and opened her eyes to find the old woman still staring at her grinning.

Clare turned her back, flipped her hair over her head and dipped her long red strands into the river. Then she rubbed the soap over every part of her head. Her fingers worked through her scalp as she smelled the glorious fragrance. She had never used anything so wonderful. Her mother made lye soap without any scent and it tasted terrible if you happened to get it in your mouth when you washed your face. Once Clare rinsed the soap from her hair, she lathered her body much the same way the woman had.

Afterward, Clare took off swimming several feet away to clean off all the suds, and then leisurely swam back to stand by the squaw who seemed to be in charge of her.

When the woman turned her gaze on her, she stepped close and reached out to touch Clare's hair. "*Ekapitu,*" she said,

Clare glanced down at her long hair draped over her shoulder covering her right breast.

The woman repeated, "*Ekapitu,*" and pointed to her hair.

"Do you mean hair?" Clare asked, gazing into the large round eyes.

The woman looked at her with a blank expression.

Clare reached over with her other hand and touched the woman's long black and grey hair and said, "Hair."

The woman said, "Hair," and shook her head.

Clare cocked her head to the side and touched the woman's hair and repeated her word. "*Ekapitu.*"

A sharp shake of the head told Clare the word didn't mean hair. Again she pointed to Clare's hair and said, "*Ekapitu,*" and giggled.

Clare's eyes flew opened at the sound. They laughed. She never envisioned an Indian actually laughing at something.

"Okay, if it doesn't mean *hair*, what does it mean?"

The woman's eyebrows shot up.

Clare lifted her shoulders and shook her head. She watched the old squaw whirl her head around, searching. When her focus landed on a bush near the river edge, she waded toward it. Clare followed.

The woman grabbed berries from the bush and held them up.

"*Ekapitu* means berries?" Clare stated, reached out and took a berry from her hand and popped it into her mouth.

The woman laughed again. She shook her head and held a berry next to Clare's hair.

"*Ekapitu,*" she said.

"Oh, *red*. It means red." Clare nodded, and took the bundle of berries from the woman and placed them on top of her head and said, "*Ekapitu.*"

The woman's laughter echoed along the riverbanks. A strange sense of amity touched Clare. This old squaw could possibly be the only person on this planet to befriend her while living in this strange world, if she lived long enough. With a finger pointing into her own chest, Clare said, "Clare Rose."

The woman took a finger, touched Clare's chest and repeated, "Clare Rose."

"Right. Now, what's your name?" Pointing a finger, she touched the old woman's large bosomed chest.

A deep wrinkle formed between the old woman's bushy brows. Another light flashed in her dark eyes, then a wide grin showed off a mouth with a missing tooth. She pointed to herself and said, "*Chhawi.*"

Clare placed the palm of her hand against her chest and after repeating her name she laid her hand against the woman's chest and said, "*Chhawi.*"

Chhawi pointed to Clare and said, "Clare Rose." She smiled and started babbling.

"Wait a minute," Clare threw up her hands with a gesture. "You're speaking too fast." Her gaze drifted beyond *Chhawi*'s shoulder to connect with their chief's black eyes. Her eyes widened at the sight before her.

He stood tall, bared-chested, revealing muscles rippling down his stomach. He wore a breechcloth covering parts she had only imagined with Sally and Betsy, until her wedding night when Jonathan stroked against her to push inside her. She bit the corner of her lip and stared. She'd never seen so much skin on a man. His long legs were brown like his chest and every area on his torso appeared tight like a horse's long, lean muscles. She'd never seen such a brown, perfect body on a man before. When their gaze connected, she followed his gaze sweeping over her hair, and then leisurely traveling down her upper body to where the water lapped against her midsection.

"Uh...my..." Clamping her mouth shut, Clare shivered when her drenched hair dripped water down her chest. Suddenly, aware of her bare breast, visible for the entire world to see, including the chief's, she quickly sank down into the water.

He'd been watching for how long, she didn't know, but she did detect a slight smile on his lips before he turned to walk away. The funny expression on his face puzzled her.

"What's his name?" She asked and tipped her head toward the chief.

Chhawi turned and stared at her leader's backside strolling toward the village.

When she turned back, Clare touched her chest and repeated, "Name."

Chhawi pointed to her leader and said, "*Chakotay.*"

"Is he the chief of your Apache band?"

Chhawi's head drew back. She frowned. With her wrinkled brown hand, she slapped her chest and said, "*Numunuu*— Comanche."

"Oh," Clare surprised tone injected a tremble through her body. "I…I didn't know. You're…" she pointed, "…Comanche." Clare bit her bottom lip, digesting the news. "You're Comanche." Suddenly, the river water grew cold, raising chill bumps on her skin.

Hurrying toward the river's edge, Clare rushed to the bundle she had dropped by the shrub. She glanced toward the village. They're Comanche. Her pa had once said they were the fiercest tribe around. She remembered the word Comanche meant enemy. Cruel and merciless at killing all they came in contact with, and now, she was their captive. Yet, they had not once raised a hand against her, nor harmed her in any way.

Quickly, she slipped into the deerskin dress and glanced back to find *Chhawi* standing in clear view of all the villagers, and not caring who laid eyes on her bare body.

Clare bent to pick up her tattered clothing and wondered if she could ever be uninhibited about her own body. She shook her head. No respectable woman shed clothing in sight of another person. No lady did such. She slipped on the soft moccasins and wiggled her toes inside the warm fur. Her gaze studied the intricate designed on the hide. Even the dress was neatly stitched with beautiful, beaded embroidery. The skill of the Indian squaw surprised her. She glanced up. Comanche squaw. A shiver shook her body.

After making their way back to the teepee, *Chhawi* filled a wooden cup with a hot drink. She shoved it into Clare's hand, and said, "Un."

"You mean take it?"

To her amazement, *Chhawi* said, "Take it."

Clare mumbled, "You're a fast learner," and took a sip. "Hmm, good," she said eyeing the old woman named *Chhawi*, who, it occurred to her, was quickly becoming her only friend and was skilled in calming her nerves.

With a satisfied expression in her eyes, the squaw turned and slipped through the teepee.

Clare took another sip, glanced around at what she supposed was to be her home for the rest of her life no matter how short. Placing the cup near the fire, she crawled under the warm animal hide and stared at the flickering fire.

A tear rolled from her eye to drop on the bedding. She had two choices, since it appeared she was going to live—for now anyway. So far, none of the Comanches seemed dangerous. If anything, they ignored her. She could either reconcile to this way of life, or try to escape. Another tear slid out, rolled over her nose and down onto the bedding.

Escape to go where? Pa's dead. Jonathan's dead. Sally's dead. More than likely, Betsy's dead. What happened to her ma?

Clare rolled her face into the soft fur and let her crying heart release the flood of tears, shaking her body with agony.

A hand touched her head in a soft caress. Clare turned her wet face upward to find the gentle eyed, old squaw sitting on the floor next to her. She flung her arms out and hugged the only friend she had since her frightful nightmare had begun. When the skinny arms circled her, Clare relaxed, quietly crying in the arms of the motherly Indian, rocking her back and forth.

"You wait, see. After many moons, you will make a new life and be happy with us."

Clare jerked back and stared at the woman. "You…you speak English."

Chhawi shrugged. "Some. You make me remember. Many seasons ago, I was like you. I live this life forced on me. I learned to be happy."

Clare's mouth dropped. "You're white?"

She nodded.

"But…you…you look Comanche."

Her thin lips spread into a sad smile. She reached up and touched Clare's face, and then glanced at her hands. "I grew old. I once had soft, white skin like you." She looked up at the sunbeam streaming through the top of the teepee and back at Clare. "Comanche life not easy. We work hard to survive, but we enjoy life and know what's important."

"You mean you were kidnapped? Like me?"

"By the Apaches."

"Apaches. When? I mean how long ago?"

Chhawi's shoulders drooped. She turned and gazed longingly into the smoldering fire pit. "Years have gone by since the last time my thoughts turned to all those years past." For several minutes she sat silently, staring into the past.

Clare studied her brown, leathered face. She was a white woman.

"I think I was ten or twelve."

Clare's eyes widened. "How…how long ago was that?"

The old woman swung her gaze back to Clare. "I don't remember anymore. My home's been with this band for many, many moons."

"What's your birth name? Do you remember?"

"My white man's name?" She shook her head and stared at a swirl of smoke making its way up the center of the teepee and out. Her low voice mumbled, "I don't recall." Lifting her head, she smiled at Clare. "I don't think I've said this many white man's words in a long time. Well, not since I made my son learn some words."

"You have a son? Is he white?"

"No, no. He's the chief."

"*Chakotay's* your son?"

Clare stared at the woman with the twinkle in her eyes.

Chhawi reached over and touched Clare's cheek. "You should decide what you want." Pushing to her feet, she stood, smiled, and turned to leave. Before she pulled back the flap on the teepee, she looked back upon Clare. Her brows pulled together. "Don't wait too long to decide. Life's like the wind, comes and goes while most times, you are unaware."

"*Chhawi*, why…why didn't they kill me?"

Her kind gaze touched Clare's hair, and then rested on her eyes. "With your coloring of hair and eyes, you're worth much if traded to the *Mexicanos*."

Clare's mouth dropped. Now, she understood. Did this band have plans to eventually trade her? She stared down at her hands. The sun had already turned them a golden color in just the short time she'd been with the band.

The only way out was to escape and risk death, or kill herself.

* * * *

Clare woke up sluggish. After sitting up for a few minutes, she slowly moved toward the opening, and stepped out of the teepee. She couldn't believe she slept for so long. The sun was sinking in the west. She had slept most of the day away. Her gaze swept the camp. The squaws were busy working in groups. Some were tanning deer hides and others were preparing meals. The children, most naked, were running around, giggling and laughing without a care in the world.

Clare tightened the lines around her mouth. *Chhawi* was right. She had to make up her mind. What was she going to do?

Chapter Five

Clare strolled up behind *Chhawi* squatting next to a dead animal. She stared down. It was a magnificent deer that once roamed the area with the other stags. All of its life snuffed out by an arrow. Its eyes were open, large eyes staring back. Lifeless.

It wasn't like she hadn't seen a dead animal before. Pa brought many a deer home after a hunting trip, but she'd never stood so close to one so soon after a kill. Pa always stayed in the barn out of sight where he did whatever he had to do for their meat.

Several other squaws gathered around with *Chhawi*, and when the old woman turned to her, she shoved a knife into her hand. Clare looked down at the sharp blade. Her brow drew into a deep furrow. Her incensed gaze shot down at the crinkled-eyed squaw. What did she expect her to do?

Chhawi squinted up at Clare and indicated with a jerk of her head toward the large, dead deer.

Clare's eyes flew wide. No. She defiantly shook her head. "No." she stepped back. "I can't...I won't...do..."

Chhawi narrowed her eyes and studied her, and then reached out and grabbed her arm, forcing her to the ground.

Clare dropped to her knees next to the carcass. Panic set in and she released short choppy breaths. Her blood shot through her veins, sending her gaze whirling around the camp, looking for a way out.

Chhawi's aged, thin but strong hand grabbed hers. Clare's head jerked back. She tried yanking her hand away, but she was trapped and moving at the mercy of a determined controller. The wrinkled hand tightened, squeezing her fingers around the knife handle. Clare watched the blade slice into the animal's chest near the ribcage. Another squaw pulled the skin up and away from the intestines, allowing the guts to fall onto the ground following Clare's knife cutting up through the chest. After the quick, proficient incision, *Chhawi* released her hand.

Clare's face crinkled in disgust. She stared down at the dark blood dripping from the knife, and then shifted her gaze back to the squaws working on the bloody innards, stripping them completely away from the body cavity of the large, dead stag. Clare scooted back and pushed to her feet. Escape. Now. She turned, ran through the camp and into the woods toward the river.

By the time she heaved a breath of air into her tight lungs, she realized the village was nowhere in sight, only the river running through the forest. She dropped to her knees and sucked in a long breath and stared up at the sky. What was to become of her?

She glanced back. No one bothered to follow. No one cared. Her gaze swung down to find her red fingers gripping the bloody knife. She'd never stuck a knife into anyone or anything, and certainly not into the guts of a dead animal.

Swallowing hard to keep the sickening rumble in her stomach from making its way up her throat, she squeezed her jaws together, took several deep breaths of fresh, clear air, and tried not to think about her queasy stomach. Leaning back on her legs, she slowly watched the river meandering down through the thick trees toward the plain.

They had chosen a beautiful spot for their village, a place with lots of water and open grassland beyond the woods. The Comanches were resourceful. She'd learned that in the short time she'd been with them. Heavens, how long had she been with them now? When had her days turned into weeks? She had lost track of time.

Clare scrambled to her feet and strolled several yards to the river's edge. Kneeling, she washed the blood from the knife, dropped it on the ground, and then swished her hands in the river. When she took a deep breath, she smelled the fresh scent of late fall lingering in the air. A chill scurried over her skin. She folded her bare arms against her chest and rubbed them to circulate warmth. Winter was near.

Reaching out, she plucked a lone berry from a bush by the river's bank. All the fruit was almost gone, everything was preparing for the cold season, even the people in the village.

Only a few short months ago, the weather had been warmer, and she hadn't a problem in the world as Mrs. Jonathan

Montgomery. Now, she experienced time flying by and on other days, dragging or standing still. Time didn't change; *she* was the one changing. Did she want to change? She'd have to if she continued to live with the Redman. If so, she'd no longer sit at a dinner table, dressed in beautiful silk, chatting with her husband over what to do about the home they were building. She'd never have a chance to ask him about the article in the gazette about his running for governor. The lifestyle of being a fine, respectable lady no longer existed. The life ahead consisted of gutting beautiful animals to exist.

She sat back on her legs, glanced down, picked up the knife, and pressed its tip against her chest. Her gaze stared down at the rippling waters flowing over the rocks. She pressed the sharp tip harder between her breasts until the jagged point cut through the deerskin dress she wore. Another slight push and the tip poked her skin, causing her eyes to squeeze shut.

Did she really want her life to end? Only a coward did such. Slowly lifting her eyelids, she stared across the river and her eyes connected with the large, yellow eyes of a huge, grey wolf.

Clare held her breath. He didn't move, just watched her. In her mind's eye, time floated to a complete stop while she studied him closely, the way he did her. He was beautiful, strong and healthy looking, and yet, a sadness reflected from his stare. She took a deep breath, dropped her arms to her side, and released the knife. The magnificent wolf blinked, turned, and disappeared into the thicket.

Even though she knew the whole episode had to be her imagination, it didn't matter, the wolf spoke to her. Not physically, but in a spiritual way, telling her…what? She shook her head and pushed to her feet to head back to camp. Instead, she turned her direction downriver and strolled along the edge, keeping an eye out for the last few berries she might find. Every once in a while, she'd glance around for the wolf, but he wasn't to be seen.

The cool air smelled clean and the sun warmed her face. She wasn't ready to go back where she'd be expected to help in preparing the animal carcass. For the last few weeks, the squaws had stopped ignoring her. She supposed they thought she'd had enough time to get over all her emotions of the past and start living the Indian life. In other words—they expected her to do her part in the everyday tasks.

Clare plucked a berry and slipped it into her pocket. She glanced back. No one followed. She turned back, plucked another berry and let her mind drift. If she had not been captured, she might be a fine lady in her new house in town. The grand house Jonathan had talked about building. He never liked the little cabin Pa had given them. Maybe one day she'd tell *Chhawi* about her handsome husband, and how he could have been governor, if the Apache hadn't killed him. Jonathan planned to build a fine house in town and, with his ferocious appetite for mounting her every night and morning, she'd probably be with child by now.

Clare stopped. She shouldn't think about what might have been. Clare Rose's life no longer existed. Now she was...was what? She wasn't Comanche, nor was she acceptable in the white man's world.

She took a step and then another, until the hard buffalo soles of her moccasins barely touched the earth. She ran with great speed from wanting to take flight into the sky, hunting for another world.

Her leg muscles trembled. Her feet began to drag. Clare heaved in another breath, but couldn't keep up with the air needed in her lungs. Her legs gave way. Collapsed, face down in the earth, she wondered why she couldn't just die. What if she didn't get up? What if she just died here? No one cared.

No, she was wrong, the old squaw cared.

Clare sat up and brushed the dirt from her deer hide dress. A piercing sting zapped her hand when blood oozed from a small scrape. *Stupid.* She frowned and turned her palms around, and stared at her golden brown hands. She no longer had a lady's white hands. Nor were her scarred hands soft and pretty, but labored hands full of scratches from picking berries, scratches from splitting firewood, and scratches from cutting animal hide for moccasins and clothing.

Clare reached up and touched her face. If her hands had become brown by the sun...what...what about her face? She must look terrible. What she needed to do was to make a bonnet to cover her face. She'd do that. If she could weave a basket, she could certainly make a sun hat. That's exactly what she intended to do once she returned to camp.

Her gaze swung around. Where the hell was she? The tall grass surrounded her. She swirled around glancing in the direction of the trees lining the river. She must have run a long way to end up in the grassy plains. Clare took a deep breath, stared out toward the grasslands, pressed her lips together, and, after a thoughtful moment, she emphatically stated out loud, "You're young and healthy. You'll not die. Now make your own journey woman, even if you have to go alone. Understood?"

She glanced down at her wedding band. None of the Indians had bothered to take it. She was no longer married. Her husband was dead. She'd be like the old squaw. She'd never marry again.

With a slight tug, she pulled her silver wedding band from her finger. After staring at the band for several seconds, she raised her hand, and hurled the ring out into the air, and watched the tiny dot drop, lost in the sea of grasslands.

Her brows pulled together. The sun was high. She headed toward the trees to return to the village when her gaze landed on the Comanche chief, standing straight and tall several yards away. His long, straight, black hair wavered in the slight, cool breeze and his black eyes drilled into hers. He held the reins of his horse and the Ranger's black stallion. She strolled close enough to connect with his tense gaze with its questioning expression.

Clare frowned, and demanded, "What?"

He stepped forward and handed her the lead rope attached to the black horse. "Yours."

Clare strived to keep a blank expression. "You're giving me the horse. Why?"

"Can you not ride a horse?"

She knew he could speak English from what *Chhawi* taught him. But, this was the first time he'd spoken to her or even noticed her, since the river incident when she had bared her body for all to see.

"Of course I know how to ride." Clare reached out, snatched the rope from his hand, walked around him and touched the horse's neck. Its long, slick body was muscular and strong, and his coat glimmered in the sun, appearing blue-black, and reminding her of the Comanche chief's long, straight black hair.

Clare leaned against the horse's head and whispered, "Hi boy. You miss the Ranger? I'm so, so sorry, but now you can be my horse. I'll make you happy. I'll call you Big Black." His large, black eyes stared into hers. His gentle eyes seemed to accept his new master.

Clare stepped to his side and tried to jump onto his back, but fell backward.

The chief laughed.

She jerked around. "Well, don't just stand there, give me a boot up."

This time the chief frowned, strolled toward her, and lifted her foot up so she could swing her leg over the horse's back. Clare held the rope, leaned forward, patted the horse's neck, and mumbled, "Let's go for a ride."

The moment she tapped his flanks, he took off in a slow trot.

The chief mounted and followed.

Clare lifted her head to let the wind and sun touch her face. She closed her eyes and moved with Big Black's gait, allowing the wind to caress her hair. How long had it been since she'd felt alive? And she did. Lifting her eyelids, she gazed over the horse's neck and watched the earth pass by…along with her past life. She smiled.

They hadn't gone far when the chief rode to her side and grabbed her lead to halt their horses. Not happy about his interruption of her euphoria riding in the wind, she followed his intense study toward an object ahead. Her gaze locked on the large grey wolf, her wolf. The one she had bonded with at the river.

The chief's motions were so slow, Clare wasn't aware of his intentions until he raised his bow and arrow and aimed it at the animal. She sucked in a quick breath and grabbed hold of his bow. His head swung to her with a surprised expression on his face.

"What are you doing?" she whispered, tears forming to cloud her vision.

Chakotay's soft voice stated, "He's wounded, bleeding, dying."

"No." Quickly she swung her leg over the horse and slid off its back.

Clare didn't think about the dangers of a wounded animal attacking. She stared into the wolf's painful eyes asking her for help. She moved toward the magnificent, grey wolf one slow step at a time. His golden-yellow eyes, dulled from pain, stared into hers, and without diverting his focus from her, he dropped to the ground, rolled on his side, and whimpered. Stepping up to his body, Clare knelt, reached out her hand, and gently touched its thick, shaggy fur.

He whimpered.

Tears swelled in sorrow for the injured wolf. Her heart cried out when her gaze rested on his blood-matted fur along his side. She whirled to set eyes on *Chakotay*. He stood near, pointing his arrow, ready to fly into the animal the moment he moved to harm her.

She couldn't stop the tears. A bleak future stood before her with no hope of ever becoming a white woman again. Heavy grief pushed the tears out in a torrent storm of rasping cries. She didn't understand, but her emotions ran over with the want of healing this animal. Not only that, she shed tears of what her life had become, tears for her fate of living instead of dying, tears for her husband, tears for her parents, tears for Sally and Betsy. All of whom she'd never see again. And, tears for her own uncertain destiny.

Gentle hands covered her shoulders and pulled her up and into his arms. Comfort, safety, and assurance spread throughout her essence, melting into her mind, telling her he'd make it all right. Wiping aside her tears, she lifted her gaze to the gentle eyes of the chief. She pleaded, "Help him."

"This creature was brought to us by the spirits. You possess special gifts. Attacking is his nature, but you are different in his eyes. Wait here and don't move or startle him."

"I won't. I...I think he understands." She turned her gaze down at the helpless wolf, and squatted next to him, waiting. A whimper escaped his large, powerful jaws, and then he closed his eyes.

Chakotay returned chewing on leaves he'd found in the brush. He frowned, looked at Clare, and bent down next to the wolf. Leaning forward, he spit the green mush into his hand and pressed the fleshy, moist leaves onto the wound.

The wolf didn't move or make a sound.

Clare watched *Chakotay* stand and walk around searching the area, until slowly, he collected several limbs and tumbleweeds. He indicated for Clare to move away to give him space to make a den for the animal. After adding several more thick branches of underbrush and tumbleweeds, he stood back and pondered over what he'd done.

Clare touched his arm. His black eyes looked deep into hers and then his gentle voice said, "He might be safe. For a while."

"Thank you."

"Come, we must leave him."

Clare wiped the moisture from her face and headed toward the horses. She stopped and asked, "Why did you help when you wanted to kill him?"

Mounting, he turned and looked down at her. "We don't kill wolves, but this one is wounded. If the spirit wants, he'll live because you gave him the chance."

"I don't understand. You kill other animals for food and clothing, why not the wolf?"

"Wolves live like Comanche. They roam free and only kill to survive. They live in bands and have families, much like us."

Clare glanced back at the thick den *Chakotay* had made over the injured wolf. "And, their only predator, like the Comanche, is the white man."

When she glanced up at *Chakotay,* his pondering expression scurried over her face. She strolled to her horse, gripped the lead, and led him to a large rock. Once she climbed up, she jumped onto Big Black.

Breathing deeply, Clare knew *Chakotay* was right. All these months she'd helped with the preparations for winter. Without wanting to, she understood the fight for survival within the Comanche's world.

With slumped shoulders, Clare followed the expert horseman ahead. When she gazed back in the wolf's direction, she said a prayer, "Please let him live."

Clare stared ahead at the chief of her band. He rode tall and confident. Oh my, what had she just said? She'd called them her band. Her pa had once talked to his friends about the Comanche skills and how they could do things on and with horses, amazing other people. They could ride faster and farther and get more out of a horse than any others. All white men said Comanche were known for being great fighters from the top of a horse. *Well, Pa, you'd be surprised at how skillful and wise they really are.*

Chakotay stopped, turned, and waited for her to catch up. She took her time, thinking about the wolf and its enemy. Clare stared straight ahead. Her mind pictured the deer back at camp where the women had gutted the dead animal. While observing the routines in camp, she'd learned these people didn't waste any part of an animal. Survival was their main quest in life.

Big Black halted next to the chief's horse. Clare glanced over at the chief and asked, "Do any of your bands eat wolf?"

"No, we're *Kotsoteka*."

"Meaning…what?"

"Buffalo-eaters."

"Oh." Clare glanced around and mumbled, "But I haven't seen any buffalo around here."

The chief's gaze swung back and stated, "Further beyond the grasslands is where we find the herds. After several more sunrises, they'll move on and we'll follow."

Wide-eyed, Clare said, "You mean break camp? This isn't your permanent home?"

He shook his head and touched his horse in the flanks to gallop toward the village. She followed alongside, listening to his particulates. "We never stay in one place for long. We follow the buffalo. Following the buffalo keeps the white man from finding us."

"That's why you need so many horses. When you and your men go out during the day, you come back with food and sometimes, more horses. Where do you get them?"

The chief's shoulder lifted. "Anywhere...everywhere. We trade, some are wild, others, we steal."

"You mean you steal from your own people? Why?"

"Not all Indians are the same." He frowned. "Are all white men your people? Don't they fight each other, too?"

"Well, yes, but...I...I...I see what you mean. So, when you found me running from those other Indians, you were on your way to steal their horses."

Releasing his hold on her gaze, he nodded.

"They weren't Comanche, were they?"

"Apaches."

"Well, they were mean. I wished you had killed them."

"Why?"

"They hurt my friend. When I found a way to escape, she was caught and I couldn't help her." Clare narrowed her gaze. "Why didn't you steal their horses after you captured me?"

"Too late."

"Why? You could have saved my friend."

"The Rangers attacked them. They don't leave anyone alive. The only purpose for the Rangers is to kill all Indians."

Clare's eyes widened. "Oh my God. If I hadn't tried to escape, I'd have been rescued by the Rangers."

He didn't reply.

"Maybe Betsy was saved after all."

She studied him for a moment, and then asked, "If you hadn't captured me and if the Rangers hadn't come along, what would've happened to Betsy and me? Are the Apaches so different from the Comanche?"

"They'd enslaved your friend for their use until they no longer wanted her, and then kill her. You're stock...sellable."

"Sold. *Chhawi* said if it hadn't been for you, I'd be in Mexico by now. I really don't understand. Why me?"

"They used your friend. You're different." The chief reached out and touched her hair, ran his fingers down a long, thick strand, and held it in the palm of his hand. "Flaming hair and green eyes are worth a lot."

"So, are you going to sell me?"

"My band steals horses for trade. You're free to go whenever you want."

Sure. Go where? "So, why do you have so many horses?"

"Before horses it took longer on foot to follow the herd. Now we can follow the buffalo in one day. The horses help us keep the white settlement from crowding in on us. With horses, the Comanche has become the most powerful warrior. We can trade for fur, buffalo skin, beads, all kinds of stuff."

Before Clare could ask more questions, he kicked his horse's flanks and rode ahead, letting her know the talk was over.

Chapter Six

After placing a few logs in the fire pit, Clare crawled into bed and snuggled down, feeling drowsy. She thought about her talk with *Chakotay*. He spoke honestly about her situation and showed her kindness. He also said she could leave anytime.

What if she did leave? She'd get lost, die of starvation, or freeze to death in the snow. Yet, if she did, by some miracle, find her way back to Silver Sage Creek, what then? Not even the Ranger would gaze upon her the way he did the day she was kidnapped. Not now, not since he failed to rescue her. Clare yawned, closed her eyes and swore, "By God Almighty, I'll never again think about the *what ifs*."

Early the next morning, Clare stood in front of her teepee. She slept late again. All the squaws stayed so busy during the day, no wonder they fell asleep early and got up early. Clare supposed at some point, she'd go through the same daily routine without thinking—never again spending hours frivolously the way she had with Betsy and Sally.

Clare stood straight, reached up, fingered the smooth twig *Chhawi* had made for her hair and pulled it out, releasing her thick, red mass to flow down her back. She gathered her hair into her hands and combed her finger through her long strands and began weaving until she made one long, thick braid, like the old squaws in the village. Later she'd ask *Chhawi* to help her do a scalp lock, which was nothing more than a slender braid decorated with colored scraps of cloth, beads, and a single feather.

When she looked up, she found *Chhawi* watching her with a sparkle in her eyes, smiling at her and nodding. Clare returned her smile, thankful for her kindness. The old squaw knew Clare had now decided to become one of them.

Several women made their way to her and handed her a basket. *Chhawi* said, "Come, we need to find the last of the berries and nuts…if we can find any. Cold season is coming fast."

After walking in silence for several minutes, Clare spotted a bush covered with berries. "Look, *Chhawi*."

"Good eye, *Keshini*."

"What did you call me?"

"*Keshini*, your Comanche name."

Clare said, "*Keshini*." After thinking it over, she shook her head. "No. It's a pretty name, but I have white man's blood in me and I can never be a true Comanche in their eyes. You know that. So call me Clare Rose. I'll keep my English name."

Chhawi studied her for a moment, spread her lips showing off her teeth with a tooth missing, and said, "*Keshini*."

Clare laughed. "Okay, what the hell, *Keshini*. What does it mean in English?"

"One with beautiful hair."

"Oh." Before Clare could say another word, the woman turned to search for more berries. After several minutes, she hollered. "Look," she motioned for *Chhawi* to hurry. "Here's a bush filled with red berries."

When *Chhawi* laughed out loud, Clare turned. "What's so funny?"

The old woman gazes into her eyes with a wonder and said, "Martha."

Clare questioning brows pull together. "Who's Martha?"

Chhawi pointed at her chest and proudly stated, "My name. Martha."

"Martha? Your English name's Martha?"

She nodded.

"Martha, can I call you Martha?"

She looked to be in deep thought for a moment, then looked at Clare and shook her head. "No, I've been *Chhawi* longer than Martha."

Clare nodded. "Do you remember anything else?"

Shuffling her feet along, *Chhawi* lowered her heavy bones down on a rock, took a quick breath, and stared out beyond the bushes toward the grasses waving in the breeze.

Clare sat down next to her and waited. Finally, *Chhawi's* soft, quivery voice spoke.

"I was only about ten years old when my parents headed west. I recall a town, can't remember its name, but we stopped there to buy supplies before moving on. My pappy was a preacher. I had a sister and three brothers."

She turned her gaze to Clare with a shocked expression. "They were all killed when we were attacked somewhere out on the plains. I remember hiding in the wagon with my little sister." Her surprised expression turned to *Keshini*. "I now remember her name. Violet."

Chhawi's thin, boney hand lifted to her mouth, and then dropped to her lap as she stared out toward the grasslands and into another lifetime. "When they discovered us, they dragged us from the wagon and set it afire. My brothers, Ma, and Pappy were dead. They took me and my little sister with them. They weren't good Indians. They were cruel and hurt me. My little sister was weak and didn't live through the first winter."

"How…how long had you lived with the Apache band?"

"Ah, let me think." *Chhawi* rubbed her forehead and looked down at the ground. "I can't recall, but it was months before the Comanches raided their camp in the middle of the night. When they found me tied to a tree, they cut my ropes, put me on a horse, and rode off with me. I have to tell you I was glad they killed all those Apaches."

Clare couldn't imagine the brutality her friend endured while forced to live with the cruel savages.

As if she'd come to the end of her life story, *Chhawi* stood. "Let us walk further downstream, we might find some nuts."

Following alongside her friend, Clare thanked God above that this band took her in and this sweet, old woman befriended her. While they walked and searched for nuts and berries, Clare chattered away, telling *Chhawi* all about her life at Silver Sage Creek. She supposed she wanted to tell someone before she forgot her life in the white man's world.

Keshini squatted near the fire pit and held out her wet hands to the warm flames. They hurt from the cold wind, and her back ached from bending over the hide for so long. When the braves returned with a large buffalo, she had gritted her teeth and with determination, helped *Chhawi* strip the hide and lay it out in order to attach it to pegs. She had never worked so hard in all her life. Stretching the hide over the pegs to dry was a grueling process. No wonder the squaws seemed old before their time. She wasn't even nineteen and already her skin appeared brown.

Keshini glanced up to connect eyes with the chief. His lips spread thin crinkling his eyes in an approval grin. She returned his smile and stood. After stretching sideways several times to get the kinks out of her back, she turned toward *Chhawi* to help with whatever needed to be accomplished. There were always never-ending tasks to complete before evening settled in.

Horse hooves pounding the earth drew her gaze in their direction. Several riders headed straight for the chief, coming to an abrupt halt. The bare-chested Indian jumped from his pinto while speaking in non-coherent syllables.

She shook her head. She'd never fully speak their language, but most importantly, she didn't want to forget her own either. The excitement in the young brave's tone kept her attention. Could it be the Rangers? What else alarmed him enough to speak in such an urgent tone causing the people to gather around him?

The chief spoke a few words, and then turned, and said no more than two words to the gathered group. Immediately, the entire village rushed about, moving in a manner of importance.

Keshini frowned. She found *Chhawi* bending over the fire pit with a water bag. The smoke curled up into the air the second the water extinguished the fire.

"*Chhawi*, what's going on?"

Her dark eyes glanced up. "*Keshini*, pack. We move camp."

"Now?"

"Now," she stated and poured the rest of the water on the pit. "Come, take down your teepee."

"Why are we moving? Are we in danger?" she asked, stepping up her pace to keep up with her old friend.

Chhawi grabbed the flap of *Keshini*'s teepee, "Buffalo moving. Here," she indicated the edge of the teepee hide for *Keshini* to grip. Within minutes, her home was packed up and ready for transport.

Stopping to catch her breath, *Keshini* glanced around and couldn't believe how efficiently the squaws worked. Within twenty minutes of the chief's announcement, the squaws had stripped their teepees, taken down the poles to tie to the horses to pull the travois, loaded all their belongings, and headed out to follow the men on horseback. She stepped next to *Chhawi*, touched her arm and stopped Big Black in his tracks. "I'll help you up."

"I walk."

"I know you can, but I insist." She stared at her friend. "Really now, you don't want to upset me, do you?" She stood solid, placed her hands on her hips and cocked her head, staring into the dark eyes looking back at her.

"Come on. I know how hard you've worked all day and I'm a hell of a lot younger than you...so, up you go." *Keshini* helped the old squaw onto the mount, then grabbed a blanket and placed it on her leg. "Here, *Chhawi*, the air's cool, take this blanket and cover your shoulders." She gave her friend a quick smile, turned, and led her horse in the wake of the swirling dust of the other packhorses. Big Black snorted under his load.

She didn't really understand where the buffalo went or how the braves knew where to locate them. In all the months she'd lived with the band, she never set eyes on one buffalo. Without asking where they were going, she followed the long line of Comanches for the next several hours. She was surprised to find they weren't the trailing ones. Glancing back, *Keshini* watched one of the squaws veer off from the band and head toward a clump of trees.

"Look *Chhawi*," *Keshini* lifted her chin toward the Indian squaw running away from the band. "Why is she leaving us?"

Chhawi's head turned in the direction indicated and studied her for a moment. "It's time."

"Time for what?"

"Her papoose."

"Baby. By herself?"

The old squaw nodded and turned her gaze back, shrugged and stared ahead. *Keshini* watched the squaw disappear into the clump of trees. Not another soul headed her way to help. After a moment's contemplation, she reached up and grabbed the water bag, handed the lead to *Chhawi* and took off running toward the trees.

Breathing hard, she entered the cool, shaded area and slowed her steps. The fresh breeze touched her damp skin, sending a chill down her spine. With furrowed brows, she stopped and listened. Not far from where she stood, she heard the bubbling brook making its way to the river and back to where their camp had once been. Then, a slight sound connected to her ears, just above the chirping birds.

She quietly headed in its direction. There on a soft bed of grass, she found the squaw squatting with her hands hugging a tree branch. Her white knuckles and labored breathing meant she wasn't far from giving birth.

Keshini bit down on her lower lip. She didn't know what to do. Near the squaw's knee lay a cradleboard and a blanket. She hurried over and quickly took the blanket. When the squaw looked up into her eyes, tears formed and her lips tried to smile, but instead, she squeezed her eyes, pushed her knees up, and before *Keshini* could move, the baby slid from the woman's womb. Calmly, the Indian squaw took her knife, cut the bloody umbilical cord, and lifted it up to *Keshini*.

Her eyes widened. What was she to do with that?

Again, the squaw motioned for her to take the thick, bloody umbilical cord.

Keshini reached with the tip of her fingers, and took it. Her gaze swung back to the squaw. She frowned and lifted her shoulders. The woman pointed to a tree. Holding out the ghastly, heavy cord, *Keshini* swallowed hard and stood, then she strolled over to a branch and hung it on a limb. When she turned back, the squaw smiled. *Keshini* didn't understand why she hung it on the tree, but she knew there had to be a reason. She'd have to ask *Chhawi*.

The mother picked up the tiny, slimy baby, reached for the water bag and washed him. Afterward, she swaddled him in the blanket and handed him to *Keshini*. Then she drank several drops of water, laid back and closed her eyes.

While the mother slept, *Keshini* held the baby close to her chest. She grinned when a sweet little whimpering sound emerged from his rosy puckered lips. The newborn's little round face was pink and chubby, and he had a head of soft, fine, black hair sticking up like feathers. *Keshini's* lips spread wider when a small sucking sound came from the tiny mouth. She'd never held such a small baby—and he wasn't even an hour old. Amazing. He was adorable.

She glanced down at the mother, sleeping with her arms under her head, exhausted. *Keshini* recalled seeing her in camp with two other little ones running at her heels. This had to be her third baby. Maybe the more you had the easier it was to give birth. Still, it had looked painful.

Keshini settled back against the log, stretched her legs out on the ground and studied the baby. Both baby and mother slept peacefully. She took a deep breath and glanced around the serene area filled with chirping birds, warm sunshine flickering on the tree leaves, and the rippling stream making its way through the woods. Her eyelids grew heavy. Filled with contentment, she closed her eyes to the tiny sucking sound from the small bundle in her arms.

Suddenly, her eyes flew open. The baby's *pia* was sitting next to her staring at her with a twinkle in her dark, brown eyes.

"Oh, forgive me, I didn't mean to fall asleep," she mumbled, and handed the baby to the mother.

The squaw grinned and held the baby to her bare breast. *Keshini* took in the small bundle nudging the mother's full breast. Once he was fed, the squaw stood, swaddled the baby and strapped him in the cradleboard. With a glance at *Keshini*, she headed out of the woods and in the direction of the band.

At least three hours, or longer, had elapsed since they had dropped behind the caravan of Comanches. *Keshini* chewed her bottom lip, fearing the going was too difficult to catch up before nightfall.

"How do you know we're going the right way?" she asked, glancing at the squaw. She could tell the mother was getting tired. Stopping short, *Keshini* handed her the water bag.

"Let me carry him for a while. I really think you need to rest."
She knew the *pia* didn't understand her. *Keshini* gestured to the
baby in the cradleboard.

"Look," she motioned with a nod toward the west. "The sun's
going down. We really should build a fire and keep the baby warm.
Please, you can't go much further." She frowned and bit her
bottom lip. The Indian squaw hadn't understood a word she said.
Giving birth appeared painful and strenuous, and if she walked any
farther, the mother might drop from sheer exhaustion.

The sound of horses drew *Keshini*'s gaze. *Chakotay*'s long,
black hair waved in the breeze, riding toward them with one other
rider. The sight of him warmed her heart.

As the chief approached, his eyes connected with hers before
shifting to the woman and the bundle strapped to her. Both
dismounted and the one, who appeared to be her husband, guided
her to his horse and helped her mount behind him.

The chief took her hand to help her up onto his horse. "You
ride with me. We need to get to camp before dark."

Chapter Seven

Keshini circled her arms around *Chakotay's* waist and when the horse jerked forward, she hugged him tighter. They rode at a hurried pace and by the time *Chakotay* led them across an extreme, desolate ocean of grass, *Keshini* realized the band had gone much farther than she had anticipated. How the Comanches could know where to go in this dry, dusty plain was beyond her. Their chief led the horses through the trees and back toward the river stream. After following along the riverbanks, they came upon the camp.

Keshini's gaze scanned the camp area site. Teepee after teepee was in place, not looking any different from their old village. No one could guess they had traveled miles and miles and arrived in the late afternoon to set up a new village.

Glancing back at *Chakotay*, *Keshini* raised her shoulders, and asked, "Now what?"

"Your teepee is through there." He took her hand and led her through the maze of teepees until *Keshini* laid eyes on her own teepee with its familiar design painted on its side. She loved the wolf painting the Comanche Shaman had painted for her the day after she and *Chakotay* returned from helping the grey wolf. "Oh my heavenly days, *Chhawi* must have put up my teepee. How sweet."

His dark eyes drilled into hers. "She knew your cause for dropping behind the band."

Keshini neared the door flap of her teepee, stopped and gazed directly into his eyes. "I…I appreciate you coming for us. I was afraid the baby might get sick before—"

"Comanche babies are healthy. She's a good mother. Tonight the child will be blessed."

"How?"

"Ceremony."

"For the baby?"

"The medicine man will light a pipe and his name will be revealed."

"Can I come?"

The chief studied her. "Don't talk. Squaws not allowed."

"I promise, even though I'm *not* a squaw." *Keshini* slipped into the teepee, leaving him standing with an opened mouth, which she was sure was about to dispute her statement.

Chhawi, squatting near the fire, looked up, and smiled. She continued to stir a pot of stew without questioning her about the baby.

Unable to hold back, *Keshini* dropped next to her and chattered, "Oh *Chhawi*, I can't believe what I witnessed today. A tiny papoose was born in just minutes and is so sweet. I can't believe how strong Comanche squaws are and after a little rest, she got up and started walking. I was so worried about the baby getting sick from the cold weather, and the mother, wow, she was getting tired, and then there was the chief. He came for us. How did he know…"

Keshini read the twinkle in her eyes. "You…you told him, didn't you?"

Her lips spread thin and instead of confessing, she handed a bowl of stew to *Keshini* and settled back with a satisfied grin on her face.

Keshini shoved in a mouthful of stew and chewed with her thoughts on the events of the day. She swallowed, and then asked, "You know, she handed me the umbilical cord and had me hang it on a tree. Why?"

After eating another spoonful of stew, *Chhawi* looked at *Keshini* and stated, "Comanche believes if the baby's cord is hung on a tree and not disturbed before it rots, then the baby will live a long and prosperous life."

"How interesting. Oh, *Chakotay* said the medicine man will name the baby. Why?"

Chhawi stood, took a blanket and handed it to her. "That's the way of the Comanche."

"So what happens during the ceremony?" *Keshini* asked, reaching for the blanket that was handed to her. She threw the cover over her shoulders with her eyes on her friend.

"Comanche's most precious gift is their children. The medicine man will pray for him and give him a name."

"Why? Shouldn't the mother and father have some say in naming their child? White men always name their own children."

When the drums sounded, *Keshini*'s eyes widened. "Can we go?"

Keshini followed *Chhawi* to the ceremony area where all the elders and chiefs were in a circle around a large fire pit. The squaws were standing in an area off to the side in the shadows.

Loud drums prolonged their beating rhythm until *Keshini*'s heart pulsated along with its rhythmic pattern. A low chant from all the Indians seemed to be repeated over and over.

What are they chanting?" she whispered in the old woman's ear.

"*Numunuu*. Meaning the Comanche are the Lords of the Plains."

Keshini shuffled in closer so she could watch and wished she could understand the words. *Chhawi* moved closer to her and whispered in her ear, "Squaws not allowed."

"What's he saying now?" she whispered back.

"*Parabio's* calling the father of the child."

"Who's *Parabio*?"

"The old Indian next to the medicine man. *Parabio* is the peace chief, very experienced and gives advice, makes decisions."

Keshini's gaze looked over at a bare-chested Indian stepping forward from the shadows and the *pia* who had given birth just hours ago strolled close behind. The father held the baby out in his hands toward the circle. The medicine man took a long draw from the pipe, passed the smoking pipe to the one next to him, and then took the baby. Each member of the council blew a swirling smoke into the heavens. When the smoke floated upward from the earth the medicine man held the baby up toward the sky.

The pipe made its way around the circle. The medicine man's Comanche words flowed from his lips in a chant-like song, all the while lifting the baby toward the north, south, east, and west. *Keshini* had never heard anything sound so beautiful.

"Tell me, what's he chanting?" she whispered without taking her eyes off the ceremony.

"A prayer for the child. Each time he lifts the child it's a sign for him to be happy and healthy while growing to be a loyal Comanche."

After lifting the infant four times, his gaze looked upon the father of the child and he said, "*Duranjaija.*"

Chhawi leaned closer to *Keshini*. "He's been named *Duranjaija*. His name foretells his future."

"I don't understand. How can a medicine man foretell a child's future?"

The old woman lifted her shoulder and in a matter-of-fact tone said, "Any child can grow up to be a great hunter and warrior if his name suggests courage and strength, even if he is sick or weak. Comanches expect great things from their children because they're the most precious gift given by the spirit."

"What does his name mean?" she asked, curious.

"A heroic son."

Touched by the deep, spiritual ceremony, *Keshini* blinked to keep her eyes from filling with moisture. The medicine man returned the baby to its father, who in turn handed him to his *pia*. A proud beam glowed from her face when she took the papoose, cuddled the baby in her arms, and walked out of the circle toward her teepee.

Keshini turned to follow *Chhawi* back to her teepee, but stopped short. The baritone voice of the chief filled the night air. Curiosity stopped her from leaving. What was happening next? Turning back she observed the powwow council where *Chakotay* stood speaking to the *Parabio* who sat next to the medicine man. She grabbed *Chhawi's* arm and mumbled, "What's going on now?"

Chhawi's gaze swung toward the council and listened. Her brown, wrinkled face appeared to be stunned and her brows pulled together. Moving close, she whispered in *Keshini's* ear. "The chief's asking permission to wed."

When an unmistakable mummer escalated around the circle, she swung her gaze back to the council. They were all talking at once in their language. Negative tones and words indicated their disapproval of the chief's request.

All fell silent when their *Parabio* spoke in a curt demanding tone. All eyes were on him, waiting.

The old woman stepped forward intently listening, and then, she shot a sharp glance her way.

Keshini had an uncanny suspicion the intense dialogue was all about her. "What's going on? Who does he want to wed?"

Chhawi's brows lifted high onto her forehead. She whispered, "You."

Keshini gasped, her head jerked back. Swinging her gaze around the circle of the most important Comanche leaders of the band, her stunned, wide eyes couldn't believe what just happened. She shook her head.

"Nooo...I'll not marry that man," she spat out loud enough for the circle of Comanches to hear every word.

Chhawi grabbed her arm. "*Keshini*, Comanche women are not free to choose the one they marry."

"Fine. Great for Comanche squaws." Her irate gaze drilled into her friend. "I am not a Comanche." If the so-called warriors wanted to dominate their squaws...well, fine, but they very well would not dominate her. She was white.

"No matter, the council decides."

"No they won't," *Keshini* lifted her voice for all to hear. Before *Chhawi* could tighten her grip, *Keshini* jerked her arm free, marched out of the shadows, and stomped into the circle of Comanches and up to their *Parabio*. She pressed her lips and squinted eyes aimed straight at him. Clenching her hands, she spoke assertively and emphasized the words she intended them to understand. "I will *not* marry a man when I'm *not* in love with him. I *choose* who to marry. Do you understand?"

Keshini swirled and pointed to *Chakotay*, "Tell him."

His brow lifted.

Aaah...*Keshini's* brows pulled tight, she turned back to the elder. "I'm not a *Comanche*, I'm a *white* woman and we do *not* have to marry because we're *told* to."

When the council's *Parabio* spoke, *Keshini*'s gaze swung toward *Chhawi*. "What did he say?"

Wide-eyed, she shook her head.

"He said you have fire in your eyes." *Chakotay's* lighthearted tone revealed his amusement at her display of anger.

Dragging her gaze from *Chhawi* to the chief, she swirled back to the *Parabio*. "Of course, I'm angry. You can't control me."

The chief spoke to the council members, who she assumed was translating her words, but when the *Parabio* answered him, laughter rang out among the councilmen.

Keshini's boiling blood heated her face. How the hell could she talk to people she couldn't even understand? She turned, shot the chief a defiant glare, and marched off toward her teepee, leaving behind her loud, echoing laughter.

Quickly slapping the flap back, she stomped into her teepee and dropped onto her bed of blankets. She wanted to cry she was so mad.

"My *Keshini. Keshini. Keshini.* "

She raised her head to find her old friend gently whispering her Comanche name while stepping through the opening. She moved to the fire pit, put a log on and sat near. "*Keshini, Keshini,* you will need to spend time in deep thoughts over this matter."

"*Chhawi*, what have I gotten myself into?" She pushed to a sitting position and studied *Chhawi* for a minute. "What are you telling me?"

"There are worse things than marrying a chief."

"Why marry someone I don't love?"

"This has nothing to do with love. Your choice could shape your life with the Comanche."

"If you don't wish to wed the chief, the *Parabio* will choose another person for you to marry. If you don't agree with another, you will spend your life alone, without child or mate. You will then become a burden on the village for you will have no man to bring you food and shelter."

Keshini watched the woman, who once had a life as Martha, push to her feet to leave her alone with her thoughts. Her shoulders slumped, realizing she once had a different life too, Clare Rose's life. She curled up under the warm hide and closed her eyes. After several long minutes, her eyelids flew open.

"Oh my heavenly days." *Keshini* threw back the hide and sat up. The harder she tried to fall asleep the more awake she became. Reaching for a log, she tossed it into the fire pit, edged her way back underneath the hide, and stared at the growing flames.

Should she marry the chief? If she intended to be one of them, she had to start her new life some way. Besides, she did like him. She might learn to love him. Otherwise, she'd grow old with the band of Comanche while working and laboring away the days. The other women in the camp seemed to be happy and enjoy their family life. Could she have the same and live a happy life as a Comanche's wife?

* * * *

Early the next morning, *Keshini* stepped outside her teepee and discovered she was the only person up and about. That was a first. While she added firewood to the pit, she squatted near, waiting for the small flames to eat away the new logs. She lowered her head into her hands, closed her eyes, and took a deep breath, thinking over her restless night. Finally, in the wee hours of the morning, she had come to a decision. She opened her eyes to the flaming blaze.

A pair of moccasin feet strolled into her vision. She raised her head to stare into the dark eyes of *Chakotay*.

How the hell did he walk so silently? She glanced around. They appeared to be the only ones stirring in the breaking dawn.

"You're up before the *taabe*."

She swung her gaze toward the east and stared at the brightness of the rising sun. She nodded and glanced back into the flames. "I had a decision to make."

"Have you?"

"Does it matter?" she asked, fixing her eyes on him again.

He squatted several feet from her, but didn't release her gaze. "Matters to me." He glanced down, picked up a stick near his foot, and poked the fire like a small boy needing to distract himself while waiting for his mother's response.

She stared at him, surprised that he cared about her decision.

Chakotay gazed into her eyes and said, "If you become my squaw, it will be because you made the choice to do so and the spirits will bless us."

Keshini frowned. "Why do you want me?"

"You have strength and courage. You are blessed with a kind heart. I will honor what you decide." He stood, tossed the stick into the fire, turned, and walked away.

She watched him. Huh. He thought she was kind. Had she changed?

She never considered herself a kind or compassionate person. She thought back about the Clare Rose Coulson girl growing up around folks knowing she was the granddaughter of the founder of Silver Sage Creek. Had she been kind or thoughtful? No…arrogant maybe, and self-centered, but kind? No.

Had living with the Comanche changed her?

She stood. "*Chakotay.*"

He stopped, turned and connected his large black eyes upon her. "I'll marry you…on one condition."

He slowly strolled back toward her, and, with a lifted brow, he waited.

Keshini pressed her lips, cleared her throat, and then stated, "I…I know Comanche warriors are allowed to have more than one wife. I'm white and always will be. Therefore, if you marry me, I'll be your *only* wife."

From the expression on his face, she thought he was about to laugh, but instead, he said, "Agreed."

Taken back with his agreement, she nodded. "Well then, that's settled, so when do you think this will happen?"

"I will speak to the *Parabio.* Soon." He walked away, indicating the talk was over.

Keshini's mouth dropped. He had nothing else to say. She stared at her soon-to-be husband until a hand touched her arm. *Chhawi* smiled up at her and gestured for her to follow.

This was the first time she'd been in *Chhawi's* teepee. Much like hers, with a fire pit in the center of the earthen floor, it was cozy, warm, and inviting. Her wrinkled, frail looking hands lifted a white buffalo hide from a large woven basket in the far corner of the teepee. She looked at *Keshini*, held the hide up against her, and smiled. "This will be your wedding dress."

"Oh, it's beautiful. A white buffalo skin. I don't understand. How do you make the hide white?"

She shook her head. "No making white skin. White buffalo...rare sight to see. Special. Only a few have set eyes on a great, white buffalo."

With gentle hands, she spread the hide over her bed, pulled out a bead pouch, and sat down. "*Chakotay's* father traded for this. I saved it for my daughter to wear on her wedding day." With several beads selected, she laid them out in a design.

"Daughter?" *Keshini*'s stunned voice was barely above a whisper. She sat near with her eyes glued to her friend.

"My baby girl didn't have a chance," *Chhawi* mumbled. Her sad eyes rested on the soft, pure, white buffalo hide. "The day before she was born, her *ahp* and several others went out to hunt for the celebration, but never made it back."

Chhawi's rough, labored hand gently rubbed the soft fur. She looked up at *Keshini*. "My baby died two days after her father was killed. No matter, it was a lifetime ago. Now, you will wear it for me."

Keshini threw her arms around her friend. "I'm so, so sorry, but you have your son, *Chakotay*."

Chhawi nodded. "He's always a true son, though not blood."

Keshini's eyes widened. "Oh, I thought..." Tears blurred her vision as she gazed upon *Chhawi* digging into the pouch for more beads, shaking her head.

After several moments of sorting through the beads of many shapes, sizes, and colors, she spoke softly, "No, his mother died during childbirth, and the chief took me for his wife to raise his infant son."

"I...I didn't know. Then, *Chakotay's* a full-blooded Comanche?"

Chhawi nodded her head, and then shot her eyebrows up and giggled.

"What's so funny?"

"You."

"Me?"

"You commanded the chief to have only one wife. I never heard anyone demand a Comanche chief do anything."

"Well. No woman in her right mind shares a husband."

Sad eyes gazed into hers. "I would have."

"I'm sorry."

"Don't. Think about your wedding. This hide will be beautiful with your red hair. Now, which beads are we to use?"

Chapter Eight

Several days later, *Chhawi* slipped the white buffalo dress over *Keshini*'s head and spoke casually in her soft voice. "During the council's powwow last night, they announced the chief's wedding ceremony will happen tonight."

"Tonight. Good heavens, can't they give a woman a little time to prepare?"

Chhawi shrugged. "For what?"

Keshini opened her mouth to object to not being informed, or given the time to back out, if wished, but quickly clamped her lips together. What was the point?

With a leather thong, *Chhaw* gathered a thin strand of *Keshini's* hair and braided a slender scalp lock to hang down the side of her face. She attached a single feather at the end of the lock, stepped back, and nodded her approval.

Keshini, once a white woman named Clare Rose Coulson Montgomery, walked out of her teepee holding *Chhawi's* arm. She sucked in a nervous breath of cool night air, glanced up at the diamond twinkles in the heavens, and wondered if this was all real. Had she been thrown into another life by mistake? Where was her world? A falling star sliced across the universe whispering its powerful force, telling her to follow the road destined for her.

Many of the squaws stood in a line near her teepee. *Chhawi* tugged on her arm and smiled at her. She skimmed her gaze over grinning squaws and past the blazing fire pits reflecting light on the entire band of Comanche Indians, and the *Parabio* who all expected to wed their chief and the white woman. Straight ahead, her gaze circled the council members and *Chakotay* waiting for her to approach.

Keshini strolled toward the circle and stopped several feet from *Chakotay*. He stood. His straight, black hair hung down his back. He stood tall, wearing a loose-fitted buckskin shirt, decorated with fringe hanging from his shoulders, and colorful beads in a wolf design covering the sleeve of his right arm.

She wasn't sure what to expect, but it certainly wasn't what happened next.

Chakotay said several words, which *Chhawi* interpreted, "Since the white woman has no family, my gifts are presented to the *Parabio*."

He stepped toward several horses tethered to a pole. "These I give to you." The chief stepped back into the circle and sat down.

The *Parabio* nodded, lit a pipe, took a long draw and passed it around the circle. Each Comanche council member took a puff before passing to the next. The last to inhale from the pipe was *Chakotay* at which time the *Parabio* nodded. The chief stood, walked to *Keshini*, took her hand, and led her to his teepee.

She glanced back at *Chhawi*. *That's it?*

Standing inside the chief's teepee, flames from the fire pit lit up the walls around them. *Keshini* stared at him. His black eyes reflected sparkles from the blaze, staring back at her. He waited.

She didn't move.

He stripped his shirt off to reveal his brown, muscular chest.

She blinked and glanced around the teepee.

Slowly shaking her head and chewing her bottom lip, she lifted her brows. She took a quick breath and spoke. "Wait a minute. That's it? We're married?"

His eyebrows lifted. He nodded.

"I'm only worth a bunch of horses? I don't even get to say a word, or even be recognized at my ceremony, which in my opinion was no *wedding* ceremony."

His massive muscular shoulders lifted. "What more is needed?"

Her feet began to pace on the soft, hide-covered floor. She stopped, faced *Chakotay,* and slapped her hands against her thighs.

"I don't know. I've been married before, you know. I wore a long white, silk dress with a beautiful head cover streaming down my back. I had a chance to confess my love and approval of the person I married. We had music, singing, dancing, and food. But, this...this..." She swung her extended arm around to indicate her frustration.

"Good heavens...I'm the bride, *me*..." she poked her finger into her chest, "...I didn't even take part or speak a word. Huh, I could have waited for you in this place and have not even shown up for the likes of this kind of ceremony."

"This is the Comanche way."

"Fine. Now what?"

Before he answered, drums started filling the night air, along with chanting from the medicine man and laughter. The band celebrated their wedding; only no wedding couple was present.

The chief grinned. "Now you have music."

"Great."

To *Keshini*'s disbelief, *Chakotay* stripped his moccasins off, and, without hesitating, he shoved his pants down and stood before her in all his gorgeous, brown essence. Her mouth dropped. Her eyes widened, staring straight at the object below. Now she'd be able to tell Sally and Betsy what a man looked like, but it was too late. She couldn't draw her gaze away, and then he turned. Not the least bit self-conscious, he crawled into bed and looked at her, expecting her to do the same.

Keshini glanced around. There was no place for her to retreat.

Well, she'd not undress the way he did. No respectable woman slept naked. Reaching down, she slipped out of her white moccasins and stepped toward the bed. She sat down, scooted her feet beneath the cover and glanced at the chief.

As if knowing her thoughts, he sat up, reached over and pulled up her dress until it slid over her head.

Keshini quickly covered her breast and slid down. Waiting, she laid flat and stiff. Remembering all that Jonathan had done, she knew what to expect.

When *Chakotay*'s hand touched her breast, she jumped. She hadn't expected him to touch her, only mount and start pumping. He didn't. His hand slid along each breast, gently and softly, touching each nipple. She shivered. *Keshini* closed her eyes, aware of a building excitement in her loins. Her uneven breath shook with excitement, triggering a reminder of the thrilling sensation she'd experienced when the Ranger looked at her with his wicked desires.

His hand slithered over her stomach. When his hand traveled down between her legs, her eyes flew opened. Wow, Jonathan never did that. His large, rough hand pushed her legs apart. She obeyed. His finger slipped inside her. Her legs jerked together.

He stopped and waited.

Sensing his patience, she slowly spread her legs open again.

The sensation of his finger inside her body hurled tingles up her stomach. Her beating heart pounded to the beat of the drums outside their teepee. Heart thumping, short of breath, awareness exploded in her body, telling her to squirm and wiggle beneath his hand. Self-conscious, but about to give in, he pulled his finger out and mounted her.

She waited for his long hardness to enter her. This she remembered from Jonathan. But when her Indian husband gently slipped inside, her body reacted in a different way. His thrusting, along with the beating drums, intensified the awe running through her blood. *Chakotay's* rhythm became the beating sounds of the drum outside their teepee. She couldn't stop her back from arching up against him in such a primitive manner, wanting him to go deeper inside her. New and exciting sensations traveled over her body. Was this what her ma had intended for her to experience on her wedding night?

In seconds, *Chakotay* released a moan. His body trembled, he went limp over her, took a deep breath, and rolled off to her side.

That's it? She lay still and listened. From his soft breathing she knew her new husband had fallen asleep.

Keshini lay still. Tears formed. What was wrong with her? What had she expected? Something more? She rolled over on her side, wiped away the tears, and vowed to not forget what she disliked about being married.

* * * *

Keshini knelt to check on the sundried deer hide. A slight grin spread her lips. Pleased with herself, she straightened and wiped the sweat from her brow. She admitted she was proud of the work she had done. Even *Chhawi* had remarked favorably on her painstaking efforts in accomplishing an excellent end result.

Though it had taken her a couple of weeks to learn the drying and soaking process, she had achieved the hardest thing she'd ever had to do. Gritting her teeth, she had tackled the bloody innards and scraped away the fat and flesh without vomiting from the stench. She even learned to rub down the pelt with a mixture of animal fat, brains, and liver to soften the hide without gagging.

Her gaze swung to *Chhawi*. The sweet, old squaw had become more like a mother. She knew if the old mother hen hadn't taken the chick under her wings, *Keshini* might never have adjusted to the Comanche ways. *Chhawi* was a good teacher and without her, she was sure none of the other squaws had time to show her how to smoke the hide over a fire to produce its light brown color, or make blades from bones and antlers, or many of the other uses the animals offered to them for their continued existence. Now, she understood. All animals were sacrificed for a reason—their survival.

Since her wedding night, *Keshini* realized her days blew by like the wind. Now holding her own, she worked hard alongside the other squaws while *Chakotay* and his braves rode out each day. By the time the hunters returned with their fresh kill, there was more to do.

Much to her surprise, marrying the chief proved to be the best advice *Chhawi* had given her. Everyone respected him, trusted him, and followed his leadership, and being his wife made her proud. She bent and dropped another log into the fire pit.

Thundering horse hooves brought her head around toward the sound of the hunting party returning. Several small children took off running past her to greet the braves with eagerness. She grinned at their excitement, stood, and waited for the Comanche hunters to halt their painted horses in the middle of the village. Quickly dismounting, they showed off their kill with pride and moved out of the way so the squaws could take over and prepare the carcasses.

Keshini stared at the chief strolling toward her. Her heart did a little flip. His upper body was bare, showing off a reddish-brown skin with rippling muscles. His long, buckskin leggings fit his muscular thighs and were held up by a leather belt tied around his waist. His feet, covered with moccasins of knee-length, buffalo-hide boots, strolled right toward her.

In all her life, she'd never seen so much skin on a man. At first she'd been embarrassed seeing the little boys running around camp without any clothes. Now staring at the chief, her husband, in his buckskin, she didn't have to wonder what an adult male looked like any longer. *Keshini* forced her gaze to connect with his wanting eyes and waited for him to step near enough to speak to him.

"Good hunt?"

He nodded, reached down, took her hand and led her to their teepee. She knew what he wanted. After every successful hunt he came back all excited and wanting to bed her.

* * * *

Keshini glanced at her husband. His eyes trailed over her naked body. A shy smile spread over her lips. "What," she asked when he continued to observe her sliding a long, deerskin dress with long sleeves over her head.

He shrugged, moved slowly off the bedding, and stood over her. He fixed his eyes on her. She had become accustomed to his approving looks after they made love.

To her surprise he touched her hair and said, "For many months you hurried under the cover before undressing. Now, you are no longer ashamed of your beauty. That's good."

She reached for her moccasin, and with a quick glance at him, she tried to explain. "Well, white women living in Silver Sage Creek never stand naked before anyone. I didn't, not even with Jonathan, my husband, or any man, or woman. It's just not proper, but...but here, things are different." She slipped her other moccasin on and turned to leave when his hand touched her arm. She gazed into his eyes.

"My squaw, the body is a beautiful gift from the spirits and should be held in high esteem. Comanches are not inhibited by all the proper standards of a civilized society." He waited for her response.

She nodded. "In many ways, your culture is far more gifted in the ways of living, and more refreshing than the white man's customs. Actually, they could learn a few things from the Comanches."

Chakotay followed her out of their teepee and took off toward the men tending the horses while she continued to her duties. She squatted and stirred the soup mixture and let her gaze roam over the village and all the activities going on. Laughter echoed from children playing and having fun, and she could hear the squaws talking in high spirits in a lighthearted manner. *Keshini* bit down on her lower lip. These people weren't silent, sullen, reserved savages, the way the white man portrayed them to be. They were men, women and children, not Indians, but human beings with deep convictions and love for their families.

Since she'd become the chief's wife, the band had accepted her in many ways, especially the squaws. They were more at ease around her, and more relaxed, chatty, and cheerful, releasing their true colors for living and loving. Even the children were no different than those at Silver Sage Creek.

Keshini stepped from her teepee, stretched her arms and scanned the village. Dawn dwindled away, allowing the rising sun to light up the morning sky with its soft, yellow reflections on wispy clouds floating high above. Thin columns of smoke crept from the smoke holes of the teepees to ascend in the still morning air while squaws casually strolled about carrying water and wood to start fires. Once again, the day's preparations for meals had begun.

She waved at *Chhawi* exiting her teepee. Several braves hurried from their teepees at the moment *Chakotay* stepped past her with a blanket covering his naked body. She smiled and watched him join the other men to head for the river, followed by some of the male children. The first time the Indians had dropped off their blankets and plunged into the icy water, she'd been embarrassed. But now, she knew it was a custom they indulged in to make them healthy and tough. She laughed at the first yelp, recognizing *Chakotay's* voice. When the rest of the braves squealed like little children the second their naked bodies sank into the ice-cold water, she giggled.

Before she could join *Chhawi*, a loud scream echoed through the camp, drawing her gaze in the opposite direction. *Keshini* took off running. The terrified scream sent her heart pumping blood faster than she could breathe. An image of Betsy flashed through her mind. By the time she passed up a multitude of teepees, *Keshini* slowed her steps at the sight of several men standing by a teepee. The teepee belonged to the *pia* she'd helped when the squaw gave birth on the trail to their new camp.

When *Keshini* took a step forward a hand grabbed her arm. *Chhawi* held her back, shaking her head.

"What is it?"

With a frightened look, she shook her head.

In lightning speed, the husband dragged his wife and his two young children from their teepee, then his rushed actions sent the flight of a burning arrow into the air landing on their home. Within seconds the flames consumed the teepee.

"Where's the baby," *Keshini* heard the panic in her own voice. She whirled, searching through the crowd. "Where's the baby?" she whispered to *Chhawi* while the fear inside trapped her breath with the awareness of what was happening. "He's dead. Isn't he?"

Without acknowledging her nod, *Keshini* swung her gaze back to the black smoke bellowing up into the sky. She stood frozen watching the flames lap up the teepee and the tiny baby inside. Somewhere in the back of her mind, she heard the grief of the mother's cry while the leaders of the band made their way from the river to gather close enough to assess the reason for the turmoil.

Keshini squatted near her fire pit outside her teepee, away from the tragedy. She stared into the dark soft eyes of *Chhawi*. She didn't even remember walking away, or sitting near the fire…as if nothing had happened.

"*Chhawi,* what happened? I don't understand. Why did they burn their teepee because the baby died?"

"If it's sickness, all had to be burned. A sickness can travel through a camp fast. Entire bands of Comanche have been wiped out by sickness."

"Are you talking about cholera?"

Chhawi shrugged her shoulder. "Any sickness, even smallpox."

Keshini had heard stories of Indian tribes being completely eradicated by cholera when she was a little girl. At the time, she didn't think much of it. Never had she considered an Indian mother's grief when her baby died. Now she knew better. She'd never forget the heartache in the grieving mother's scream.

She listened. The village was quiet and some distance away the men had congregated, murmuring in low tones. Now what? Fever outbreaks leave many dead. She turned her gaze on the squaws standing near their teepees waiting for instructions.

When their heads swung around in the directions of the plains, only then did she hear the sound of an approaching horse, riding into camp. He barely stopped the horse before sliding off its back and sprinted straight toward the group where the chief stood.

Keshini pushed to her feet. Something had transpired. Something critical.

Before *Keshini* could question the old woman, an elderly Comanche who they called Chief of Peace, stepped from the group and with a raised voice, spoke.

"What did he say?" She whispered to *Chhawi* without taking her eyes of the elder.

"Come, time to move."

Not a moment to spare and no time to question, *Keshini* knew she'd have to wait to find out what was really going on and why the urgency to move again. Her gut told her it wasn't the buffaloes.

Like the wind sweeping down from the canyon, and with amazing proficiency, each squaw did her job. They moved very quickly and quietly, without a sound. Not even the small children cried out. Within twenty minutes they had packed up and headed out toward the mountains.

Keshini wasn't fast or skilled like the Comanche women, and though she had managed to adapt to her new life in so many ways, she still had much to learn. Reaching up she gripped a pole with all her might causing the teepee to tumble. Once the poles lay on the ground, she dragged them to her horse.

"Whoa, Big Black, don't move, I'm supposed to tie the poles on either side of you, so…so, don't move. Ohhhh…" The poles slipped from her hands. She jumped back.

Big Black turned his head with the whites of his eyes glaring at her. She glared back with her shoulders drooping and arms hanging straight down, she wrinkled up her nose at the horse.

"I know, if you could talk, you'd tell me how to do it." She took an exasperating breath and bent to pick up a pole. Suddenly *Chakotay*'s hands reached in front of her and took the pole from her hands and in seconds had tied the poles onto Big Black. Without a word, *Chakotay* gave her a slight smile and walked off. She turned her gaze at Big Black looking at her. "I know, load the travois so you can get going."

Once the last bag was tied securely, *Keshini* looked around to see if any one needed her help. She could tell *Chhawi* was struggling with her poles. After watching *Chakotay* tie hers, she figured she could do the same. Running to aid her friend and with both their hands, they were able to accomplish the task in no time. Once the bags were tied securely on the packhorse, they headed out of camp to catch up with the others, trailing somewhat behind.

Keshini's brows drew together in a tight line. She glanced back. Why the urgency? Rangers. What if they found them? Her heart skipped a beat. What if her Ranger found her? Would he take her home? Home to what? How many deaths had to happen for her to be rescued? She stepped up her pace. They needed to hurry.

The traveling day stretched out until the sun drifted down behind the mountain. The woods thickened with a hushed darkness, and yet, they kept moving. *Keshini* could tell her old friend was tired from her slumped shoulders revealing a weariness they all felt. She was glad all the squaws were given horses to ride instead of walking alongside the packhorses. They continued onward. She wanted to tell her husband to stop, but he knew more than her of their danger and how far they needed to travel. All night, if needed. The children had to be hungry, but not a cry sounded from their mouths.

Keshini halted her horse when she noticed the caravan slowing to a stop. Up ahead she could hear a low murmur from a rider making his way down the line. She waited. Without speaking to any one person, he rode closer, giving an order. Thankful, *Keshini* understood his blissful words, "Rest. Sleep on the ground."

She dismounted Big Black and quickly moved to *Chhawi* to help her down from the horse. Her frail, boney body leaned into her hands. *Keshini* grabbed a blanket off the back of the horse and spread it out near the poles. She helped the *Chhawi* down onto the blanket and in no time her eyes closed in a deep sleep.

Quickly retrieving her own blanket, she covered *Chhawi,* and then lay down beside her. Her body quivered. Wow, every muscle tingled from exhaustion. She stared up into the dark sky; with its moon drifting down in the west, twilight hovered near.

Chapter Nine

Keshini leaned her tired shoulders against a tree and took a deep breath. Traveling with little rest had finally come to an end. Why did it take so long to find a safe site? All she wanted to do was return to a normal life and quit moving so often. It was hard. But nothing about a Comanche's life was ever normal. Her shoulders slumped when her gaze scurried around the village. The fever continued to spread, mostly attacking the very young and the elderly. She couldn't remember the last full night's sleep she'd had. Nursing the sick kept the healthy ones busy day and night. Now, the only thing she wanted the most was to crawl beneath the covers and close her eyes to drop into a deep sleep.

Far too many had fallen sick. The fever had now claimed the young mother of the baby who had died first and her two little ones, leaving her husband alone without any of his family members. She'd lost count of the elderly deaths during the last three weeks. The medicine man was summoned to one teepee after another throughout the days and far into the nights.

Keshini leaned her head against the tree and looked around for *Chhawi*. Come to think about it, *Keshini* hadn't set eyes on her dear friend for several hours. She frowned. Every minute of her time, along with *Chhawi*, she spent trying to give aid to the sick, day and night. Her friend appeared tired and drawn yesterday. No one could keep up such pace without rest, especially *Chhawi*, as she was old. *Keshini* heaved in a deep breath, pushed her tired muscles to her feet, and hurried to her friend's teepee.

"*Chhawi*, are you in there? Can I come in?" *Keshini* waited. A soft moan sounded from inside. Her brow wrinkled. Pushing back the flap, she stepped in. A panic button flipped her heart cadence upward the moment her gaze landed on the frail body lying on the bedding. Her entire body shook.

"Oh no. Why didn't you call for me?" Quickly she grabbed a water bag, rushed from the teepee, and hurried to the stream.

"What's wrong?"

Keshini stopped short to the sound of her husband's voice. "*Chhawi* has the fever."

His troubled expression swung toward the squaw's teepee.

"*Chakotay,* are there more sick ones?"

His gaze turned on her. A solemn nod and worried expression told her the fever was spreading rampantly throughout the camp.

Tears gathered to blur her vision. "Will it ever end?"

"I'll get the medicine man."

"Please hurry." She took off. How were they to survive this sickness?

For the rest of the night she sat next to *Chhawi*. Using a damp cloth, she wiped her forehead and covered her with more blankets when the chill took over, shaking her body badly. *Keshini* gently raised *Chhawi's* head and touched her lips with medicine water trying to force her to swallow. She coughed and spewed out the liquid before it was able to do any good.

By the middle of the night, *Keshini* slipped out of the teepee and looked around. She wasn't the only one awake. Several braves sat around the fire pit, murmuring in a low pitch, while some paced in front of their teepee waiting to see if their loved ones made it through the night. A young mother at the far end of camp clung to a tiny, wrapped body, desperately crying when the father forced the baby from her arms.

Keshini searched the faces hovering around the fire pit. No sign of the medicine man among the braves. She hurried toward a small group sitting around the campfire and found *Chakotay.* She didn't take her eyes off her husband's approach.

"Where's the medicine man? You were supposed to get him to *Chhawi's* teepee. She needs more medicine."

Chakotay took in a deep breath and pushed it from his lungs and stood. He appeared to have the weight of the world on his shoulders. His head hung low and without a word, he took her hand and led her back toward *Chhawi's* teepee. He stopped in front of the opening and faced her. "*Keshini,* our medicine man is dead."

Her head drew back. "But...but, who's to care for the sick. Who knows what medicine to give them?"

"Do what you can. Help her make her way into the new life with ease. "

"No, she'll not die." *Keshini* jerked her hand from his and slipped inside the teepee. Kneeling by the old woman's side, she folded her hands and whispered, "Please Great Spirit, if you exist, let my friend live." A tear rolled down her cheek. She dropped her head onto the bedding and whispered, "Please, please, please."

A gentle hand rubbed her hair. She lifted her tear-stained face to stare into weak brown eyes. Thin frail lips tried to smile and when her wrinkled small hand reached out, *Keshini* placed her hand in hers. Then, *Chhawi,* her white-Indian friend named Martha, took her last breath.

Tears bumped into each other streaming down *Keshini*'s cheeks. Blinded with grief, she dropped her head, threw her arms over her most precious friend in the world, and wept. What was she to do without this dear, dear friend? She never told her she loved her. She did, she truly, truly did.

Sometime later, *Keshini* looked up to the sound of the teepee flap opening, expecting to see *Chakotay*, but instead, the Indian she always called Chubby entered. When his gaze touched the body, he quietly stood still and motioned for her to come.

She shook her head. She certainly didn't want to try and help another sick person when there didn't seem to be any hope. His sad expression furrowed his brow. He turned and left. She rested her head near the old woman's body and closed her eyes.

Later, a gentle hand touched her shoulder. With swollen, red eyes *Keshini* looked up into the eyes of *Chakotay*. "Come, we must take her to rest."

"Where?" she whispered, staring down at the still body.

Keshini rode on Big Black, following the long procession ahead of her. Their Chief insisted *Chhawi* lay to rest with many others in a cave hidden far into the mountain. She wanted to bury her in the ground and put a cross over her grave, but *Chakotay* denied her wishes. All the words she argued did not change his mind. *Chhawi* was to be buried the Comanche way. She finally agreed. *Chakotay* was right. The old squaw had lived a Comanche longer than she had ever been a white woman.

When they return to the village, *Keshini* expected the people to burn *Chhawi's* belongings the way they had done the others. But no one made a move to do so.

"Why haven't you and the others burned *Chhawi's* teepee?" She whirled around, but the only seemingly individual to understand was Chubby. His sad eyes said it all.

"Is it because she was a white Indian? Huh?"

He stared into the fire pit.

"I know that's what you call us…all of you do." *Keshini's* piercing rant drew many of the braves, gathering around to hear.

"You," she pointed at the circle of Comanche, "kidnap us, and then expect us to learn your customs, but without actually accepting us. Well, the old woman took on your Comanche ways, learned to live your way, and even took a husband according to your traditions. And, so have I. Not only did she live the Comanche way, you even had the gall to call her *Chhawi*, a Comanche name."

Keshini whirled and marched into *Chhawi's* teepee, grabbed her few belongings, and rushed out into the opening. She piled everything in the fire pit. After waiting for the items to set ablaze, she turned back, pulled the poles down and ripped the teepee and dropped the bundle on the fire. Her disgusted glare turned on each one, and then she returned and hauled the poles over to the fire.

Tears blurred he vision when she stared down at the poles in her hands. The harder she tried to break the long poles, the more her tears flowed. Chubby walked over and took the poles from her. She looked up into his understanding face and stepped back. He took his hatchet and split all the poles and handed each piece to *Keshini* to throw into the fire.

The blaze shot out, burning all the remains of the white-Indian who had befriended her and helped her adjust to the Comanche ways. *Keshini* dropped to her knees and stared into the flames, and without shame, she let the tears flood her face in grief for the squaw she loved and who had meant so much to her.

A small, timid hand touched her shoulder. *Keshini* turned her gaze into a little girl's dark round eyes. Her comforting gesture was so sincere she knew she had cared for her friend, too. Chubby pushed the child aside and motioned for *Keshini* to follow him. She frowned and glanced at the child.

Chubby pulled her arm.

Despondent, she rose to her feet, wiped her face, and followed him. He didn't wait for her, but expected her to follow him to her own teepee.

Keshini's heart sputtered to a stop. She caught her breath and gave Chubby a questioning glance, but she knew…*Chakotay* had come down with the fever. Before rushing inside she ordered, "Get water."

He took off.

The chief had fallen prey to the sickness and *Keshini* desperately tried to save her people's chief. When Chubby entered she quickly took the water bag and motioned for him to leave before he became another victim. Giving *Chakotay* what was left of the medicine water proved easier than with *Chhawi*. He drank and kept it down, but when his body started shaking with the fever, she didn't know what else to do. She held deerskin up against the fire to heat the hide, and then covered *Chakotay* to warm him. He moaned and tossed about. His trembling became worse and out of control. Chills shook his entire body. Desperate to save him, she slipped beneath the covers and held his naked body against hers. Frantically, praying for the Great Spirit to use her body heat to help him heal.

In the darkest hours of the night, his fever shot up, burning his body. Crawling out from beneath the covers, the only thing she could think of was to put a wet cloth against his face, neck, and rub his chest down with cool water. Finally, he calmed down enough to sleep, and then a few hours later, his body shaking started all over again.

Two days she stayed by his side. If it hadn't been for Chubby, she wasn't sure how she'd last. He constantly peeked in on her several times throughout the day and night bringing water and the small amount of medicine remaining. On the third day, *Keshini* fell asleep holding *Chakotay* in her arms.

Keshini slipped on her moccasins, bent and listened to *Chakotay's* slow, relaxed breathing. For the first time in two days, she stepped from the teepee and glanced around. She didn't know who to talk to since no one except *Chakotay* understood English.

She strolled throughout the village and studied her people. Who could she talk to? How many more had died from the sickness? Had all the old and young died, leaving the healthiest behind? Please let it come to an end.

She squatted near a fire and warmed her hands. Why hadn't she grabbed a blanket to throw around her shoulders before taking leave of their teepee? *Keshini* felt a slight tug on her braid. Turning her gaze, she recognized the young girl who comforted her after *Chhawi's* death. Her small hand reached out and touched her hair again.

"What's your name?" *Keshini's* soft voice asked. This was the first time any of the children dared walk up to her much less touch her.

The small girl pointed at her and said, "Clare."

"Yes, how did you know?" The girl grinned, but didn't say anything.

It had to have been *Chhawi.* She glanced around. *Chhawi* probably told everyone her English name and no telling what else they knew about her. For the length of time she'd lived with them, she didn't know any of them. Only *Chhawi.*

Keshini nodded and pointed at her chest and said, "Clare, but call me *Keshini.* What's your name?" She pointed at the small girl's chest.

A woman reached down and took the child's hand. *Keshini* stood and gazed into her eyes. When the woman said, "*Lillooset,*" and looked down at the child.

Keshini repeated, "*Lillooset.*"

The small one grinned.

When the mother handed *Keshini* a water bag and indicated for her to drink, she took several swallows and handed back the water bag. "Thank you…ah…*нra.*"

The squaw took her hand. *Keshini's* eyes widened and allowed the squaw to lead her to a teepee. She stood outside the opening while the squaw ran in with her daughter who had scurried ahead of her. In no time, she exited with a bowl full of stew.

"Oh my, how thoughtful." *Keshini* blinked away the tears blurring her vision.

The woman pointed toward their teepee and babbled so fast she didn't understand the words, but understood what she wanted her to do. *Keshini* nodded, took a step back, smiled and turned in the direction of her teepee.

When she slipped quietly inside, she found *Chakotay* sitting up. "No, no, no, no, you can't get up. You have to rest." Hurrying to his side, she knelt before him and handed him the broth. "Here you go, this will give you strength."

"I must see to my people. They need me."

"Not at this moment. Eat."

He looked at her with a lazy, raised brow. She lifted the bowl to his lips.

"I took a walk around camp. It appears the worst is over. I can't be sure how many passed on, because I can't find anyone to speak my language."

"I will teach you our language." His voice sounded weak, though he tried to appear strong for her sake.

"After you're better, now sleep until tomorrow." Taking the bowl from his hand, she helped him under the cover, and in a short while, the chief was sleeping more peaceful than he had in the last couple of days. She stepped out, took a breath of fresh air, and decided to stay outside for longer than a few minutes.

She spent most of the late afternoon gathering firewood and boiling what little meat they had left. Silently slipping back into the teepee, it appeared her husband hadn't moved, but breathed in a restful rhythm. Feeding the fire for the night, she took off her fringed dress and moccasins, and slipped beneath the cover next to her husband. He was warm. Cuddling down against his bare skin, his warmth seeped into her body. For a long time, she stared at the flickering fire licking at the logs, before finally allowing her eyelids to close in a deep sleep.

* * * *

Keshini woke before sunrise, dressed, and stepped outside the teepee. *Chakotay* needed to sleep and rest for a while longer. Once awake, she knew, duties to his people called, no matter how weak his body. After scanning the camp, she stepped near a woman stirring a mixture in a pot hanging over the open fire. When the squaw looked up, she mumbled a Comanche word. *Keshini* didn't understand indicating with a shrug. The squaw squatted near and glanced inside the pot. She repeated the same words.

"Meat. Meat?" Her eyes widened. *Keshini* glanced down and said, "There's no meat."

She stood, looked around, walked to another fire pit where a few more squaws were cooking. They had no meat either. The sickness had prevented the men from hunting.

Once again *Keshini's* gazed out over the camp looking for the braves. Drawing her gaze back to several squaws standing around the fire, she touched one's arm and asked, "Where are the men?"

They stared back.

"Braves?" she demanded, swinging her arm around to indicate the area.

The women started blabbing all at once. Holding up her hands, she shook her head. "Right, they're out hunting buffalo. Could take days. I'll be back." Quickly running toward Big Black, *Keshini* stopped to pick up a bow and arrow near her teepee and hurried to mount her horse.

Riding deep into the trees, she finally halted Big Black, and silently glanced around the dense, dark forest. She slid from the horse, hesitated, and stood still. Her fingers squeezed the bow. She shuddered. This was crazy, what the hell did she think she could do? She only knew she had to do something to help. If her people continued to eat not much more than berries and nuts, they'd surely have a reoccurrence of the fever, and eventually, wipe out the entire village. Even though the men were out hunting, she knew they could be gone for days before they succeeded and headed back.

The sound of a deer caught her senses. Her head swirled in the opposite direction. Tiptoeing forward, she squinted to get a better look between all the deep foliage. There he stood, looking around. He was young, but fat.

Keshini placed the arrow in the bow, pulled back on the string and stared into the eyes of the deer. She waited. He took off. Her arms dropped, tears gathered so fast she could no longer see the running deer. Quickly wiping the moisture from her eyes, she stepped over a fallen branch and continued to move quietly through the forest.

There he was again. This time she didn't hesitate. Raising the bow, she pulled back the arrow and released it without taking her eyes off the animal. He dropped. She stood frozen in the spot staring at what she had just done. Now what was she supposed to do?

Hurrying to her trophy, *Keshini* knelt, reached out and touched his chest. His labored breath struggled to take in air. She glanced into his eyes. Large, gentle eyes stared back, asking *why*.

"Oh, I'm so sorry." Tears flooded over her eyelids, down her face, touched her lips opening to release a wailing cry. "I'm sorry, I am sorry."

Not wanting him to suffer any longer, she pulled the knife from her belt, and whispered, "Thank you for feeding us. If there's an afterlife for animals, I pray you will be there." Then, she quickly ran the knife over his throat.

Keshini leaned back against a tree, folded her arms over her legs and pulled them to her chest. She dropped her head and released a loud cry for the living animal she had just killed.

Finally, running out of tears, she took in a shuddering breath and hollered for Big Black. When he made his way to her, she took a rope, tied it to the deer, mounted and headed back to her village.

The moment Big Black trotted into their village, she didn't have to holler at the squaws. At the first sight of her, they came running. Untying the rope from her horse, they immediately started gutting and preparing every part of the deer. One of the younger squaws came up to *Keshini* the moment she dismounted. *Keshini* could tell she was thanking her for what she had done for them.

As it turned out, the hunting party didn't return for three mornings. The braves entered the village with successful kills, bringing home three large buffalo, but *Keshini* could tell they were stressed and anxious about something.

"Why did it take so long for the men to bring back the buffalo?" she asked *Chakotay,* thankful he was getting stronger with each day's passing.

"Buffalo moving on. Winter feed is sometimes hard to find, so the herd moves more."

"So are we breaking camp?"

"Soon."

Chapter Ten

Two days later, they broke camp. Many were still weak and recovering from the fever, but they knew the weather was threatening and winter closing in on them. To make it through the winter, they needed to follow the buffalo before the snow covered the plains, or got too deep near the mountain bench to travel.

Big Black snorted under the load he carried while *Keshini* walked along at his side. Swirls of dust danced behind packed horses following the line of Comanche. Most all horses were used to carry packs and those people recovering from the fever, leaving a few to walk. Going was slow. So far, cold wind blew constantly, and the bellowing, grey clouds promised moisture soon.

She walked alone. She missed her friend.

Now there was no one to talk to except her husband, but he was busy leading the band. A chill ran down her back. Strong wind bit into her skin, stinging. With a jerk on the deerskin, she pulled it snugly over her shoulders and pulled Big Black to a halt. Her hand flew up to wipe away a tiny white flake. Squinting against the cold, she took a quick glance from under her hooded deerskin. She blinked away more snowflakes. Why couldn't the white storm wait until they settled camp? She wiggled her toes to keep them from getting numb and glanced down. The moisture covering the ground made it hard to keep the wetness from seeping into her moccasins.

She blinked away tiny, white specks blowing into her face and peeked through her eyelashes at the other women. Surely they were exhausted, too. Their heads hung low, hides pulled tight around their bodies, moving forward in slow, steady paces. No one ever complained; no matter how worn-out, tired, and worried, they moved forward, trusting their leader to follow the Great Spirit's guidance to the place for them to settle for the winter.

The entire band showed signs of fatigue, no wonder, traveling for two straight days tested their strength and stamina. *Keshini* slowed to a sluggish pace and shivered. Gripping the lead tightly, she took steps forward. Big Black followed. "Come on boy, we can't get behind." Her voice was lost in the wind. Cold crept into her body, draining her energy. She hated winter and this was only her first winter with the band, and she had no idea things could be so hard and rough.

Big Black stopped. She glanced up. The long caravan stood waiting. She breathed a sigh of relief, waiting like the others. They all needed to rest.

The flakes were getting bigger and heavier. She squinted through blowing snow and recognized Chubby speaking to some of the squaws ahead. No sooner had he spoken, but the band of women broke formation and scattered. *Keshini* stood staring. They talked too fast for her to know what was going on. She waited.

Some of the babbling squaws disconnected the travois from their horses and began the laborious process of setting up their teepees. It appeared they had finally found a place to set up their village.

Keshini's gaze studied an area not far from the stream, and yet, large enough space within the Quakes and oak brush. The stream was close by, plenty of trees to shade them and protect them from the wind, and visible below was the wide-open plain where the buffalo roamed, she hoped. What she really wanted to do was to go off near the woods and be by herself. But, her husband was the chief and needed to be alongside his people.

Within a short time, *Keshini* had set up her teepee and knelt to dig a pit near the opening. A boy touched her arm and mumbled. He pointed to her teepee, said something, and then pointed to the sky. He spoke again.

She turned the palms of her hands up to indicate her dilemma. "I'm sorry, I don't understand." Smiling, she glanced up and nodded. "I know a storm's brewing."

"He's telling you to dig the pit inside the teepee first."

Keshini's head swung to find *Chakotay's* slow saunter advancing toward her with a black buffalo hide wrapped over his shoulder, flapping in the wind.

"Why?"

"The snow's coming and the meals will need to be prepared inside where it's warmer."

She nodded, nodded at the boy, stood and stepped toward her husband. "Is this place suitable for our teepee?"

Without taking his eyes off her, he said, "It will do."

"Well, I wasn't sure. After all, you are the chief. I wasn't sure if there were some regulations for placing your teepee. *Chhawi* always helped me set up our teepee. I never thought about where…until now." *Keshini* looked down. Sorrow consumed her for a moment. Her gaze swung out toward the plains.

With drooping shoulders, *Keshini* searched the terrain, squinting through the blowing snow. They had moved farther south. *Chakotay* told her this was their last move until spring. Where then? Farther south again? Farther from the white man's world? Where were they in comparison to Silver Sage Creek? They'd moved, what, twice now, no three times. Were they still in Texas territory, or were they closer to Mexico? There was nothing for her eyes to see expect rivers of grasslands running onward and onward until meeting the sky. And, danger, she was sure, from *Mexicanos*.

She'd heard her pa talk about Mexico and how they raided and killed the Indians. She trembled. The thought of anyone killing *Nemene* sent a nervous tremble through her blood. She shivered.

"You are sad?"

She glanced up at *Chakotay*. She'd forgotten he was standing at her side. She shrugged. "I just wondered how far south you'd keep moving us. Don't you get tired of moving so much?"

The wind whipped her hair against her face. *Chakotay* reached out and gently moved the long strand and gazed deep into her eyes. Before she could say anything, he swung his head toward the plains.

"We move when the Great Spirit moves the buffalo. We're never weary of following or hunting. We go where the buffalo go, until…"

Keshini glanced up into his face when he paused, and frowned. "Until what?"

His dark, serious eyes turned on hers. "White man forces us to move."

"Why? I don't understand. Why can't there be peace among the white man and Indians?"

"To make peace with the white man is to become white Indians, to become like an arrogant society, believing their ways are the civilized way. White men think they're sovereign over the Great Spirit. They hold nothing but empty promises. What I've witnessed, they can be more savage than the Indians I have fought. We will continue to resist the white man's domination. We'll not give up our culture."

She lowered her head. His words made sense to her now, since now, she was a white Indian. Glancing back toward the open plains, she took a deep breath. "Will we ever go toward the horizon?" she asked nodding her head toward the tall grass meeting the sky.

"In due time."

She glanced down at the spear in his hand and up into his face. "Is it time?"

"We must hunt. *Pia utsui mua.*"

She raised her shoulders and shook her head.

"Cold rains and snow with winds coming. What the white man call the month of December. This is the last hunt until the *tahma mua.*" He grinned. "What you call the new spring moon…April, when the green leaves appear on the trees and the sun warms the earth. Tonight the council will decide when we leave for our final hunt."

"How long will you be gone?"

"*Wahaatu* or more." He held up two fingers.

Keshini understood. "If you don't come back for two days, where will you stay? Do you need more clothes?" she asked, taking in his long buckskin pants, knee-high moccasins, and the thick buffalo hide covering his shoulders.

"The Great Spirit has the power to make us strong and show us where to find shelter and food. The mother of all spirits will guide us."

"Mother of all spirits?"

"The Earth," his tone indicated she should have learned by now how important Mother Earth was to the Comanche. He turned and walked toward his fellow hunters to join the elders in their teepee where the fire burned peyote while they discussed the winter ahead.

Turning, she stepped inside her teepee, knelt down on her knees, and started digging a pit in the ground next to the fire pit in the center of the room. Once dug, she lined it with the buffalo stomach to use for a cooking pot, which *Chhawi* taught her to do. Then, she filled it with water and placed the heated stones from the fire pit in the water to heat to a boil. She had been taught to roast or boil their meats over the open fire. Once the water boiled, she added the last of the Juniper berries, nuts, honey, and a tallow to add a little flavor to the buffalo meat.

While she waited for the meat to cook, she picked up a soft, tanned buffalo hide she'd been sewing for moccasins and attached a hard rawhide sole for better protection during the winter months.

By the time the meat was ready to eat, *Chakotay* stepped into their teepee, and looked directly at her with a dark look in his eyes.

"We leave before the sun rises." A slight smile spread his lips. He strolled over and sat near the fire. With his legs folded in front of him, he leaned over, took a bowl and poured liquid from the water bag. Retrieving a small pouch from his pocket, he untied the gathered top and dropped several small grayish mushroom buttons into the water. He then placed the bowl into the hot ashes, glanced at *Keshini* and reached out his hand for her to sit next to him.

"Now we eat and then give thanks to the Great Spirit."

Keshini folded the hide, placed it inside the basket, and moved across the room. Without saying a word, she scooped a bowl full of stew from the pot and handed it to him. After filling her bowl, she sat next to him and ate in silence.

The wind howled around their teepee, bellowing the sides out and in from its strong gusts. The tall trees surrounding the village sang in a light whistling sound from the whipping force of the wind blowing through their branches.

By the time they had eaten, the liquid in the bowl sent swirls of steam into the air. *Chakotay* leaned over and with the protection of a hide cloth, picked up the bowl and took a taste. After several sips, he held it to *Keshini*.

She glanced at him and obediently took the bowl and sipped. Her face crinkled. The truly bitter liquid slid down her throat. She coughed. "What…what is this?"

"We now wait for the spirit to join us."

To her surprise, *Chakotay* started chanting. He closed his eyes and lifted his hands to the heavens. His words made no sense to her, but their mystical sounds and his voice soothed her mind. While chanting, he held his hands high, rocking back and forth. His long, straight black hair draped over his shoulders from his motion.

He stopped and without looking at her, he chanted a prayer in English. "Great Spirit, give us blessings under your sky above. Lead us into a bounty hunt to return with enough for all *Numunuu*. We will give back in return for what you give us. Your hunters will kill only to eat. Our life belongs to you, Great Spirit. You know we need only buffalo, water, and grasses to feed our horses. There is nothing more from the Great Spirit we need, but to live life as you intend."

He took a drink and handed the cup to *Keshini*. She wanted to refuse, but once she glanced into the chief's eyes, she knew refusing the drink showed disrespect to his Great Spirit. By the fourth or fifth sip, she was beginning to feel the effects of the mushroom-shaped button he'd put into the water.

Keshini took a deep breath to clear her thoughts before she could ask, "What are we drinking?"

"A ceremonial herb called peyote."

"No." She pushed it back into his hands. "That's what the Apaches used to drug me and Betsy."

"We do not use peyote for a drug. It's only used for religious purposes. Do not worry, there's not enough in the drink to make you lose control."

"You're wrong. I can't think straight. My mind's foggy. This is no different than drinking a bottle of whiskey."

"We do not partake of the white man's spirit water. It is evil."

He stood and held out his hand. *Keshini* reached up, placed her hand in his and let him pull her to her feet. She swayed toward him and giggled. "I have to tell you, your peyote stuff is definitely a bad button."

With his help, she made her way to the bed, but had to sit while he slipped her moccasins from her feet and lifted her dress off her shoulders. She allowed him to pull back the deerskin covers so she could crawl in and wait.

Fire crackled in the pit, sending shadowy images over the teepee walls appearing like large ghosts, swaying back and forth with each gust of wind. *Chakotay* slipped from his leggings and quickly pulled his shirt from his body.

Keshini stared at his rippling stomach muscles. The reflection from the fire lit up his skin to a beautiful, golden brown sheen. For the first time ever, she wanted him to make love to her, to say words of love in her ear, to declare his love to her.

Keshini fixed her gaze on her husband's body crawling into bed. She wanted him to touch her. To make passionate love to her.

She closed her eyes. "Whew! *Chakotay*, your peyote drink makes me feel warm and fuzzy all over." She grinned, scooted next to his side and hugged her arm over his chest. Her breast pressed into the solid muscles along his side, triggering a pleasing sensation shimmering over her body. His skin against her nipples sent a quiver down through her abdomen. She'd never experienced such a splash of stimulating senses. She liked sleeping naked. Skin on skin made one want to do the act, an act she had thought repulsive at one time.

Her hand rubbed over his muscles rippling down over his stomach. Daring to travel further, she slithered her palm down until she took hold of his long, hard shaft. His breath sucked in and before she could feel and touch him more, he mounted her and slipped inside so fast she couldn't react. No passionate words, no touching, no kissing, and after several quick thrusts, he moaned, rolled over and fell asleep.

Keshini lay stiff, gazing up toward the top of the teepee where an opening allowed the smoke to pass through. She followed the slight grey stream drifting up and out.

She pressed her trembling lips together to dwarf the need swimming within her body. A lone tear escaped the corner of her eye. Slowly she took a long slow breath, clamped her jaws tightly, and to rid her body's needs, swallowed hard, rolled her back to her husband's deep soft breathing and listened to the howling wind.

* * * *

A sour taste woke *Keshini* with a start. She jumped out of bed, wrapped her naked body in a blanket, and rushed outside the teepee toward the trees. Barely reaching a concealed clump of trees, she bent over and spewed out the bitter sickness in her stomach. After throwing up the vinegary matter several more times, she began to feel somewhat better.

Daring to make her way back to her teepee, she remembered the sickness had killed so many only a short while ago. What if she was getting the fever? She didn't feel hot, only sick to her stomach. Then, she recalled her night of peyote. That's what made her sick. Never again. *Chakotay* could drink his stimulating liquid, but, religion or not, she had the right to refuse. She didn't care if it was a religious ceremony tradition—it wasn't hers.

Keshini stopped at the opening of her teepee and glanced around. The weather had turned worse. Clouds had darkened into large, grey pillows. Very few squaws ventured from their teepees. Her gaze scurried toward the corral. From the mounts remaining, she knew the hunting party had taken their leave. A couple of days, maybe more before they'd return. *Chakotay* never woke her to let her know they were heading out. The moment she entered her teepee, she dropped on the bed, covered her naked body, and fell back to sleep.

Late afternoon arrived by the time *Keshini* woke. Again, her stomach went queasy when she pulled up. Dropping back on the bedding, she stared over toward the flames. She frowned, waited until the queasiness subsided, and then pulled to her feet. Her shoulders slumped. Squatting, *Keshini* picked up a log and dropped it onto the smoldering fire. She shivered.

The wind had become silent. Along with the grey sky above, her thoughts were overcast with sadness. Why, because she missed her husband when he left to hunt? Yes, she did. And, she missed *Chhawi*, her best friend. Indian friend, anyway. Betsy and Sally used to be her best friends. Fear squeezed inside her brain and trampled over her heartbeat. What if she forgot her life before this one, once old like *Chhawi*? And, like *Chhawi*, forget her own English name.

She grabbed a stick, poked the fire licking the log and spoke out loud, "My name is *Clare Rose Coulson*, I was born in Silver Sage Creek, on November 24, 1840 and married Jonathan Montgomery on July 2, 1858 when I was a woman of eighteen years."

She paused, and then stated, "I had a birthday last month. I'm nineteen." *Keshini* dropped the stick onto the fire. "I'm a nineteen year old squaw." She hung her head, and then, stood and crossed the room to her bed. Snuggling down in the deerskin, she closed her eyes and drifted into a deep sleep.

A shiver ran through her body, waking her. Only a few sparks flickered in the fire pit, barely giving any light in the dark teepee. Crawling from beneath the covers, *Keshini* hurried to throw more wood on the cinders, squatted, leaned over, and took in a big breath to blow several times to help start the flames lapping the wood. With her eyes on the flames growing, she picked up a blanket, threw it over her shoulders, and glanced at the bellowing walls. She shivered. She hated winter.

The howling wind blew stronger with each gust. The snow was on its way. Unable to find a reason to stay up, she crawled underneath the hides and watched the fire build, warming her teepee. *Chakotay* always made sure the fire never went out during the middle of the night, but he was gone. She missed him.

Chhawi, you were right. Marrying the chief had been the right thing to do. He's good to me. She giggled. I suppose he's like all males, he wants to mate more than I do, but I suppose it's meant to be when one's a wife. I guess it has something to do with breeding. I wish you were here to talk to, *Chhawi*. I miss you.

What if she did become with child? There was no reason to think she couldn't. Did she want to have a child in this harsh terrain? Why not? Didn't all the children in the band appear happy, laughing and enjoying their life? The only life they'd ever known.

Why wouldn't a child be happy? There was always food, warmth and love. Love. Yes, love. These people were a family band showing care and love toward each other. She now believed in her heart they loved her. She loved them, even her husband, though he'd never said the word. He was gentle and kind to her.

She loved him too, but not the kind of love her ma had for her pa. Jonathan said those words all the time, well, not so much after they married. *Chakotay* was different.

He treated her with…with what? *Keshini* thought a moment, trying to figure out why her Comanche husband was a better husband than Jonathan. Maybe, one day she'd figure it all out.

Maybe she hadn't been married long enough to know if Jonathan could have been a better husband. No, their short marriage had shown her a personality she hadn't seen in him before they had married.

A child, huh. Which, *Chakotay* or Jonathan, showed signs of being a good father? Something deep inside of her told her the Comanche chief, already a great leader, showed the best qualities of being a wonderful *ahp.*

She giggled. She'd used a Comanche word for father without thinking about it. Did she want to be mother? A lazy smile covered her lips. The word for mother was easy. *Pia.* The children ran throughout the camp hollering at their *pia.*

A mother, hmm…Keshini yawned, closed her eyes and before drifting off, she whispered, "I'll let you decide Great Spirit."

Chapter Eleven

"*Pia, Pia.*"

Keshini turned her gaze to the small child running toward her. Her lips spread into a wide smile. *Pia*, the one Comanche word she loved the most. She never thought giving birth to a little human could be so rewarding. With opened arms, she squatted. "Come to *Pia*." The dark-haired child rushed toward her with a delightful giggle.

She swung him up into her arms, squeezed him against her chest and stood. *Samarjit* looked so much like his father with his shiny, black hair and golden skin. The only difference was his green eyes. The elder chiefs said he was a special Comanche warrior destined to do great things for *Numunuu*, because he was of two people. The *Parabio* and the elderly chiefs named him *Samarjit,* meaning *victorious in war*. But, she only wanted to protect him from those people bordering on so much sadness and cruelty.

"Come on, say goodbye to your *ahp*. We must send him off with the Great Spirit to watch over the hunting party and return with many buffalo."

The moment she set eyes on the chief, *Keshini* experienced a proud rush, knowing her husband and the father of her son sheltered, fed, and protected them and all his people. Three years ago, *Chakotay,* swollen with pride, had strutted around the village like a peacock announcing the birth of their son. Reaching out, he took his boy into his arms.

"My little brave, you are the chief while I'm gone. Watch over your *pia*. We will return in two or three days." His gaze swung to her and then down to her protruding abdomen.

Keshini touched the swell in her belly and felt the heat rise up her neck. She knew what he was thinking. They'd be blessed with more children. He told her the Great Spirit rewarded him with a loving family by giving him strength to protect them and the entire village.

A small thump beneath her hand drew her gaze. She grinned. Without hesitating, she reached out, pulled *Chakotay's* hand, and held it against her stomach. When she gazed up into his black eyes, she read his emotional amazement of the life within her belly. Secretly, she hoped to give him a daughter this time. A daughter could wear the white buffalo dress *Chhawi* had made for her wedding day.

He quickly glanced around and pulled away his hand. *Keshini* laughed. The Comanche men never wanted to appear weak or submissive to their wives. She knew better. All the family men showed so much love for their wives, but in a crowd they had to appear domineering.

"I'm glad you're taking Big Black. He loves to run and I never get a chance to ride." She reached up and rubbed the horse's black nose, and then took her son from *Chakotay's* arms, and said, "Say goodbye."

The quiet boy grinned, waved at his father, and reached out to pat the horse. *Keshini* stepped back and held *Samarjit* close until the band of Comanches rode off to accomplish yet another hunt.

"Down." The boy squirmed in her arms.

"My little one wants to play, huh?" The instant his feet touched the dirt, off he went to find his playmates. She smiled and headed back to the fire pit to finish the meal she had begun.

Though the sun was shining in the east, the chill in the air spoke of winter too close for her comfort. She didn't like cold weather. Staring ahead at the squaws working diligently near their teepees, children running in playful laughter, and the elders smoking their pipes in little groups, her mind drifted. During the wintertime, Ma and Pa sat inside their cozy, warm home, and she had cuddled in front of the hearth and listened to her ma's soft voice read from the Bible. If she still lived in Silver Sage Creek, she…

Keshini's gaze swung to her child. She couldn't go back. Not now, not ever. As a white Indian, she had a family and her destiny was being a white Indian until the day she died, like *Chhawi*. She'd die with the name *Keshini*, the one with the beautiful hair.

Keshini pulled the heavy fur hide close around her shoulders and glanced out beyond the grassland sea quivering against the cold wind. The men had been gone for three days, long enough to return with their kills. Once they arrived there'd be so much to do, which she was looking forward to, for their supplies had run low. After the first two days, the squaws had no hides to sew for winter clothing and meat for stew. They were all ready to dig into the kills and prepare every strip of carcass needed before the winter storms closed them in for several months.

Keshini continued to stare through the sea of grass toward the horizon. She worried about *Chakotay's* decision on moving in the spring and knew he also had conflicted thoughts. If they moved farther toward the sinking sun, they'd leave harsh winters behind. But, traveling farther south drew them closer to the Mexicanos and in the open pampas grasses, unprotected.

"Go horsy."

Samarjit waved at her the moment she glanced around. He rode on one of the old horses used to teach the young boys how to ride. She grinned and waved. An elder walked along side, speaking.

Every little brave, at the age of three years, became acquainted with the skills of riding. She was amazed to see how he loved horses and showed no fear. *Keshini* waited until the elder chief approached. He stopped and waited for her to reach up and pull the boy from the horse.

"Time to eat. Are you hungry?"

"Yeah."

"Give the horse a pat on the nose and tell him you'll see him later."

Samarjit reached up and touched the horse's nose and said, "Bye, bye." She smiled at the elder before he turned and walked away leading the horse.

Keshini placed *Samarjit's* feet on the ground. She giggled. Half the time he spoke English words and Comanche words in the same sentence. With his little hand in hers, she led him inside their teepee. He sat near the fire with his legs folded in front of him and waited. *Keshini* scooped a bowl of broth for each of them and squatted next to him. Once he gulped down the soup, he yawned, crawled onto the bedding, and closed his eyes.

Her gaze lingered on him for several minutes. Thank you, Great Spirit for blessing me with such a remarkable child. She blinked, covered her mouth in a wide yawn and listened to the soft wind sending its cold waves toward them. They'd had a couple of days with the sun's warmth, but according to the squaws, they'd soon be enclosed in winters' freezing arms. Being with child easily tired her. She stretched out on the bed of hides next to *Samarjit* and pulled the fur over them. Her body needed rest, too. The baby took more out of her than when she carried her little boy. Her eyelids closed. Maybe, when they woke, *Chakotay* would be home.

A terrifying scream and a gunshot jerked *Keshini*'s eyes wide. Had she been dreaming?

Another gunshot.

No.

Scrambling to the opening, *Keshini* peeked out.

Frantic squaws rushed from their teepees with their children in their arms, holding tightly to little hands, all but dragging their tiny feet along the ground, running toward the forest. A group of elders held their bows and arrows in their hands, ready for fight.

Another shot rang out.

A child dropped to the ground. A squaw knelt and gathered the little one into her arms and the scream of grief echoed throughout the village.

Another shot blasted through the air to slam into the mother's back. She dropped with her child in her arms.

Keshini covered her mouth. She glanced back at *Samarjit*. He stared at her with wide, tearful eyes, but he hadn't said a word. She peeked out again, and this time, she recognized the enemy.

The Rangers didn't let up, but fired from their pistols, blasting shot after shot. Bullets slashed through the air toward targets trying to run for cover. Even the children were fired upon like jackrabbits. *Keshini* took a step back inside the teepee. Swirling around, she grabbed a blanket and wrapped her son's entire body. "Baby, do not speak or cry, for *Pia*, can you? Please keep your lips together and do not release a sound!" With tearful eyes, he nodded.

Hurrying toward the opening she peeked through the slit. Her people were running in all directions trying to reach the woods. Holding her precious package, she hurried to the opposite side of the teepee, lifted the corner and crawled out. After a quick glance around, she took off running for the dense forest beyond the camp. If she could just get into the heavy wooded area, she'd find a safe place to hide.

Before her steps carried her far enough, a long, strong arm from high above a horse swooped her up. Trapped in his arms, *Keshini* hung onto her bundle. The horse turned back toward the village center.

The gunshots had ceased. There was no more screaming. The Ranger released her, allowing her to stand next to his horse. She whirled to run. "Try and you'll regret it, missy," came the gravelly voice of the Ranger.

She glanced up and looked straight into the barrel of his six-shooter. She glared into his eyes, stood firm, and held her son to her chest.

Samarjit had not cried out the entire time. She had to keep him safe. Her gaze took in the village of dead women, children and elderly men sprawled out on the ground. Silent tears rolled down her cheeks.

"Hey, Cap'n, found a white woman."

Keshini glanced up at the man with his gun pointing at her. Her arms tightened around her son. The approaching horse drew her gaze. The man on a white horse pulled to a halt and quickly jumped to the ground. *Keshini* fixed her eyes on the familiar face. A face from her past.

"Well, I'll be damned. It's the Coulson woman."

"Are you sure?" asked her captive.

Pulling her gaze from his crystal blue eyes, she scanned the camp of dead bodies. The tears streamed silently down her cheeks. "Why?" her low sickened voice put a frown on his face.

She looked back at the Ranger that once had tried to rescue her. Now, he was rescuing her again. Only she didn't want to be rescued.

"You had no right. No purpose? There was no reason to kill women and children, or the old. Why?" *Keshini* stepped to the man with the gun aimed at her. "Kill me. Now," she demanded.

Captain Burchett reached for her.

She jerked back.

"Captain, we better hurry before the hunting party returns."

The Ranger gazed into her eyes.

Her brow furrowed deeply and turned to the unholy sight before her. Her breath hitched when her gaze touched a small body lying face up, lifeless. She moved slowly with tears silently flooding over her eyelids. Holding *Samarjit* with one arm, she squatted, reached out to the tiny little girl and closed her eyes and whispered, "*Lillooset.*"

Before she could stand, the Ranger quickly stepped to her, took her in his arms and heaved her onto his horse, mounted behind her and circled his arms around to hold the reins.

"Let me go. Let me go, please," she begged.

The bundle in her arms squirmed. She glanced down. "Please." A tear rolled down her cheeks to drip onto the blanket covering her child. She cuddled him up against her breast to let him know she'd keep him safe. Moving to the rhythm of the horse beneath her, *Keshini* bit down on her trembling lower lip, and tried to calm her breathing to help her son to fall asleep.

She looked around at the Ranger with the soft blue eyes. "Please," she whispered. His gaze connected with hers. He blinked and then swung his focus ahead, showing no signs of emotions in his expression. A thought of demanding him to let her go, to return to those they left behind entered her mind, but she knew he wouldn't understand or let her.

The heavy beard hugged his face and his long flaxen curls escaped the dingy, white cowboy hat, worn square on his head. He'd never said a word or acknowledged the child in her arms. With each swaying motion, her body pressed closer to the man holding his arms against her sides. She'd been rescued and he figured he'd done a good deed.

Keshini turned her head straight, bit down harder on her lower lip, and leaned back against his chest, moving with the motion of the horse. Her Comanche life had come to an end. Only the Great Spirit knew what her next life entailed.

What lay ahead? Did her ma still live? What reactions to her should she expect from the white people? Her jaws tightened. Whatever safety measures it took to keep her Indian family…her half-breed son and the baby she carried, safe, she promised to protect them with her life if necessary. She looked down at the small bundle in her arms. He was just a small little boy with brown skin and black hair. Dear God, what kind of life lay ahead for him with the white people?

Five days later, with tired bodies and dirty faces the Rangers and their rescued white-Indian rode into Silver Sage Creek. *Keshini's* tired shoulders drooped. Finally given a horse of her own, she held *Samarjit's* exhausted little body for so long her arm tingled from his weight. He'd fallen to sleep several miles back and she didn't have the heart to move him. Nights without a fire worried her, for she didn't want her son to get sick, but the Rangers kept a keen eye open for the Comanches and fires can be seen for miles. They figured once the hunting party returned and discovered the bodies, and the white woman missing, they'd track them down.

Keshini had kept looking, waiting, and hoping, but *Chakotay* and the braves never showed. And, now, ahead lay a town she had been forced to leave and forced to return to. What was she to do, or where was she to live? Why did the Ranger bring her back? Had the Great Spirit discarded her?

Keshini straightened her shoulders and sat tall on the horse, forgetting the weight of her child sleeping on her arm. For the last five days she had dreaded what lay ahead. Now the moment had arrived.

When the Ranger slowed his horse, she did the same and followed close behind riding down the center of Silver Sage Creek. Faces turned in their direction. Many stopped and stared. The pompous women shook their heads, while the men gaped at her bare, brown legs dangling from beneath the buckskin dress she wore and the moccasins covering her feet.

Her blank gaze skimmed over faces she was sure recognized her red hair, and knew instantly, she was the Coulson girl—a white-Indian survivor.

Keshini fixed her eyes straight ahead.

Yes, she was a survivor. Even if the entire town shunned her and her son, she'd make sure *Samarjit* was a survivor in the white man's world, too. This, she was sure, might prove to be harder than learning to live the Comanche way.

Her gaze linked with the Coulson Mercantile sign. To keep the tears from gathering, she blinked several times and took a deep breath, all the while aware of more townspeople gathering along the boardwalk, gawking at her and the child in her arms.

The Ranger led her to the steps of the mercantile and halted the horses. His head turned toward her. Clear, blue eyes connected with hers for a split second before he glowered at the curious people gathering near the storefront.

Keshini watched him dismount and then step up onto the porch and disappear into the store. He seemed to care. Why? Why didn't he just drop her at the store and leave? For days, he'd kept an eye on her and her son, watching her every move, being the one responsible for her return. He never said a word, but always near, her personal sentinel. For some unknown reason, he did make her feel safe.

Aware of all eyes on her, *Keshini* glanced down toward the end of the boardwalk. Outside the swinging doors, looking in her direction stood the saloon woman, Ruby. She hadn't changed. Hurriedly, her gaze took in the familiar shops. It appeared nothing had changed in the town or the people. Only her.

Without looking directly at anyone else, *Keshini* turned her gaze back toward the doors of the store. No sooner did she hear someone's feet running, her father appeared. He stopped short and stared at her.

Keshini's mouth dropped. Pa's alive and looking well. Reading his dismayed expression, she swallowed hard dispelling her stunned gaze, leaving her face unreadable and emotionless, she hoped.

He didn't say a word, but stood gawking at her in disbelief. Finally, in a voice just above a whisper, he said, "Clare Rose."

A name she hadn't heard in many years. She tilted her head and returned his stare. *Clare Rose*. Well, she supposed it was her name…again.

"Clare Rose," screamed a proverbial voice from the past.

Keshini blinked away the moisture trying to form. Her mother rushed from the store, and for a second in time she detected a spark of happiness flash across her face, but it disappeared so fast *Keshini* couldn't be sure. Her ma stopped next to her pa, grabbed his arm and covered her mouth with her other hand. Neither came any closer, nor did they appear overjoyed at seeing their only daughter.

Samarjit squirmed, and sat up. Instantly, their expression changed to horror when they laid eyes on the child she held so protectively. Irritation swelled inside her chest. Sucking in a deep breath, she said, "Hello, Ma, Pa."

When they didn't reply, the Ranger stepped from the boardwalk and reached up to help her from the horse. Holding her son tightly, she slid down, turned from his arms, and faced her parents.

Now, a growing crowd of inquisitive townspeople pushed closer to see the white-Indian woman who had lived with the Comanches. She held her head high and swung her gaze around the gathering horde. Most showed pity on their faces, or was it repulsion for living instead of dying? She couldn't tell. She turned her gaze back to her parents.

Her mother's wrinkled brow deepened when her eyes trailed down her clothing, and back up to her braided hair filled with colored strings and feathers.

"*Pia*."

Keshini glanced at her son squirming in her arms. He wanted down. He was tired of being in her arms for so many days. She wanted to let him down to run and explore his new town, but she couldn't let him go. Holding onto him kept her mind lucid enough to ignore the rude folks gawking at her while they waited for her parents' reaction. She waited too.

Why didn't they show some kind of long-awaited delight at a child coming home? She glanced back at the horse. God help her. She wanted to run.

The Ranger cleared his throat drawing her gaze. He stood next to her, twirling his dingy, white cowboy hat, with a confused frown pulling his brows together. He looked up at her parents, seemingly uncomfortable with all the silence.

"Mr. Coulson." His voice, slightly edged with anger, ordered, "We should go inside."

In contrast to his tone, he softly curved his hand around her elbow to lead her up the steps, onto the boardwalk, and through the front door.

Once inside, she jerked her arm from his grip and turned to wait for her parents to enter. Her pa closed the door and flipped the open sign to close. He slowly turned toward her.

"Well, Clare Rose, I can surely say, I'm bowled over at seeing you're alive...and...and here."

"I can tell."

Samarjit squirmed drawing her pa's eyes to the bundle in her arms.

She hugged him to her chest. "Is it okay if I let him down? He's been on a horse for days and needs to stretch."

Pa swung his hand out toward the hardwood floor and nodded.

Keshini bent and put his little feet on the floor and removed the blanket from his bare-chested body. She supposed she should be grateful the Ranger had suggested putting him in a breechcloth instead of leaving him naked like all the Comanche children his age. When she straightened she caught her mother's wrenching disgust splashed across her face with her eyes fixed on her belly.

"You're...you're with child," her sickened tone reflected her repugnance of her daughter actually allowing such an unforgivable act.

Keshini's gaze dropped to her protruding abdomen. She rubbed her round belly and looked at her ma. "Yes." She placed her hand on her little one's head, and smiled. "And, this is my son, *Samarjit.* Your grandson."

No one in the store missed her mother's quick intake of breath before she covered her mouth again.

When neither said a word, she turned her back to her parents and gave the Ranger her full attention. "Well, Captain—"

"Do you intend on keeping *him*?"

Keshini's gaze darted back to her pa. Facing them, she squinted through angry eyes and demanded, "Who?"

"That…" He pointed to *Samarjit.*

His cold, condemnation turned her blood into a frozen lake. "*He* is my *child.* Your *grandchild.*"

"But…but…but," her ma's pitched voiced sputtered her disapproval. "Clare Rose, he's…he's…he's an Indian."

Clare shook her head and took a deep, trite breath, knowing very well this was only the beginning. "He's Comanche and mine, which also makes him white."

What had she expected? Certainly, not for her pa to be alive. She glanced at him and knew what the look in his eyes meant. Not only his eyes, but also the townsfolk's eyes…they thought…better she died instead of returning a white Indian with half-breeds.

She bit down on her bottom lip, gathered her son into her arms, and swung her gaze to the captain.

She was taken aback. Captain Drury Burchett's harsh glare aimed at her parents, seemingly riled and annoyed by what was being said.

"Well Captain, what now?"

With clenched jaws and firm set mouth, he dragged his gaze from her parents to her.

"Captain, if you'll give me a horse, I'll gladly return to my village."

"No!" hollered her ma.

Keshini's head whipped around, astounded to hear her ma's adamant reply.

Her grip on her pa's arm turned her knuckles white. "Henry, we can't let her go back, she's…she's our daughter."

The anger in his eyes subsided for a brief moment.

"Ah…look, ah," her pa combed his fingers through his hair and, without looking at her or *Samarjit,* he mumbled, "Alyson's right, you can't go back. We…we still have the land and the cabin. Why don't you go there?" He swirled around, took a lung full of exasperating air, and turned back to meet her gaze. "Maybe you could work here. I need someone to stock shelves."

"Yes, Clare Rose, you can help here and live at the cabin. But, but, you'll need some clothes," she added, taking in her buckskin dress and moccasins.

She looked into her parents' faces and pitied them. It wasn't their fault. Didn't she have the same reaction to the Indians before she became one of them?

She turned to the man who had returned her to another life, and stated, "Captain, your duty is over. You've brought me back, now I no longer require or want your assistance."

Ignoring her request, he pushed away from the counter and with his stare directed at her, he asked, "Where's this cabin?"

"About half hour ride south of town," her pa answered.

"Come on. I'll take you there." His tone indicated a final decision for which she had no say.

Hugging *Samarjit* close, she turned and spread her lips into a slight smile. "Pa, I thought you dead. It's good to see you well."

The doors slammed open violently, rattling the glass in the windows. Heavy boots stomped into the store.

Clare glanced around to set eyes on the man entering. Shock vibrated through her body with such a jolt she nearly dropped her child. She stared into the miserable expression of Jonathan Montgomery. Like her pa, she never dreamed he'd be alive.

"It's true. You've returned."

In a quiet calm voice, she said, "Hello Jonathan." Immediately, she recognized the hatred and disgust in his glare. She stood firm and hopefully stared back with a blank face.

His indignant glare traveled down to her swelling belly, and then to the small boy in her arms. "My Lord Almighty. You have an Indian child and one on the way." With a revolted scowl, he said, "Why did you come back with that?" His head jerked toward the child. "Why?" he asked again staring at her belly.

"Why? You'd rather I be dead?" The strength in her voice surprised her, considering her jumbled nerves twisted into a knot the moment he had stomped through the door.

"Huh." His squinting eyes trapped hers. "Better dead than carrying a beast in your belly. If you had to come home, why did you bring that…that little savage?"

Clare squeezed *Samarjit* close. Wide-eyed, she lifted a brow and drilled her gaze into the man she now loathed. "He's not a savage. He's a three-year-old baby. My baby. So is this one." She patted her stomach.

The captain stepped to her side. Before she glanced up at him she noticed his fist formed a tight ball. "Please Captain, can we go now?" His enraged scowl aimed at Jonathan, warned Clare to keep things under control. "Please Captain, now."

Grudgingly, he took her elbow and led her out the door. Clare didn't give her parents, or Jonathan, another glance. Once the Ranger helped them both onto the horse, she squared her shoulders, pulled the reins, and headed out of town without another fleeting look at a single person. *Samarjit* hugged his small arms around her neck, bringing swelling tears to her eyes.

Chapter Twelve

When Clare Rose finally laid eyes on the dilapidated building in the distance, she pulled back on the reins and halted the horse. She glanced at the Ranger. During the entire ride, he hadn't looked at her, or questioned her about her parents' attitude at her homecoming. Maybe now he understood why she didn't want to return.

She cleared her throat drawing his attention. "There's the cabin. Now, you may take your horse and leave. *Samarjit* and I will continue on foot."

Before he could reply, she slid from the horse, put the little one down to walk, turned her back to the Ranger and strolled toward the cabin holding her son's hand.

"Wait."

Clare glanced back. "Yes, Captain Burchett."

"Keep the horse." With those three words, he turned his horse in the direction of town and rode off.

Bewildered by the Ranger's demeanor, Clare waited until he rode out of sight before walking back for the reins to lead the horse and her son toward what would now, from this time forth, be their home. Within a stone's throw, she stood still on the dry, dusty ground, staring at the unfinished cabin.

Jonathan had never bothered to roof the second room of the building. The years had turned the logs grey and the windows were boarded up, but the door was left wide open.

Dropping the reins, she softly gripped her arms around her bulging abdomen and stepped close to peek inside. A small field mouse scurried across the dusty floor. The only things left in the cabin were cold ashes in the fireplace and the cast iron stove, everything else she and Jonathan had had to start a home was gone. Her gaze rested on the now empty space in the corner where once a bed accommodated her and her husband, reminding her of a time long ago.

What a disappointment her wedding night turned out to be—
not what she had expected. Jonathan pushed into her like his life
depended on...on what...what her ma called "reaching his peak".
Surely women never reached a peak. Afterward, he'd rolled over
and went to snoring. *Chakotay* touched her more and had gentle
hands compared to Jonathan.

Clare chewed on her bottom lip to keep from gasping, and
stared into the empty space. With a curt shake of her head, she
blinked away the memories and took a good look around. From the
appearance of things, Jonathan abandoned the place right after she
was taken. He never wanted to live outside of town and made it
known to her and everyone else he'd have a big house in town one
day.

Keshini, Keshini, when you were a young woman, you were
very, very foolish to think the only thing you wanted in life was to
marry.

"*Pia*." The small, strong voice interrupted her ruminating over
the past. "Yes, my little brave?"

"Is this our home now?"

He was wise beyond his years. She worried about him. Not
once had he asked about the cruel raid on his people, the
murdering Rangers killing his playmates and the elders, or why
they now live in the white man's world.

"We'll make it our home and be happy sweetheart."

"I wanna go back."

Clare squatted, circled her arms around him and hugged him
close. "I know dear, but *Pia* needs us to stay here. We will be safer
here. One day, I will take you back to visit. Can you help me make
this our home?"

His small round eyes looked beyond her. "We have a wood
teepee for a home."

She grinned. "Yes." Clare turned her head and looked at the
cabin in a three-year-old child's eye. He'd only known teepees,
and now, walls of wood.

His dark head of hair framed his round face. His green gaze
shot from hers to the woods, he pointed. "Look, a rabbit."

Clare watched her little one scurry off after the grey, furry
rabbit. Her shoulders slumped while the tears blurred her vision.

He'd miss his little playmates…and…his way of life—a journey of uncertainty. She lifted her head up toward the heavens. "Great Spirit, please help us. He's not to blame for the journey he'll have to take. Please make him strong and wise in order to live in a world where he'll never belong." A chill ran down her spine. Cooling air announced the afternoon quickly moving into evening. They needed something to eat. Pushing to her feet, Clare dug into the pouch hanging around her neck. Hum, enough biscuit for her boy and the nearby creek served them with plenty of water. At first light, she'd hunt for food.

"*Samarjit* help me gather fire wood."

"Fire pit in wood teepee?" he asked, running toward her.

Clare giggled. "Not tonight. Are you hungry?"

When he nodded, Clare sat on the ground near a tree, leaned back and took a deep breath. They needed a good rest, for tomorrow they'd face a long workday. She stared at the cabin, handed a biscuit to him, and mumbled, "Our wood teepee will need a roof before the snow comes."

Samarjit turned his eyes upon the building and frowned. "Ruff," he repeated with a frown.

Clare pointed toward the cabin and explained. "Top."

He slowly nodded, but his frown told her he didn't quite understand.

Realizing they had sat for a long spell, Clare took *Samarjit* by the hand and strolled down to the creek. After quickly washing him off, she dried him with the blanket and headed back to the cabin. She needed to get the wood collected and a fire going.

A pathetic whimper whirled her head toward the corner of the cabin. She stepped back. A black wolf stared back at her with pleading eyes. The animal limped closer to her and dropped at her feet. Before Clare could stop *Samarjit*, he knelt beside the animal. With some vigilance, Clare reached for *Samarjit* and pulled him to her side. He whined.

"*Pia. To'sarre* hurt."

"No my little brave, he's not a black dog, He's a wolf, *isa*."

Clare stared down at the animal, contemplating what to do when she swung her gaze toward the woods and stared straight into the eyes of a large, yellow-eyed, grey wolf. How could it be, was he her wolf, the one she and *Chakotay* had saved? It was. She knew it was him, knew it in her heart. He wanted her to help his mate.

She squatted and gently rubbed her hand over the animal's long body. Dark matted fur on the back of her neck revealed a wound. Looking closer, she found a small hole filled with dry blood. She'd been shot with a small caliber gun. Clare looked the animal in the eyes. Her large, yellow eyes stared back with a plea Clare couldn't resist.

"Let's see what we can do for you." Clare gathered the skinny animal into her arms and stepped into the building. Making the animal comfortable near the fireplace, she stood, and glanced around the empty room. A small tin can lay discarded near the backdoor.

"*Samarjit*, bring *Pia* the tin cup." She pointed

Eager to help, he pitter-pattered across the room, grabbed the tin cup and carried it back to his mother.

"Thank you sweetheart. Now stay by the door and watch her while I run and get water from the creek." He nodded.

Not at all sure of how to help the wolf, but knowing she had to, she hurried out of the cabin and down to the creek. The look in her sad eyes begged her to help. And, how could she resist the plea from her mate. She glanced around. Watching somewhere close was the grey wolf.

Kneeling, she filled the cup with ice-cold creek water and turned to head back. Her heart bumped her chest, stopping her breath in midstream. Inches from her stood the Ranger. "Captain Burchett, why…why have you returned?"

His gaze dropped to her belly. Clare watched when he raised his hand and rubbed the half-moon scar on his cheek.

While on the long ride home, she had noticed he'd touch his scar every time he'd look at *Samarjit*.

"Sir?" she demanded.

Clearing his throat, he slowly shifted his gaze up to hers. "I…uh…I brought back a few items you might need for the night," he stated.

"Such as…"

His shoulder lifted and his head tilted to the side, "Blankets—"

"I have a blanket."

"You'll need more blankets...and...food."

Clare sucked in a long breath and studied him for a moment. His blue eyes didn't stray from hers. With a slight smile on her lips, she said, "Thank you, Captain."

Drury dragged his gaze from Clare's face and looked toward the half-built cabin. A curious brow lifted. "Do you really intend on living in that?"

Of course, where else? Glancing down, she stepped past him without a reply.

"Where's your son?" The Ranger's deep voice indicated his closeness.

"He's with a wounded animal in the house," she stated without turning her eyes on him. Ignoring him, she hurried to the cabin where she found *Samarjit* still standing in the doorway. She entered and knelt next the animal.

Captain Burchett squatted near to take a good look. "That's a wolf. You're lucky he didn't attack you."

"*Pia*—help the *sarrie*."

Clare looked at her son to reassure him. "She's not a dog, little one, she's a wolf, and *Pia* will help."

"She's been shot," Clare glanced up at the Ranger. "Since you're still here, you might gather firewood and get a blaze going while I gather some herbs."

He pulled his gaze from the wounded animal to her, stood, stepped through the door and disappeared. Clare pushed to her feet. "Come, little one. Let's find some healing herbs in the woods. Maybe there'll be some around here like there were at home." Home. Yes, the village had been her home. She missed them. She missed *Chakotay* and the village life.

Clare glanced down at her son. He missed his *Numinu*. Dismissing the treasured images creeping into her head, she focused on her search for the right plant. "Come, we need to hurry, dark will soon overtake the sky."

By the time the captain had a blaze going in the fireplace, Clare had crushed the plant and set it aside. She stared at the wolf, knowing there was a slim chance of her surviving, but she had to try.

"Since the bullet hasn't killed her, infection has surely set in, so we need to get the bullet out before using the medicine."

Clare glanced down at the knife strapped to the Ranger's belt. From her indications, he pulled it from its leather holder and handed it to her. She held it over the flames and when she turned to the animal, Captain Burchett was kneeling over the wolf, examining its wound. He spread the fur away from the entry wound and looked up. "I'll hold his head while you remove the bullet. Unless you want me to."

"No, I can do it."

His gaze swung to her son. "Think you can help me hold his head while your ma tries to remove the bullet?"

"Her."

"What?"

Samarjit grinned. "She's a girl."

Glancing at the boy, a small chuckle slipped from the captain's lips. "Can you hold her head?"

The boy nodded.

"If he...*she,* growls, run."

Samarjit nodded.

Clare listened to the Ranger. He sounded like it didn't matter *Samarjit* was a half-breed. Yet, she knew better. Several times, she caught him looking at her son with the same puzzling look in his eyes as her parents.

When his gaze swung to her, she diverted her glanced down toward the animal. She had the feeling he knew what she was thinking.

With the soft tone he'd used on *Samarjit,* he instructed her, "If she growls, she might start after you. If so, you'll need to put an end to her with the knife. Understood?"

She nodded. Leaning over the animal, she gently rubbed her side. "Be brave *isa,*" she whispered in a calm tone.

Clare carefully cut into its neck until her fingers touched the small metal imbedded in the muscles. She glanced into the wolf's eyes and recognized the suffering pain, but the brave wolf didn't move or make a whimpering sound.

Captain Burchett's gentle voice continued to speak, appeasing the boy and the wolf. "What's your name?"

"*Samarjit,*" he whispered, not daring to take his eyes off the animal.

"*Samarj…Samarj…*what if I just call you Sam?"

"Sam." *Samarjit* repeated and frowned.

"You can call me Drury."

While digging the shell from the wolf's neck, Clare smiled slightly at her son's nonverbal reaction. She took the bullet and threw it into the corner of the room and quickly picked up the herb. After soaking the plant for a few minutes and allowing it to absorb enough water, she packed the wound.

Sitting back, her thankful gaze swung to the Ranger. "The plant will draw out the poison. Hopefully, the medicine will kill the poison spreading through her blood stream. Then, she will live."

"How can you be so sure?" he asked, bewildered the wolf hadn't died already.

"The Great Spirit brought the grey wolf here so his mate could live."

Clare looked up at the Ranger's questioning baffled expression from her statement. She smiled. "Until you live with the Comanche, to understand is beyond your comprehension."

The wolf whimpered and licked the boy's hand. A wide grin spread the young boy's lips, showing off pretty baby teeth. He looked up at his mother with shiny eyes.

The Ranger dropped back against the wall and smiled at her. "What does *isa* mean?"

"What?" Clare frowned, picked up the can, and poured the remaining water over her bloody hands.

"You said, 'be brave *isa*'. What does the word mean?"

She stood. "It a Comanche word for wolf." Clare glanced one more time at the animal, turned, and headed for the creek to wash the rest of the blood from her hands. After plunging her hands into the water several times, she shook them dry, stood, glanced toward the wooded area, and looked straight into the yellow-eyed grey wolf.

She smiled. He turned and disappeared into the dark, thick forest.

Hurrying back to the cabin, she found both the Ranger and her son sitting near the wolf, neither saying a word. The wolf appeared to be asleep. Clare stepped in, squatted at *Samarjit*'s side, and looked up at the captain. Her brows pulled together. The sadness in his expression puzzled her.

He returned her gaze. "I'm sorry I failed to rescue you."

Ah, now she understood. She shrugged. "That was a long time ago. Besides, the Comanche band was good to me."

His forehead puckered. "How can you say such? Comanches are savages."

"No. The Apaches that took me from Silver Sage Creek were savages. They killed Sally and Betsy. At the time I figured they had killed Pa and Jonathan, too. I found out later, the only reason they hadn't killed me was their plan to trade me off to the Mexicans."

"So what you're saying is the Comanches are better savages."

"No. They're not savages."

"You don't mean that—they kidnapped you."

"They saved my life. And, not one Comanche stopped me from running if I had wanted to escape."

"Then why didn't you?" his bitterness cut into her words.

"And go where? The inhospitable surroundings would have killed me before I ever found my way back to Silver Sage."

He took a deep breath, jerked his white Stetson from his head and ran his fingers through his dark blonde strands. "I suppose you're right. I just don't understand how you can defend those vicious animals."

Ignoring his accusing tone, she said, "Not all Indians are the same. Hell, many white men are violent and brutal in ways I'd call wild and savage, too."

His eyes widened. She wasn't sure if it was from her words, or the cuss word she used. It didn't matter. She was somewhat livid at his accusations.

"Did you not ride in several days ago and kill women, children and the harmless elders? Some were my son's relatives."

"Children grow to be killers."

"How can you think of my child in such a way?"

"Every time I look at your belly, I'm reminded an Indian defiled you and needs to be killed."

"I wasn't defiled. I married him of my own free will. He's *Samarjit*'s father."

Drury jumped to his feet so fast, he caused the wolf's head to rise, and a growl snarled from his curled lips.

"How could you marry an Indian? Respectable women would rather die than commit to a Redskin."

"How did you become so callous and so full of hatred toward all Indians…they're human beings, too."

With a deep, enraged tone, his angry glare drilled into hers. "All Indians need to be rounded up and put on a reservation so the government can control them. They're all savages."

Clare hugged her son and in a low demanding voice said, "Get out. Get out. Leave."

Drury glared at the boy, turned, and walked out of the cabin.

Clare didn't move until she heard his horse's hooves fade in the distance.

Chapter Thirteen

Clare's tight lips released a grunt as she strained every muscle in her arms upward shoving two heavy flour bags onto the upper shelf. She dropped her arms, turned, took a deep breath, and searched the room.

Where did he go now? She strolled toward the back door of the mercantile and glanced down the alley. Her son sat in the dirt, splashing in a small puddle left over from the morning rainfall. She chuckled quietly, stepped from the door, and squatted next to him.

"*Samarjit*, what are you doing?"

He looked up and grinned. "P*ia,* call me Sam."

She laughed. "All right, *Sam.*" Well, he did live in the white man's world, she reasoned, he was right and should be called Sam. "Are you making mud pies?"

He nodded and slapped his hand in the muddy water and giggled.

Clare lifted him up into her arms and stood. "Come on, baby, let's wash up and have a bite to eat. Are you hungry?" He swung his arms around her neck. "Whoa," she laughed out, "Don't touch mommy, you'll have mud all over me."

He leaned back and with a devious giggle placed a small muddy finger next to her cheek.

Clare drew her head back and laughed. He was getting bigger and taller and harder to carry, especially with the growing baby inside her. She plopped his bottom down on a stool, straightened, and touched the mud on her cheek. "You little stink, you got me. Just for getting mud on me, you have to stay put so I can wash your hands, and then, maybe *Pia* will give you some cheese and crackers."

After wetting a rag and turning back, she hurried to grab his arm, barely stopping him from climbing down for yet another interest that caught his eye. With a quick swipe against her cheek to clear the mud, she turned her attention to Sam's hands and face, and then she reached up and took down a bag of crackers, cheese, and berries, which he devoured in a few short minutes.

"Now, my little one, you need to nap while *Pia* works."

Sam crawled down from the stool, looked up at her and puckered his dark brows above his green eyes. "Not sleepy."

Clare yawned. "Really? Are you sure?" She yawned again, covered her mouth, and gazed into his sleepy eyes.

Sam yawned, rubbed his full tummy, turned and ran toward the shelves where he crawled underneath onto a pallet. Clare reached for a blanket, bent down, gently covered him, and in no time he was sound asleep, looking like an angel.

Returning to the large worktable, she completed the task of folding several different gingham fabrics to display in the storefront window. Gently, her hand rubbed over the floral, cotton material. She could make a dress and clothes for Sam. Why not? She'd made all her deerskin dresses. *Chhawi* had taught her. One day, Clare Rose, you're going to make a gingham dress and be a fine lady again.

"Clare Rose, get in here. Clare Rose."

Her pa's demanding tone cut through her daydreaming. Clare raised a brow. No, she had passed the period in her life of becoming a fine lady.

"Get in here. Clare Rose."

She frowned, dropped the fabric on the table, shot a quick glance at her sleeping son, and then stepped to the door. Not once since she'd started working at the mercantile had she been permitted in the storefront during the hours customers meandered through the aisles shopping for store goods. They hadn't said, but she knew her parents didn't want people to see her or Sam, and especially, her growing belly.

"What is it Pa?" she asked, searching the large room stocked with goods on tabletops and shelves that climbed to the ceiling.

"Over here."

Clare moved toward his angered voice and peeked around a shelf. "Pa, did you fall? You know you shouldn't be climbing." Dropping to her knees, Clare struggled to help him to a sitting position. "Goodness, are you hurt?"

"Stop your sniveling. I'm fine. Help me to my feet."

"Henry…what happened…Henry, have you been climbing again?"

Clare glanced around. Her mother rushed up, bumped her aside and took Henry by the arm to help him stand. Clare observed them making their way to a stool. Her pa had a slight limp, but otherwise, he appeared all right.

"Should I get the doctor?" she offered.

"No. No doc." He frowned at her and glanced down at his foot.

"Henry, maybe you should see doc. Your foot's swelling."

"I said no."

Clare watched him study his foot, wiggled it back and forth and announced, "See, I can move it. No doc."

Neither one looked at her. They treated her like she didn't exist. With a slight headshake, she turned to see why he'd been climbing. She was sure he didn't think she could tell how much he'd changed since the town had been attacked four years ago. He pretended he was healthy, but he wasn't. His back hunched, and a few times she'd noticed his face crinkle with pain.

She glanced down, spied a bundle of whips on the floor, and glanced up at the pegs sticking out from the wall hanging with leather straps. So that's what he was doing.

Quickly gathering the leather horsewhips and without hesitating, she climbed the ladder several feet off the floor, and then, reached up and hung the whips in a neat order. After climbing down, she paused to take in the scene before her. Alyson was on her knees examining Henry's bare foot and neither bothered to look up at her. Hopefully, one day, they'd forgive her for returning. But, she had her doubts. Leaving them alone, she hurried back to the storage room.

When her gaze swung down toward the far end of the room where Sam should have been sleeping, his pallet was empty. "Sam where are you? *Samarjit.*" Clare whirled around, searching the room. The back door was opened. Not the mud puddle again. She grinned, shook her head and hurried out.

Her brow furrowed. He wasn't playing in the alley. Her instincts told her his little, curious mind led him to explore. Where did he go? She had never given him freedom to go around town. He'd get lost. The only thing he was familiar with was the backroom of the store, Mr. Hops' livery stables, and the surroundings of their cabin.

Her heart bumped against her chest. "*Samarjit*," she hollered. She listened. Nothing. Taking off she ran down the alley toward the main street. Wide-eyed, and in a near panic, she searched among the horses, buggies, wagons and the crowd of folks coming and going. Trying hard to lay eyes on a small black-haired boy appeared futile. He was nowhere in sight. Clare blinked to clear her watery eyes while her head whirled in every direction. *He's so small; he couldn't have gone far.*

* * * *

Drury Burchett, holding a shot glass in his hands, leaned forward with his elbows resting on the dark mahogany bar. He never touched the whiskey to his lips, but his intense stare focused on the golden liquid swirling in the glass.

He yanked off his hat, threw it on the bar, wiped his forehead, and then continued to stare into the glass at the swirling liquid, allowing his mind to picture the strong redheaded woman.

Hell, she'd rather live with Indians than be back in Silver Sage Creek. His finger rubbed the rough scar trailing down along his cheek. Quickly, lifting the glass, he swallowed the golden brown liquid and slammed the glass down.

"Here you go, Cap'n," offered the bartender. He filled Drury's glass before he could refuse.

Without looking up, Drury picked up the glass, and, once again, he stared into the liquid, allowing his mind to enter into a partition that needed a bolt. He couldn't seem to stop thinking about her. If there's a God in Heaven, He knows she's right. We're all hypocrites. Even her parents thought she should have died, like all the townspeople. Yeah, he had read their faces the first day they rode in. Being a white Indian with a half-breed, and one growing in her belly, most folks thought she'd been better off dead. But, she wasn't.

She was full of life, determined, strong, independent, and gorgeously beautiful. He'd never met a woman as independent and strong-willed as Clare Rose Coulson Montgomery and…and, whatever her Comanche name was. Drury rubbed the ridge trailing down his cheek.

Flaming red hair framed her face in a glow of golden, brown skin, deepening the green color in her large eyes. Her skin was appealing and added to her exquisiteness, and yet, her coloring was an indication of where she'd lived for the past four years. He'd seen her arriving at the livery stables in the mornings often enough to know she hadn't conformed to the respectable women's ways of Silver Sage Creek. Not with what she wore every day. The old farmer hand-me-down flat, crown hat shaded her face so people couldn't see the sadness in her expression, or angry arrows darting from her gaze. Who'd blame her? Neither parent helped, except to work her for little pay, probably more than likely out of guilt. Her hand-me-down, oversized shirt and trousers were their intentions to hide her belly, rather than to have her parade around showing off the growth inside her.

He squeezed his hands around the glass until his knuckles turned white. *That's right Burchett, don't forget, she's got a growing child inside her. And, it's an Indian. Hell, what was she going to do with another one?* Why was he so taken with her?

"What's got my big, bad Ranger so riled up he hasn't noticed me standing here for the past ten minutes?"

Drury turned his gaze to Ruby. He took a swallow from the glass, pushed to his full height and suppressed a smile, but before he could reply, the bartender hollered, "Hey, Ruby, you serving Injuns now?"

Ruby pulled her probing study from the Ranger to the bartender who indicated with his head toward the door.

Drury turned to acknowledge Ruby, but her gaze stared past him. He glanced around and recognized Clare's boy. What the hell? Where was Clare?

"Oh, he's adorable." Ruby rushed forward and squatted in front of Sam. "Where did you come from, little man?"

The bartender wiped the counter and mumbled, "He ain't no little man, he's Injun."

Drury aimed a scowl at the bartender and slammed his glass down, sloshing out the liquid. Turning his back, he leaned against the bar and watched the boy's green eyes, like his mother's, shift from Ruby to him, and then to the piano. In a quick start, his bare feet carried him to the stool, which he proceeded to climb onto.

Ruby laughed, stood and followed him. "Want to play?" Gently, she took his hand and placed it on the keyboard and pressed.

Sam's eyes widened. He grinned and slapped the keys to make another sound. Ruby laughed when Sam giggled out loud, threw up both hands, and quickly banged on the keys. He looked at Ruby. She smiled back. He pounded the keys several more times.

"Well, well, well...lookee here, Rangers. Ruby, ain't he the Injun boy belonging to old man Coulson's white Injun daughter? What are you, a redskin savage lover now?" Laugher rang out.

Ruby swung around to set eyes on four Rangers walking through the swinging doors. Taking in a deep breath, she frowned and lifted Sam off the stool. "I better get you home. Your ma's probably looking for you."

Without a glance in the Rangers' direction, she carried him out of the saloon, put him down, held his hand, and strolled alongside him toward the mercantile. Once near the storefront, Ruby set eyes on Clare and immediately recognized the panic in the mother's face.

"*Pia.*" Sam hollered, grinning.

Clare whipped around. Air pushed from her lungs the moment her gaze fell on her son. She couldn't stop the smile from spreading over her lips and she didn't miss the saloon owner's hand holding his. The moment Ruby released his hand his bare feet headed directly for her.

"*Pia.*"

Clare knelt down with opened arms. "Sweetie, you scared *Pia*. You took off. Please don't leave me again."

"*Pia.*"

She hugged him tightly, pushed to her feet with some difficulty, and gazed into the eyes of the woman she used to talk about with her friends. "Thank you."

"My pleasure. He's a darling little one."

"Where did you find him?"

The woman's quiet laughter flowed from her bright red lips. "Come a wondering into my place and took a shine to my piano."

"I'm so grateful to you for bringing him to me. He's growing so fast, and his curiosity keeps me busy just keeping up with him."

"I'm sure. You're lucky you have him with you."

Clare studied the woman's congenial smile. Ruby was a pretty woman and looked to be close to her age, at least not more than two or three years or so older than her. Her soft, dark eyes revealed a compassion Clare hadn't expected. She smiled at the woman, and something in the way she looked upon Sam made her ask, "Are you a mother?"

Ruby's gaze shifted from Sam to her, but she hesitated for a brief moment before smiling. "I have a daughter. She'll be two next month. She's with my mother in Atlanta."

"So far away. It must be hard." Clare didn't miss the sadness sweep over her face when her eyes dropped to take in Sam. "I'm sorry. You must miss her so much." When the woman didn't answer, Clare turned toward the alley, and said, "Again, thank you."

"Mrs. Montgomery."

Hearing her married name, Clare turned her gaze back, shook her head and said, "Please, Clare will do fine, after all I don't really think I'm considered married to Jonathan Montgomery any longer."

Ruby took a step near. "Why?"

"Look Ms—"

"Oh please, call me Ruby."

Clare shifted Sam onto her other hip and faced the woman. "Look at me."

Ruby's gaze traveled down her oversize shirt and man's pants and rested on her swelling tummy. "You're with child."

Clare nodded. "No man like Jonathan with his position, wealth, and power wants a woman with half-breed children. I'm sure I've been the talk of the town."

"I don't pay no mind to gossipy women around here. I get along better with men than women any how."

That, she was sure, was an understatement. Clare looked her in the eyes realizing she probably didn't have a female friend in the entire town.

"If you don't mind me asking, were the Indians cruel to you…is…is…that why you have the child?"

"No. If I had a choice, I'd return to the Comanche band."

Ruby's head jerked back. Her eyes widened. "You don't mean that."

"I do. I married the chief. The band treated me good. They're loving people trying to save their lives in a culture the white man is bound and determined to banish."

"But, they're savages."

"No, not the band I lived with. The Apaches who kidnapped me—yes, they're savages, but not the Comanche band. They loved and took care of me for four years. They were more my family than my own ma and pa."

Clare heard a quick breath intake from behind her. Ruby's gaze shifted beyond her. Clare glanced over her shoulder and connected eyes with her mother. She stood in the mercantile doorway, stiff with arms to her sides, her face drained of all color. Her miserable expression made Clare sad, but she spoke the truth.

"Ah, Clare…"

Clare drew her gaze back to Ruby.

"I…I…ah…you have a sweet boy." Before Clare could say another word, Ruby turned and hurried toward the saloon.

Clare swung her gaze back, but her ma had disappeared into the store. Sucking in a breath of regret, she smiled at Sam and slowly walked down the alley toward the door. "You want to go home, Sam."

"Home."

"Mommy just needs to collect a few things and we'll walk over to the livery."

"Horsey."

Clare stepped inside the door and almost stumbled over a large, brown flour bag filled with items. She quickly put Sam down and opened the string. Her eyes widened at the items packed inside. The bag contained bread, clothing, extra blankets, and…and staples she and Sam had done without, like sugar, flour, and…coffee. Glancing up, she fixed her eyes on her pa standing in the doorway. Tears blurred her vision.

His rough voice shot at her like a bullet, "Left over items, didn't want to throw 'em out. If you can use 'em, take 'em." He turned and disappeared.

She hurried, swiped at a fallen tear, then grabbed the string, pulled it tight, and looked around for Sam. He stood in the doorway leading into the store, staring at the man walking away from the same spot—his grandpa. "Sam, come, we need to get home." Without a word, his sad frown followed her to the stables.

Mr. Hops, the small, short, skinny liveryman, smiled at Clare's approached. "You got a big load there, missy." He led her horse out and stared down at the bulging flour sack. "You better borrow a horse to get your supplies home."

"Thank you Mr. Hops, but I can manage."

"Nonsense." He disappeared into the stables and in short order, led an old mare out with a worn brown saddle thrown over its back. "You can bring her back in the morning."

"Thank you, Mr. Hops. You're a special man." Clare smiled her appreciation and waited for him to tie the bag onto the saddle and lift Sam up.

"Here you go boy. She's a gentle old one and good for you to ride."

"I'll return the mare first thing tomorrow, Mr. Hops."

He nodded. "You be safe now, you here?"

"Will do, sir," she replied.

Their daily ride into town and out again was long, a good half-hour, so she always tried to leave early enough before the sun sank low. She glanced up at the clear sky with the sun sinking low in the west. Soon the weather would turn cloudy and cold, and she wasn't sure how to deal with the winter freeze. Especially, the long ride into town, and yet, leaving Sam alone in the cabin all day wasn't an option. She'd have to think about it later when the weather actually started cooling down.

She glanced at Sam. His grin from ear to ear put a smile on her lips. He loved being on his own horse for a change. If anything ever happened to him…ah, she couldn't think about such. Thank the Great Spirit for Ruby. She liked Ruby. So did Sam. Maybe, just maybe she and Sam could have one female friend in town. Clare let a small giggle bubble up from her throat. Several years ago, she felt Ruby beneath her, not worth knowing, and now she was a good friend.

Hmm, Captain Drury Burchett was Ruby's friend. Maybe, he was somewhat more than a friend. She'd noticed them together before her other life. Rest assured, he was certainly different.

The last time they'd talked he'd been angry at her for having an Indian child. Yet, he'd shown a gentle side by giving her a horse, and he had arranged for her to keep him at the livery stables while she worked for her parents. If the Ranger hadn't given her the horse, she and Sam would be walking to work every day. Clare smiled. Mr. Hops proved to be a saint, one the Great Spirit blessed. He allowed Sam to play in the stable and help with little chores that his small hands could handle. Sam had formed a friendship with the man and Clare approved. He was a good white man.

Working at the mercantile had given them enough money to buy the extras they needed for the cabin and clothes for her boy. Clare glanced at him, dressed in a pair of cotton pants and a shirt. He looked like any boy, except his hair was long and black. He sat tall on the mare, showing a great amount of pride. For such a young one, he outshined any white boy when it came to riding. He looked so much like his father. She didn't have the heart to cut his hair. He was half Comanche and she didn't want him to forget.

Clare's gaze drew toward a loud crowd of townsfolk shoving their way toward the jailhouse and the hanging platform. What the hell were they heated about? She slowed the horse until he came to a halt. Seemingly angry, the crowd shouted incoherent garbled words.

Her eyes widened. Knots tightened her stomach muscles. There on the platform was a young Comanche boy tied by his wrists. A man stood nearby, ready to drop a noose around his neck.

Trying to keep her voice calm, she glanced at her son, and said, "Sam, stay here. Don't move." Her stare drilled into mirrored eyes, silently telling him to obey her. He nodded and held the horse's reins tightly.

"I'll return soon." Clare slapped her legs against the horse's belly and slowly walked him toward the swarm gathering around the platform. Her gaze studied the captive. His wrists were held together by a blood soaked rope. His legs oozed blood from large cuts and scratches, showing evidence of being dragged. The young Indian's bruised face filled with terror while tears spilled down his cheeks. He was a mere boy. Someone's child.

Anger swelled inside. With a snap, she kicked the horse and rushed headlong into the crowd. Halting in front of the platform, she hollered, "You hypocritical sons-of-bitches, what the hell do you think you're doing?"

Her cursing words shocked the angry mass into silence. All eyes stared at the white Indian moving toward the platform.

"He's an Injun," screamed a goaded voice from the onlookers.

She visibly gasped, rushing bloody heat from her lower body up into her face. If she had a gun, God help her, she'd shoot them all.

"What do you mean, woman? He's a savage."

"You want to kill him because he's an Indian, with no thoughts to who he is and what he wants? He's just a boy."

"Boy or not. He's an Injun. We know what he wants, we know. You should know—look at what happened to you. He deserves to die. They all deserve to die. Of all people, you should want them dead, too."

Clare stared into their faces and swung her gaze around the crowd, people she'd known all her life. Men and women, boys and girls, all faces of God-fearing people standing before her with hatred in their hearts.

"You self-righteous, self-centered, arrogant people. You think *all* Indians are the same. You're wrong. Look at you. *Some* of you are bad folk and *some* Indians are bad. But you're not *all* bad, neither are *all* Indians. Some have families like you. They work hard, love their children, and believe in a higher being. They're peaceful people. Don't bunch them together."

"Yeah, they raided and murdered many in our own town, woman."

She stared up at the hangman spitting out spiteful words, causing many to mumble and shake their head in agreement. She sucked in a quick breath to calm the throbbing neck vein heating the blood charging through her body. Clare jerked her reins to move her horse closer to the platform.

Taking her time, she stared many in the eyes before her controlled, non-accusing tone lifted for all to hear. "Your own white people just murdered my son's kin. Was there any justification in brutally murdering old women and children, anymore than the white man's women and children the Indians murdered? No, there isn't. When will it all stop?"

An arrogant man, with a long, grayish beard, stepped out of the crowd and looked at her. She shivered. The hatred in his eyes turned them a hellish black. Someone shouted "Indian lover," putting an ugly smirk on the ornery man's lips. Before she could react, he reached up and grabbed her off her horse. "We should hang her along with the Injun."

Clare clamped her jaws, tried to jerk free from the cowboy, but his grip tightened around her arm. Her frown deepened when she stared up at his ugly, toothless grin, which sickened her. She squinted at him, went limp, and in one swift move, she reached down, pulled a knife from her leather leg strap, and shoved it far enough into his ribs for him to feel.

"You stinking son-of-a-bitch released me…" her threatening low voice brought his stark surprised expression staring down at her. Suddenly, Clare kicked him between his legs where her ma had once told her was the best place to bring a man down. It did. Without hesitating, she jumped up on the platform, held the sharp edged knife toward the hangman. He stepped back, giving her room to cut the rope from the boy's wrists.

She whipped around to stare into the crowd, sucked in a hard breath and spat out her frustration. "You're no better than the raiding parties, murdering just for the sake of killing. You're worse. No…you're inferior compared to them, because you consider yourselves *civilized*. God help you."

Not thinking about the outcome and reacting spontaneously, she jumped from the platform pulling the boy with her, all the while holding her knife toward the crowd. No one moved.

With one hand, she tried to help him on her horse, but the weak boy fell back into the arms of a man. Clare threw up her hand slicing the knife through the air. Her eyes connected with the cold, blue, angry eyes of the Ranger holding the boy. Quickly, he picked up the kid and swung him over her horse, stepped back, and swooped her up onto the horse behind the boy. She gave him a hurried look, pulled on the reins and hustled the horse quickly toward the place where she had left Sam. Without stopping, she motioned for Sam to follow and headed out of town.

After riding several minutes and constantly glancing over her shoulder, to make sure no one followed, she finally took a deep breath to keep the tears at bay. Pressing her lips tightly, Clare patted the boy on the back and whispered. "You're safe now."

Sam's wide-eyed expression stared silently at the Indian boy. From where she had left him, she was sure he'd seen and heard everything. A shiver ran down her spine. God, what if the madness had gotten out of hand? The mob might have turned on Sam.

Clare shook her head, took another deep breath, and silently thanked the Great Spirit for protecting her son and the Ranger. Whatever possessed the Ranger to help, she was grateful. She'd never known such a complicated man. Still, he came to her aid, even with anger reflecting in his cold blue eyes, why? Why bother helping her, especially knowing how he hated Indians?

Chapter Fourteen

By the time Clare reached her cabin, the boy had lost consciousness. Sam tried to help his mother drag his dead weight into the cabin. Once inside Clare laid him on a blanket and gently washed his wounds. With the same herbs she had used on the wolf, she packed his raw wrists and covered his battered body to rest.

Clare sat back and observed the young brave. His right eye was discolored and puffy. His jaw was swollen. How could anyone hit a child? He wasn't considered a child in the white man's eyes. She reached over and gently shifted his long black hair away from his face. He was so young, just a boy, not more than fourteen, she was sure. But the right age for the Comanche elders to send out to prove himself a brave warrior.

Sam crawled up onto her lap. "*Pia*, Comanche?"

She hugged him close and shrugged. "I don't know dear. I think so."

"Take him home, *Pia*."

"When he gets better, little one."

Why was he so close to Silver Sage Creek to get caught? She frowned and stared at his markings along his forehead and down his cheek. Did he belong to her band? *Her band.* Her band no long existed…none, in time.

A horse snorted through its nose. Clare's head swung toward the door. Quickly, she shoved Sam to his feet and stood. Bending, she grabbed her knife, glanced at Sam and pointed toward the corner of the room. Silently, she placed a finger against her lips. Sam backed up against the wall and waited.

Clare moved stealthily forward and peeked around the opened door. Her tense shoulders relaxed. Holding the knife in her hand, she stepped out with fixed eyes on the Ranger. "You frightened us Captain. What are you doing here?"

His eyes followed her hand shoving the knife back into its leather leg band. "Remind me not walk up on you in the dark," he noted, staring at the weapon strapped around her pant leg. "Do you even know how to use that?"

Before he could blink, she stooped, retrieved the knife and flung it beyond his horse into a tree trunk. "Without hesitating," she said. Grinning, she stepped past him, strolled to the tree, reached up, pulled the knife out, and turned. "Now, Captain Burchett, what…" Her gaze locked with his. She froze.

The look in his eyes sent butterflies flitting through her stomach, leaving her breath short. Her mind reversed back in time when those same sensations had stirred an emotional need within her from the first moment he'd gazed upon her. Unable to move, she watched his approach.

His gait advanced, like the yellow-eyed wolf heading toward its mate. When he stopped, the gentle touch of his hands rested on her shoulders, while the warmth of his breath feathered over her face. She couldn't breathe. Her heart pounded against her breasts. The want in his gaze matched the now familiar flutter in her stomach, the sensation only he had caused. Her gaze swept over his parted lips closing in to touch hers.

His lips were soft and playful, leaving her breathless. The more his kiss consumed her, the more she pressed against him, triggering bumps over her skin. Her skin ruptured into a hot mass making her body tremble with a yearning so deep, her legs weakened. Before collapsing to the ground, she curled her fingers into his shirt, fighting the uncanny desire to throw her arms around his neck. He pulled back. The look in his eyes shot another heat flash through her body. She stared at his lips, wanting him to kiss her again. His gaze drifted over her lips and up into her eyes. The desire building inside her triggered an emotional need she'd never experienced before. He step back, lifted a brow and for the first time in years, she once again gazed upon his smile transforming his entire face into a beautiful man. Even his scar dissolved, disappearing into the transformation of his smile.

Her anticipation grew, wanting to taste his lips and take pleasure in the arousing sensations that only he had ever caused to happen within her body. He leaned against her, lowering his head to touch her lips again. When he paused his breath feathered her lips, and then he pulled back and glanced down at her swelling abdomen.

Suddenly, he stiffened, stood tall, and took a step back, putting space between them.

His changing manner didn't go unnoticed. Clare frowned. This man knew happiness at one time in his life, enjoyed living, so what happened to change him? Clare took a deep breath, swallowed hard, cleared her throat, and asked, "Well Captain Burchett, what was that?"

In his deep, sultry voice, he said, "Call me Drury." And then, with no mention of the kiss, he turned, took her by the elbow, and led her toward the cabin door. "Where's Sam and the Indian boy?" he asked.

"Inside." Clare stepped through the door and glanced at her son. He took a step toward her and stopped when Drury walked through.

Sam grinned from ear to ear and ran to the Ranger with open arms. Surprised at his reaction, Clare observed the shocked expression on Drury's face when the boy hugged his legs. She bit her bottom lip, remembering what he'd said the last time he was in the cabin.

Reaching out, Clare touched her son's shoulder. "Sam, fetch water for the boy, will you, sweetheart?"

Drury's eyes shifted from Sam to the Indian resting on a blanket. The boy rolled his head to the side and stared at the Ranger.

Clare glanced up. Hatred had already seeped into the Ranger's gaze. Feeling protective, she hurried and knelt next to the wounded boy, and gently covered his shoulders. Turning, she gazed up at Drury. Emotions darkened his eyes; even his scar appeared elevated.

He raised his hand and rubbed his scared cheek. "What will you do with it? You can't keep it here." Drury's hard glare aimed at the Indian boy, and then back at her.

"He, the boy, stays until he's well enough to make his way back to the band." She pulled her gaze from him and carefully moved his hand from beneath the hide to examine his wrist. Sam ran in with the water bucket. She quickly picked up a small bowl of plant mixture and added the water.

Drury turned, stomped out of the cabin and headed toward his horse.

Clare smiled at Sam. "Give the young brave some water while I talk to the Ranger." Clare hurried out the door.

"Drury," she hollered, before he mounted the horse.

Slowly he swung his head in her direction, faced her, and squared his shoulder while holding the reins.

Clare strolled forward and stopped directly in front of him. "Why?" She stared into his blue angry eyes. "Why is your hatred for all Indians so deep? I…I know I should have no mind, but I'd like to know why you're so full of hate."

His brows puckered while his gaze took hold of hers, and then lingered on her lips. He stepped back, pulled his Stetson squarely on his head to shadow his furrowed brow, turned, and mounted his horse. His eyes, cold as stones, swung down at her and in a restrained tone, he said, "Indians took my wife and daughter, then left them dead."

Clare squeezed her hands together and didn't take her gaze from the man riding off into the distance. Now, she understood. Grief could be unbearable and if left to fester, destroy the person's very soul.

The one thing she couldn't understand was her reaction to him. She was baffled by the churning emotions that flared up when he came around. Could there be something more that she wanted from him. What? Another kiss? Clare bit down on her lower lip. The look in his eyes had made her feel…what? Wanted. And…and the touch of his lips was…was warm, inviting. Yes, she had wanted to kiss him, too. She'd like him to try again. Neither one of her husbands had ever kissed her the way he had moments ago. She didn't know how to react to being kissed in such a manner.

Two days later, after a long day of working at the mercantile, Clare rode up to the cabin door. Sam had fallen asleep sitting up against her. Gently holding her child in her arms, she slid down from the horse. When she stepped into the cabin, her first glance landed on the bedding in the corner. The Indian boy was gone.

With ease, she laid Sam on the blankets and hurried out. She glanced around. Sure enough, the boy had left, evidently, well enough to return to his band. She hoped.

Clare stepped to the packhorse Mr. Hops had once again loaned her, and she untied the bags, dropping them to the ground. The large, canvas flour bags were heavy to carry, what with how big her belly was growing, but she managed to drag them into the cabin. Shaking her head, Clare once again, was rendered speechless when she found that her pa had packed up some goods for her to take home. He'd said they were unsellable for store goods, but she might be able to use them. Whatever he'd given her, she was thankful for his generosity.

She and Sam didn't have much, but what they did have was each other and she was thankful for that. All she wanted was to make a good life for both her children who through no fault of their own, belonged neither in the white man's world, nor the Indian's. The thought saddened her.

"*Pia.*"

Clare looked around to find Sam rubbing his eyes. She smiled the moment his bare feet ran toward her.

"You're awake. Are you hungry? The sky's still light enough to gather some berries. Wanna go with *Pia*?"

He nodded. "Where is…" he turned and pointed to the buckskin bed in the far corner.

She lifted her shoulders. "I suppose he must have been well enough to go home. Come on Sam, let's go pick berries and mommy will make a pie." Clare grabbed a basket in one hand and her son's hand in her other and headed toward the woods in search of wild blackberry bushes she had run across when out looking for fresh meat.

"*Pia*, there…" he pointed, "a bush."

"Wow. Look sweetie, the berries are plump and ripe. Be careful not to prick your fingers. The branches have sharp thorns." He picked a berry and dropped it into the basket. She smiled. "That's the way. Now, let's see if we can fill the basket with enough to make a pie."

The clopping sound of an approaching horse, not more than a hundred feet from them, alerted Clare. She grabbed Sam's hand and pulled him down with her, squatting between the blackberry bushes. Slowly, she peeked through the limbs, watching the rider draw close enough to recognize. Her quick intake of breath brought his horse around facing in their direction.

Chakotay searched the area. Quietly, he turned his horse to leave.

"Wait," Clare hollered, hurrying out from the bushes. "Please, *Chakotay*, it's me, *Keshini*.

The Comanche chief swirled his horse around and stared. When his gaze dropped to the boy, he slid from the pinto and onto silent moccasins, he strolled toward them. "*Keshini,* you live. *Samarjit.*"

She nodded. Sam took off running. His excited face expressed such happiness in seeing his *ahp* while giggling all the way into his father's arms.

Chakotay hugged *Samarjit* close and turned to Clare.

"*Ahp*." Sam's thrilled tone sent Clare's moist gaze to her son, and then back to *Chakotay*.

"Come," the chief motioned.

An angry voice echoed from the wooded area. "Over my dead body."

The sound of Drury's deep voice swirled Clare's head around.

The Ranger stepped out into the opening with his pistol pointed at the Indian. "Put the boy down."

Chakotay didn't take his eyes from the Ranger while slowly lowering Sam. The boy hugged the Comanche's leg.

Recognizing the enraged grimace covering Drury's face, panic bubbled up Clare's inners when her gaze dropped to the pistol in his hand. "Sam." She hollered, terrified her son stood in harm's way.

"Drury, don't. Don't shoot." She ran to his side, grabbed his arm and tried to push his hand down, but he shoved her away. His eyes never wavered from the Indian.

Nor did *Chakotay* take his eyes off the Ranger.

"Please Drury, please." Suddenly lightheaded, she gasped for air, searching for words to convince him. "Drury, please, he could have killed you, but he didn't, remember when you tried to rescue me four years ago."

Drury didn't move. A flicker of doubt and confusion crossed his expression. "Ah hell, Clare, you want him to kill me, or you and the boy. He glanced down at Sam hugging his enemy's leg, then back at the Indian.

Clare shook his arm. "Please don't shoot him, he…he's Sam's father."

"Hell, woman." Drury looked the Comanche in the eyes. With Clare's hold on his arm, he lowered his gun.

The Indian touched *Samarjit* on the head, turned and mounted, looked back at Clare, waiting. Clare dropped her tight hold on the Ranger's arm, ran forward, bent down and picked up Sam. "Come *Samarjit*, you need to say goodbye to your *ahp*."

"Why?" Sam asked.

"Because he has to go away." Clare blinked back tears and stepped near *Chakotay*. His heartrending expression cried out to her. "*Chakotay,* we can't go with you. It's too dangerous for *Samarjit* to live with his Indian family right now."

"Bye, bye *ahp*." Sam's voice choked and tear streamed down his chubby cheeks, and his little body shook with sorrow for an *ahp* he'd never see again. But he didn't make a screaming sound. Clare couldn't hold back the tears when she looked into the sad, black eyes of the Comanche chief. The unspoken words of goodbye were final. After a quick glance in the Ranger's direction, he reined his horse around and rode off.

A silent, mournful cry weakened Clare's legs dropping her to the ground. Tears flowed for her Comanche husband, for her son's father, and the chief of the soon-to-be extinct Comanche band.

Sucking in a deep breath, she gave Sam a hug, and then struggled to her feet, turned and glared at the Ranger. "What the hell are you doing out here hiding behind the trees?"

"I wasn't hiding. I was tracking a savage and planned on shooting him if you hadn't surprised me."

Her squinting glare aimed into his angry ones. "You'd murder him without giving him a chance. Just the way you did all those women, children, and elders in my camp."

"Murder. You can call it murder when they're the murdering, thieving savages."

"No. Not him. Not my band."

"Your band. Little lady, I'll never be an Indian lover, like you." He glared down at Sam, turned, and disappeared into the woods.

* * * *

Drury took the reins from his tethered horse, mounted, whipped his horse's flanks, and rode hard for a long time, heading toward his ranch. Finally, aware of his horse's labored breathing, he slowed to walk his stallion to give him a breather.

Drury shook his head. Hell, he'd lost control and was taking it out on his animal. His blood still boiled from the confrontation with an Indian he should have killed. Hell, what words? The son-of-a-bitch never said a word to him. More like, a silent war of words went on between them. Clare was the mouthy one. He glanced around wishing he could shoot something.

Hell, he should never have kissed her...that white-Indian woman. Once an Indian lover, always an Indian lover. Hell, she kept proving how much she loved them.

Why did she have so much control over him? Why didn't he just kill the son-of-a-bitch Indian? Hell, it shouldn't matter he's the one who saved his life. He took Big Black, didn't he? And his boots. Hell, why should it matter he's Sam's father. Shit, son-of-a-bitch, he was Clare's Indian husband. Hell.

Chapter Fifteen

Clare picked up a box of blue, satin fabric, the color of Drury's crystal, blue eyes, eyes spiraling with desire when he looked at her in his confident way. How could she forget his kiss? Her tongue slipped out and moistened her lips.

Clare squeezed her eyes, opened them, and glanced up at the ceiling. She had to forget him. Forget the emotional reactions her body had toward him. He hated Indians, including Sam. She shook her head and glanced down at the material. It was no use.

"Ow." Clare caught her breath, bent over and pushed hard against her abdomen until the sharp pain subsided. She straightened and took a deep breath trapping the air inside her lungs falling against the table in another excruciating pain. Finally, the pain settled down leaving her breathless. "What was that?"

"*Pia* hurt?" Sam's tone held a slight panic.

Clare sucked in several short breaths, turned to Sam's worried face and gave him a slight smile. "Not now. I'm fine, you can go play." She pushed away from the table, pulled out the blue fabric, and prepared to roll it onto a board for display in the store. She glanced back. Sam hadn't moved from the doorway.

"Really, sweetheart, *Pia's* fine. Do you want to go to the livery stables and see Mr. Hops? Maybe he'll let you help him with some chores."

He nodded, turned slowly, stopped, and looked back. He frowned.

She feigned a slight grin, took a step toward him, and then doubled over when a sharp pain pierced through her abdomen. Dropping to her knees, a low agonizing grunt escaped her lips before she could trap it.

"*Pia*," Sam ran to her and put an arm on her shoulder.

Clare glanced down, wetness rolled down her inner thighs. Dark red blood soaked her pants. Again, pain stabbed into her gut. She tried to hold up her protruding belly. Her baby. No. Unable to stand, she collapsed onto the floor. The last thing she remembered was her son's running feet.

* * * *

Ruby sat across the table from Drury. Her red lips parted, sending him a bright smile. She savored her moments with this man who could never give his heart to her, but she was happy to settle for his attention, no matter how infrequently. She studied him and the never-ending pain in his eyes, pain she had tried to sooth without success.

Oh, he loved her, in his own way, but for him to release the past, to love completely, took a stronger woman than her, and she didn't know if there was such a woman.

"Did I mention that darling little half-breed came into my saloon again last week?"

His stark blues aimed at her.

"Yup, he strolled in and stood in the doorway looking around. He's full of curiosity. I think he wanted to play the piano again."

"Shit." Drury grunted and shook his head. "Where was Clare?"

Ruby noticed he called her 'Clare,' but didn't let on. "Evidently, he strayed from the mercantile and found his way here. After talking to him for a few minutes, I took him back to the store. Inquisitive little fellow, wanted to know why people came inside when no one was playing the piano."

Drury took a big swallow of whiskey and mumbled, "It's beyond me why she wanted to keep the half-breed."

"Captain. I'm surprised at you. He's her son—"

"An Indian's son."

"No mind, he's her son, her child, her baby, so is the one growing inside her. Whether you like it or not, another half-breed's on its way. Soon, from the looks of her." Ruby frowned and shook her head. "Cap, the boy's half white. Ain't his fault he's got an Injun for a dad. How can you take what happened to your family out on a small half-breed?"

Drury slammed the glass down on the table, stood, shot an angry glare at Ruby, and turned to leave. His steps halted.

The subject of their conversation ran through the doors with tears streaming down his face. He headed straight for Ruby's open arms.

"Sam, what's wrong?"

"*Pia.*"

"*Pia?*" Sweetheart, Ruby doesn't know what you mean."

"Mother." Drury said. "Where's your *pia*, Sam?"

Sam's tear-stained face gave Drury a fleeting look and quickly pointed out the door.

Ruby jumped up, grabbed Sam in her arms, and without a glance at Drury, she rushed out the swinging saloon doors. Drury followed closely behind.

Ruby hurried down the boardwalk to the front doors of the mercantile, all the while looking for Clare. Holding Sam on her hip, she ran through the front doors of the store and straight toward the back. Not once did she give the Coulsons a glance.

"What's this?" demanded Mr. Coulson, his eyes following Ruby carrying the half-breed. Both owners of the mercantile turned their eyes on the Ranger close behind Ruby, disappearing through the door into the storage room.

"Clare," Ruby called. "Oh my God Almighty." She quickly put Sam down and knelt, touched Clare's shoulder, and whispered, "Honey, is it the baby?"

"Ruby...Ruby," Clare mumbled, "I'm...I'm bleeding." Clare tried to sit up, but her weak body fought against any movement.

"Leave her be."

Ruby ignored the demanding voice of Mr. Coulson while trying to assess Clare's situation. The instant her gaze landed on the bloody pants, she knew what she had to do.

"Drury, hurry, we have to get her to my place."

Drury didn't hesitate to gather Clare into his arms and quickly head out the backdoor. Ruby followed with Sam clutching her hand tightly. On the way out the door, she shot the Coulson's a scowling glance. They hadn't moved, or even asked what the problem was, with no care for their daughter's dilemma. Anger swelled inside her.

Why, oh why? She'd never understand their way of thinking. For hell's sake, she was their daughter, having their grandchild. It didn't matter that their only child had lived through such atrocious circumstances. To them, it only mattered that she had returned to embarrass them. One thing she knew for sure, regardless of their attitude toward their daughter, the Coulsons didn't like her befriending or helping Clare. A saloon owner. They couldn't see past her so-called sinful life. Why couldn't people get to know her for who she really was…a businesswoman, a person no different than them?

Ruby hurried to catch up to Drury as he carried Clare across the street, to the back of the saloon, and up the stairs to Ruby's quarters. Once on the landing, he waited for her to open the door.

"You better get the doc, Drury."

He nodded, stepped inside and placed Clare's limp body on the bed. Without another word, his boots echoed out the door and down the wooden steps.

Ruby's brows pulled together so tightly a pounding headache throbbed at her temples. She wasn't sure what to do before the doc arrived. Sam perched on the edge of the bed next to his ma. He leaned over, placed his head next to his mother, and with his little brown hand, he patted her belly. Tears stung Ruby's eyes. Hell, she couldn't remember the last time she shed a tear. Water. That's what she'd do. Put water on to boil.

In no time, the doc rushed through the door with Drury hot on his heels. After one quick look at Clare, he glanced at Ruby and shook his head. "Out. Take the boy and wait."

Ruby nodded, reached for Sam's hand, and said, "There's boiling water on the stove." The doc nodded, but his focus rested on his patient. Calmly, but quickly, he opened his medicine bag, retrieved his instrument, and shoved the stethoscope into his ears. She slipped out with Sam and glanced at Drury's worried expression.

He took a step down on the staircase and sat. Sam did the same. Sitting next to Drury, he leaned his head on his arm. For a second Ruby thought she saw compassion in the Ranger's eyes, but when he glanced up at her, a mask had covered his deepest feelings.

By the time the doc exited Ruby's apartment, Drury was pacing at the bottom of the stairs, fit to be tied. The worried frown on the doc's face sent Drury's feet flying up the staircase, two at a time. Ruby picked up Sam and waited for the doc to quietly close the door.

"She's sleeping now. I'd let her rest for a couple of days." He shook his head and studied the boy in Ruby's arms. He reached out and patted Sam's head. "You're a mighty fine looking boy. You'll have to take care of your ma."

Sam nodded.

He turned his gaze on Ruby. "Can't imagine the hardship he'll endure in this town." He pulled his glasses off and turned his sad gaze to Drury, and then back to Ruby. "I doubt the baby will make it. The heartbeat is mighty faint, so you best keep an eye on her for the next several days. She shouldn't get out of bed." He headed down the stairs, mumbling, "Don't want to lose both mother and infant. Fetch me, if you need, otherwise, I be back in the morning."

Ruby stared at Drury. All color had drained from his face leaving the half-moon scar visibly more red than normal. "She won't die, Drury, she's strong. Any woman that's been through what she's experienced won't give up too easily."

Concerned eyes stared back at her before glancing at the boy. He bobbed his head, turned and headed down the steps. "I'll be around if you need me."

****

Clare tapped the horse in the flanks to hurry his gallop toward the cabin. She'd been at Ruby's for the last five days and knew time grew near. Foremost on her mind, was getting to the cabin before her little papoose entered the world.

Sam rode the packhorse belonging to Mr. Hops. Her son handled the old mare with expertise. She was so proud of him. He had stayed by her side day and night with a fretful look in his eyes, and she had no words to console him.

Clare bit down on her lower lip. The cabin was just around the corner, thank goodness. She was beginning to feel a deep ache in the middle of her lower back, which wasn't a good sign.

By the time she fed Sam and put him to bed, Clare knew something was wrong. Her pains were sharp, but nothing like the familiar birth pains she endured at Sam's delivery. Throughout the night, Clare walked the floor until the cramping stopped long enough for her exhausted body to sink into a deep sleep.

Slowly lifting her eyelids, Clare found Sam next to her with his elbows on the bed and his head resting on his hands. A streak of sun, peeking through the window slits, fell across his shiny blue-black hair. She smiled, looking into his moist, green eyes.

"You been sleeping a long time *Pia*."

Sitting up, she kissed his cheek and said, "I was. You hungry?"

He nodded.

Unable to sit still, Clare moved constantly throughout the morning, except when the excruciating pain constricted her whole body. The pains continued to get worse with each contraction lasting longer than the one before. What worried her was the sharpness and knife stabbing sensation. And, the baby hadn't moved.

When the time arrived, she gathered up a blanket, water and a knife and waddled to the door.

"*Pia.*"

She glanced at Sam.

"It's time."

"Yes, dear. I will call for you when the baby enters our world. Wait here for me."

He nodded, followed her to the edge of the porch, and kept his worried gaze on his mother until she disappeared into the forest.

Clare slowly made her way to the area she had picked out, well into the thick forest, but close enough to the cabin for Sam to come running if needed.

She squatted, held onto a branch and pushed with all her might. Before she could relax between contractions, another took hold and with little strength left, she sucked in a deep breath and pushed until the vessels in her neck protruded. Sucking in another deep breath, she pushed and the baby slid from her womb.

Not a sound came from her tiny mouth. Clare had known the Great Spirit had taken her. Tears slid down her cheeks while she cut away the umbilical cord and tossed it aside. Hanging it on a tree wouldn't help her baby now.

Sobs escaped her lips as her gaze touched every part of her daughter's perfect body, covered in a protective substance. She gently wiped away the coating and wrapped her tiny girl in the blanket, and then gathered the black-haired infant into her arms. Holding her close against her heart, Clare rocked back and forth, while grief pushed one tear after another from deep inside her soul. Clare Rose didn't exist, but *Keshini*, a white Indian who had moments ago given birth to a beautiful Indian baby girl. She leaned against a tree and like a ghost in the forest, let her shoulders shake from her silent cries.

Ruby pulled on the reins to stop the buggy. She glanced around. All was quiet. Her brow wrinkled. She didn't like eerie quietness. And then, she fixed her eyes on Sam strolling from the corner of the cabin with his head hung low. When he looked up, she could tell he'd been crying. Quickly she jumped from the buggy and rushed to gather him into her arms. "What is it Sam. Where's your mother?"

He pointed to the cabin. His round dark eyes looked intently at her. "Baby with the Great Spirit."

* * * *

Drury strolled into the Silver Sage Saloon, glanced around the room, and jutted his chin at the bartender. "Where's Ruby?" he asked, moseying up to the bar.

"She rode out early this morning toward the white trash Indian's cabin, mumbling something about making sure the half-breed bastard baby didn't die. You ask me, she'd be better off...half-breed too." He shook his head. "Consarn—it's beyond me why Ms. Ruby's taken a shine to them kind."

Drury glanced toward the door, ignoring the loutish words and tone the bartender spat out. The late afternoon sun was sinking in the west. Drury leaned against the bar, tugged his Stetson from his head, and ran his fingers through his hair.

What if she didn't return until morning? He couldn't wait to find out what had happened. His gut told him something was wrong. Without a word or a glance at the man behind the bar, he stomped from the saloon and mounted, turning his horse toward Clare's cabin on a fast gallop.

Finally, pulling back on the reins, he slowed his horse to a trot and stared straight ahead. His gaze took in the scene. A large fire burned in front of the cabin and Clare's horse stood near the door. Ruby's horse and buggy waited along the side of the cabin.

Ruby dropped a log on the fire, turned her gaze up into his face and shook her head. He dismounted and with wide strides, hurried to her side.

"The baby was born dead. She's in there…wrapping the infant, preparing for some kind of ceremony."

The surge of guilt flashed through him the second he realized his first thought was relief for the baby not living. He quickly turned away from Ruby, hoping she hadn't notice.

Clare stepped out of the cabin with the small bundle in her arms. She lifted her gaze to his. His heart dropped. He wanted to take her in his arms and tell her the heartache lessened with time, but he knew, in reality, it took a long time in coming. Evidence of grief splashed over her face and the dark circles under her eyes revealed her suffering—all of which he understood. Losing a child slashes one's heart to pieces and gnaws deeply at your entire being.

His gaze shifted to Sam. Quiet and solemn, the child's hand gripped a fistful of Clare's buckskin dress, holding on for dear life. His sad eyes were red.

Drury hadn't considered Sam's grief for a sister, or the tragic incidents in his life. If Clare died, he'd be all alone. He hadn't thought much about him, but from Sam's drawn, sad face, he surely had. The child was sensitive, like his mother.

Clare's small family sat on the ground near the fire. Sam huddled up against his *pia*. Without speaking, their intense stare into the fire seemed to be consumed by the flames for several minutes. Both the child and mother appeared to have slipped into another dimension, listening to someone or something beyond the white man's comprehension.

Drury glanced at Ruby. She raised her shoulders and sat on the ground across the fire pit from the grief-stricken family. He did the same. Like Ruby, he also didn't understand the Comanche ceremony, yet the ritual seemed necessary for Clare to perform. But, he did understand the wrenching despair he experienced when he found his own child dead.

Clare started to chant.

Drury swallowed a large choking lump. His eyes burned. He blinked several times to keep the tears at bay. Hell, he hadn't cried since he found his wife and daughter murdered. God, hadn't Clare suffered enough?

After several minutes of chanting, Sam's wee voice joined hers. While chanting, Clare lifted the baby to the heavens, first in the direction of the north, then the south, east, and west. She held the tiny bundle straight up toward Heaven and stopped chanting.

The second Clare's despondent voice spoke, a tear slipped down Drury's cheek, rolling over the long scar. He strained his ears to hear through the crackling firewood, the words she spoke.

"Great Spirit knows the reason we cannot journey through this life with this precious one. Today, she will be called *Kiche*, meaning *spirit in the sky*. Great Spirit, give her an easy trail along the path to the other Comanches and her people."

Again, she and Sam chanted unfamiliar words, but for Drury, the beautiful sound consoled the pain he suffered for them, and himself. When she finished, Clare cuddled the newborn in her arms, stood, and walked toward the horse.

Ruby grabbed his arm. He stood, helped her up, and mumbled, "Stay here, I'll go with them."

"Where is she going?"

He shrugged. "Bury the baby."

He had no idea where she headed, but he knew he couldn't let them out of his sight, so he mounted and followed slightly behind them in order not to interfere with their burial ceremony.

Clare held the tiny, still infant in her arms with Sam hugging her waist riding behind her. She never said a word, nor did Sam. They rode for what seemed forever, far up into the mountains. Finally, Clare halted her horse near the mouth of a cave.

Drury waited for her and Sam to enter what he supposed was to be the baby's burial site.

They rode back in silence. He glanced at Clare several times. She still had not said a word upon their return. Relief spread through his cold body when they finally approached the cabin. Complete darkness had set in, making it hard to see the trail to her place. He could see Ruby standing near the fire. She had kept it burning for the few hours they had been gone.

Before he dismounted, Clare slid from the horse's back, took Sam, and entered the cabin.

Ruby hurried to Drury. "Where did you go? You been gone a long time."

He shrugged. "They buried the infant in the mountains. I guess it's the Indian way."

Clare stepped from the cabin carrying the baby's wooden bed that she had made several months before and tossed it onto the fire. Sam followed with the bedding blankets, and then they sat down and cried. The anguished cry of heartache flowed from Clare's lips, crying for a baby girl who was lost to her.

Unbeknownst to Drury and Ruby, she cried the way she had cried the night *Chhawi* had died. Clare rocked back and forth, shedding tears while singing a song she had learned in Comanche words. Sam sat in sorrow with tears flooding his cheeks while gripping his *pia's* arm.

Chapter Sixteen

Drury couldn't stop thinking about Clare being alone, so far out of town. On Clare's insistence, he and Ruby had left early the next morning to head back to town. One week had passed since she had ordered them to leave. She said there was no reason for them to waste their time watching over her.

The instant he pushed the swinging saloon doors open, Ruby hurried to him. "Drury, Clare hasn't been in town and not even her parents seem concerned. I asked them about her, but they hadn't bothered to ride out. When I told them the baby died, they were glad and never once asked if she was well. Please, Drury, you've got to go see her."

He knew Ruby was worried. He was too. "I'll go now."

"Oh, Drury." she flung her arms around his neck, knocking his hat off his head. She stepped back, glanced around, and then at Drury. "I'm much obliged."

He reached down, picked up his Stetson, placed it firmly on his head, and tugged it low. With a quick nod, he stepped out of the saloon. Hurrying to his horse, he mounted, letting his gaze land on the mercantile sign.

Just for the hell of it, he dropped by the mercantile on the pretense of buying a saddlebag for an assignment the governor was sending him on. He spied Mr. Coulson behind the counter and Mrs. Coulson nowhere in sight. He hoped she'd gone to help Clare. Stammering about, hunting for the right words, he turned to the sound of Mrs. Coulson's voice the moment she exited the storage room.

"Mrs. Coulson, I thought you were gone."

"And why, Captain Burchett?" she asked, placing a roll of fabric on the table.

"Maybe because your daughter has fallen ill."

Alyson didn't say a word, just stared at him.

He shook his head. "I forgot you don't have a daughter. How could I forget? Your treatment toward your own daughter is deplorable. The Indians kidnapped her, and now your daughter no longer exists. Little do you know she's a better person than you who claim to be a God fearing person."

"How dare you speak to my wife in such a manner, Burchett."

Drury's gaze swung to Mr. Coulson. His blood boiled. He turned so fast, he bumped into Mrs. Waterford who had, from the look on her face, heard every word. Tipping his hat, he mumbled, "Sorry, ma'am." He quickly left the store and struck out for Clare's cabin.

He couldn't make his horse gallop fast enough. Drury looked up in the direction of the sun and realized it wasn't far from the evening setting in. Good thing he could see the cabin in the distance.

Halting in front of the door, he quickly dismounted, tied the reins on the porch pole and looked around. Not a sound, nor a flickering light from inside the cabin. His worried brows pulled together. After another look around, he stepped up on the porch and softly knocked his knuckles against the heavy wooden door. He waited, and then, slowly pushed the door open. He peeked in and directed his gaze toward the corner of the room.

Drury's heart swelled, catching his breath. Clare lay sound asleep on the buckskin bedding. Her hair spread out over the covers–a red crown surrounding her face. A strong, beautiful face. Her son lay with his head on her shoulder, sleeping soundly.

The only part of the boy that reminded Drury of Clare was his green eyes. Expressive green eyes, so much like his mother's. His face appeared sweet and innocent, but a Comanche face still baring a resemblance to his Comanche father.

Drury quietly closed the door, rubbed his scar along his cheek, took a short breath, then strolled over to take a seat on the step. What was he doing? Without meaning to, he had developed an emotional need to protect her and the boy.

Drury rubbed his hand over his face, reached up, pulled his worn, black cowboy hat from his head, and combed his fingers through his hair. Emotionally defeated, he stood slowly, grabbed his saddle off his horse, and led him over to a tree to secure the reins for the night. Dropping the saddle next to the tree trunk, he stretched out on the ground and settled his head on the saddle, looking up at the stars. Breathing deeply, his thoughts turned to the family he'd lost—lost at the hands of the raiding, savage Indians.

Drury folded his arms over his chest and closed his eyes. If he had any licking sense of smarts, he'd get up and head back to town. Then, she'd never know. What was he doing here anyway? Helping? She didn't have anyone else giving a helping hand, except Ruby.

Ruby's giving spirit always reached out to those in need. Thoughtful, even to those ugly people saying mean things behind her back. He knew what people said about her. So what if she was a woman with a saloon business. Didn't matter. She was good, good hearted, and a good businesswoman. He yawned and closed his eyes.

"Captain Burchett."

The mellifluous, sweet voice drifted down from the heavenly stars and into his senses.

"Captain."

A feathery touch brought his eyes wide open. Clare had squatted next to him. Her hand rested on his arm.

"Captain, what are you doing here?"

He stared at her through the moonlight. He must have fallen asleep. Pushing to a sitting position, he blinked away the need to yawn. "I…ah…I came by to see if you needed anything. It was late, so I settled here for the night. I hope you don't mind."

"No, not at all."

He couldn't take his eyes from her. The clear night allowed the pale light from the moon to stream down on her face. A glow surrounded her red hair like an angel. An angel he wanted. An uncontrollable tremble covered his whole body. He quickly cleared his throat and sat up.

"Drury, you'll get cold out here. Maybe you should come inside. I have an extra hide you can sleep on."

He studied her. "No, I'll be fine. Not my first time to sleep under the stars." Besides, trying to sleep so close to her wasn't a good idea, especially since she occupied his mind all the time.

"If you insist," she replied and stood.

Her gaze touched him for several seconds before she finally turned and walked back inside the cabin. He took a deep breath, but before he released it, she hurried out again, carrying a heavy blanket. His head jerked back when she spread the blanket over his legs and up to his chest. He hadn't expected that. And then, she squatted next to him and turned her gaze up into the sky.

"The Great Spirit created a beautiful sight to behold, don't you think?"

"Yeah," he mumbled, but he couldn't drag his gaze from her moonlit face. When she looked down at him, he stared at her lips. She was so close, all he had to do was move in and kiss her.

"Why do you befriend me when you clearly dislike the fact I have an Indian child and that I believe the Indians are human beings with rights?"

Her straightforwardness brought him out of the trance he'd slipped into along with the caprice of kissing her. He shrugged, glanced away and searched his mind for an answer to her question.

"I don't know. Maybe, it's because no white man has ever taken the time to know who or what Indians are. Right from the get-go, we hated them."

Clare settled next to him and glanced up into the twinkling heavens. "I believe when we fear something or someone, we form defensive opinions to feel safe. Sometimes it's easier to detest than to go out of our way to learn."

"Our hatred opinions were easily proven with savages raiding, raping, and killing the white man."

She turned her gaze back into his eyes. "Should I hate you and the other white men, because you killed the band I lived with for four years and learned to love?"

For the first time in many a year, the surge of guilt stirred inside his blood. Avoiding her eyes, he mumbled, "Point taken."

"My son will have a hard way to go with people thinking the way you do. He'll never belong in the white man's world." When he glanced at her, she trapped him in her vision until she spoke. "The Indians will accept him more readily than the white man."

"Why's that?"

"They believe the Great Spirit, or if you want to call Him God, has a purpose for all those born of goodness."

"Well, He—" Drury glanced up into the night sky of billions of stars, "—must have known you were a good person to allow you to live through all the unfortunate sorrows you've had to witness."

Clare shook her head. "I wasn't such a good person. I thought like you. I feared Indians, all Indians and thought all were savages, until my new life with them. Now, I'd like to think God has changed me for the better."

"Believe me, you're the best I've ever met."

Clare's brows pulled together while she studied him. "Well Captain, I best go inside." She stood. "Goodnight."

Drury couldn't release his gaze from her shadowy figure strolling toward the cabin until she disappeared inside.

* * * *

The next morning, Clare awoke later than she expected. The sunlight streamed through the boarded windows to rest on her son's face. Her gaze touched his brown skin, black hair, and long lashes that were closed to the cruel world outside. He was so innocent and she wanted to keep him so for a little longer. She stretched back and stared up at the ceiling.

Last night had moved into the late hours by the time she returned to bed. Did the Ranger leave this morning or was he still hanging around? Clare breathed in a deep breath and tried to shake off the growing passion he twisted inside her. His taciturn charm fascinated her and stirred her body in a way she'd been unaware of with her husband.

Husband. Huh. Which one? She already had two. Was she looking for a third? Hell no. Never again. She didn't need a man to raise her son or feed them. And, the last thing she needed was a man humping her continuously. Marriage was for their pleasure only. It was for Jonathan anyway. *Chakotay* was different, a gentle man, but still there had never been anything pleasant. She supposed she'd never understand her mother's desires for her pa.

Back when she was close to her parents, she remembered the look in her ma's eyes when she looked upon her pa. Love shone all over her face for him. For her, too. Yet, the same look had yet to appear in her parents' eyes whenever they looked upon her now. It was something else…more like…what…shame, pity. That's it…pity; they were ashamed she lived instead of died. Ruby was the only other person in the entire town who didn't appear to pity her or be too ashamed to be her friend.

Clare pulled her hair from behind her neck and stretched her arms. Drury didn't look at her with shame and never with hatred in his eyes like when he looked at an Indian. Nor had he ever rubbed his scar when looking upon her. Thank goodness he kept his hatred-filled glare from surfacing when he looked into her child's eyes. Sam's astute observation of people made him aware of how the sight of him offended some people. It saddened her to know he'd learned such unkindness at an early age. Hopefully, Drury kept his hatred hidden when around Sam, if he hadn't, Sam knew.

A perplexing man he was, her Ranger. Oh my lardy, she'd thought of him as her Ranger. Well, he did reach out to her whenever trouble confronted her. Even causing her emotional reactions to jumble into knots the moment he gazed upon her. His study of her seemed so intense at times, jarring her searing nerves into an unfathomable desire for him, something she'd only experienced once, a longtime ago, before Sam was born. It was the last time she'd had peyote with *Chakotay*, when the heightened desires triggered inside her body had surprised her. She had wanted something from her husband, but, as usual, disappointment lingered long afterward.

Clare stepped outside the cabin and glanced around. He was nowhere to be seen, but his horse fed leisurely on wild grass near the spot where he'd slept last night. Clare headed down to the stream to wash up and bring back a bucket of water for Sam. She swung her head in several directions, but there was no sound or sight of the Ranger.

Squatting, Clare sat the bucket aside, gathered up a handful of water and splashed the cold wetness against her face sending shivers over her skin. Picking up the bucket, she filled it with the clear, cold water and stood.

"Here, let me carry that."

Swirling to the sound of the Ranger's voice, Clare watched the man stroll toward her. Within a foot of her, he held out his hand

and took the bucket handle. Clare took a step and with a quick glance up at him, she asked, "Did you have a peaceful night?"

"Not bad."

Within several feet of the cabin, he stopped. Clare looked back. He stood staring at the roof.

"You'll need a roof before winter sets in."

Clare looked up at the unfinished roof. "Yeah, Jonathan had never bothered to complete it after...no point now. We'll make do."

When she turned her gaze back, Drury's crystal blues deliberately studied her again. "What?" she injected with a demanding tone.

An eyebrow lifted. His lip curled up at the corner, reminding her of a day long ago when he tilted his hat at her and rode off. The day the Indians raided the town, killing Sally, wounding her pa, and kidnapping her and Betsy.

He shrugged. "Just wondered if that Montgomery fellow was still your husband."

She shook her head. "I spec not. He hasn't said so, but I'm sure he'd rather die than have a white Indian for a wife."

"Why do you call yourself a white Indian?"

"I am. Why not? In many ways, I'll always be *Keshini* and not Clare Rose. I spent four years with the Comanche and I belonged. I don't fully belong to the white man's world...not like I did once before."

She turned and quickened her steps.

"Well, it's best you don't belong to Montgomery."

She stopped, turned, tilted her head to the side and squinted. "Why?"

With a matter-of-fact tone, he stated, "You deserve a better person than a man more interested in himself than others." And then he stepped past her to carry the bucket into the cabin.

He strolled in, stood still, and looked around, taking in the sparse furniture in the one room cabin. Sam rolled over and sat upon the deer hide bedding. His sweet grin spread over his whole face when he laid eyes on the Ranger.

Clare hurried to his side. "Morning little one." She smiled and gathered him up in her arms. When she turned, the Ranger had left without saying a word.

"Well Samarjit, I think he's a little afraid of you." Quickly giving her son a kiss on the head, she said, "Hungry?"

* * * *

Clare wiped her brow and continued to load the canned goods onto the shelf in the mercantile storage room. A buckboard loaded with supplies had arrived following the stagecoach. Talk of a locomotive coming through the northern part of Texas was on everyone's lips these days. She ignored the rumor. Progress always took several years, especially to reach Silver Sage Creek. But, still supplies delivered by rail instead of the long-awaited buckboards and stages could make a huge improvement.

A soft knock sounded on the backdoor. Clare frowned, glanced at Sam napping underneath his favorite shelf, and strolled to the door. Slowly opening it, she peeked out, grinned, and stepped back. It was good to see Ruby. Her ruby red lips spread in a bright hello.

When Clare didn't say a word, Ruby said. "Well, it's definitely on the cool side out here, aren't you going to invite me in?"

"Oh yes," Clare mumbled and stepped back. "I'm surprised to see you."

Ruby stepped inside and glanced around. When her gaze fell on Sam, her eyes twinkled with such sincere joy Clare couldn't help but feel a deeper friendship toward her.

"I wanted to see how you were doing. I saw you ride into town this morning. Clare, don't you think it's kinda early for you to get back to work? You still have to be somewhat weak, from…well, you know."

Clare nodded and admitted, "A little. Thank you for inquiring. But, you can see," she waved her hand toward her son, "I have a small one to feed." Turning her gaze back, she said, "Ruby, how about something to drink? Pa keeps coffee on the cast iron stove in the front corner of the store."

"No, no dear, I just wanted to visit for a minute, then I'll have to get back to my business."

Clare gestured her hand toward a stool near the shelf where Sam was sleeping. After Ruby sat, Clare pulled a stool close and took a seat. She connected with Ruby's friendly eyes.

"Honey, I hope you don't mind, but I have a few things I need to find a home for, so I sent someone out to deliver the items to your place."

Clare's head pulled back, her eyebrows lifted. "Like what?"

"Oh, let me think…ah…ah…a bed, a table and couple of chairs, an old chest of drawers, a trunk for storage, and…and…just a couple of other items. Drury tells me you're in dire need of furniture. Please accept them. I don't need any of the things I sent out. I want you and Sam to have them."

Clare's jaw clamped tightly and swallowed hard to keep the tears from forming. "Are…are you sure you don't need them?"

Ruby reached out and patted her leg covered with old cotton pants. "Sweetie, if I needed them I'd keep them and not consider giving them away."

Clare jumped up and threw her arms around her friend. "You are so good to me and you really shouldn't, you know."

"My heavenly days, why shouldn't I?" Ruby frowned at Clare and sat back on the stool.

"People will hold it against you. No one has given me the light of day since I returned." Clare glanced down at her hands resting in her lap. "I've been told I should have died, rather than live a life with Indians, much less return to live among the white people."

"Hell, you need pay no mind to such preposterous talk. Besides, they said the same words when they brought back that Betsy woman four years ago."

Clare's eyes widened. "Betsy. She's here. Alive? No one's mentioned her. I assumed she died."

"Oh she's alive all right, except not in the right mind. Guess those savages weren't nice to her like they were to you."

"Where, Ruby, where is she living?"

"Somewhere right outside of town. I understand Ranger McCoy takes care of her. Anyway, people wagged their evil tongues about her for months, and then they seemed to forget about her. Supposed something else came along to gossip about—if they don't find someone, they usually return to me." Ruby grinned. "I like to give them something interesting to discuss, otherwise, don't you think their lives are kind of boring as hell?"

Clare looked her straight in the eyes and giggled.

Ruby laughed out loud. "You know something Clare, you're better off without the town's pompous son-of-a-bitch."

"Ruby." Clare's eyes widened hearing another cuss word coming from a woman, and out loud too. She giggled, remembering the few times she'd uttered such words.

"I know, I know," she gave Clare a hug, turned her gaze on Sam and mumbled, "Sometimes my mouth gets me in trouble. Suppose I spend too much time around ruthless, drunken cowboys." She smiled and strolled to the back door.

"Who were you referring to as pompous?"

"Oh, you know, Montgomery, the arrogant, cock strutting son-of-bitch."

"I see." Clare wasn't sure how to respond to her remarks and yet, deep down, she agreed.

"Give your little one a hug when he wakes up."

"I will. And, Ruby..." Clare touched her arm and gave it a slight squeeze, "...thank you."

* * * *

When Clare reached the cabin toward evening, she couldn't calm her heartbeat. She and Sam might have a real home after all and if she saved a small amount of the money her pa paid her, she might be able to brighten it up. Halting the horse in front of the porch, she quickly lifted Sam down and let him run in first.

"*Pia*, look," he hollered and pointed. He sounded excited. Hurrying, she pulled a bag full of food from the horse and ran inside. Her feet came to a sudden halt in the doorway. The room was filled with furniture. So much more than Ruby had indicated.

Chapter Seventeen

"*Pia.*"

"Yes, my child?" Clare glanced at Sam, who was helping her gather firewood. Her gaze softened at the sight of her son dragging a large stick that was bigger than him. He seemed to have grown so much in the last few months and was certainly getting taller.

"*Pia*, what's church?"

Clare dropped her armful of tree branches on the pile of wood stacked against the side of the cabin. She turned with a frown. "Church. Where did you hear about church?"

"In town." His innocent dark eyes looked into hers, waiting for an answer.

"Well…" Clare sat on the porch step and stared down toward the stream. "You know how the Comanche speak to the Great Spirit?" She glanced at Sam's bobbing head. "Well, the white men go to a building they call *church* and worship their Great Spirit, who we call God."

"Are they the same?"

"You mean Great Spirit and God?" Clare slowly nodded. "I suppose. If you call the Creator either Great Spirit or God, they are the same, just called a different name."

"Why don't we go to church?"

Clare's shoulders lifted when she took a deep breath. "Well, I like it here." Her hand gestured toward the woods and stream, "I like feeling our Great Spirit right here with us in this place because it's our home and we're happy here. Are you happy little one?"

"Not all the time."

Her brows pulled together. "When are you not happy?"

"I see others in the town running and playing."

"You mean other children? When did you see them?"

"Outside, by the corner of the store, but they don't speak to me. Sometimes they point and laugh. Why? *Pia*, why?"

Clare reached over and hugged him. Tears swelled, blurring her vision. She bit down on her bottom lip. His questions were just beginning. How was she to protect him?

Galloping horse hooves drew their gaze toward the trail leading to the cabin. Two men on horseback approached. Once close enough, Clare recognized the Rangers.

The moment Sam set eyes on them he jumped up and took off to meet them. She wiped away her tears and followed.

"Hello, Captain Burchett." Sam hollered, waving his hand at the Rangers, who were halting their horses and dismounting.

Clare took note of her son's excitement. She smiled and let her gaze settle on the captain, who barely gave her child a glance, but managed to nod in his direction before turning to her.

Her jaws tightened. Before she could spit words his way, the other Ranger stepped up and said, "Hello there, young man, and what's your name?"

She glanced down to find a huge grin splashed on her son's face. At least this Ranger showed an affable greeting toward Sam, unlike the slight nod from the man her son evidently admired the most.

Clare giggled softly when Sam placed his hands on his hips, stood with his feet apart to look up at the man, and in a strong voice he said, "Sam. What's yours?"

"McCoy."

Sam accepted the man's hand and laughed out loud when the Ranger shook it like he was a big man.

Clare's brows shot up. A long time had passed since her son had actually laughed out loud.

Turning back, she squinted and said, "Captain Burchett, what do we owe you for this unexpected visit?" She heard the venom in her tone when she directed it toward the man who could irritate her to no end, and yet, stir her blood for some ungodly reason.

His brow wrinkled up slightly. He studied her for a split second. "We're here to fix your roof."

Had she heard correctly? Here he stood, plainly ignoring her son, and yet willing to give her a helping hand.

"Hello Clare, I'm McCoy, do you remember me?"

Clare reeled her gaze back into the face of the man she remembered being smitten with Betsy. "I believe so."

"Come on McCoy let's get the roof in place. Need to get it done before the rains come."

Speechless, Clare couldn't believe they aimed to put a roof onto the second room of her home. She didn't know what to make of the man continually coming to her aid.

McCoy tipped his hat at Clare and said, "Ma'am, he's right. Best we get started."

Clare's gaze followed the men gripping the reins of their horses and disappearing around back of the cabin toward a pile of planks that Jonathan had intended to use for the roof.

"Come on, Sam, the Rangers will need a hearty meal when they finish, so let's go decide what to cook for them."

Another rider approached. Clare took a step up onto the porch and looked around to see who was coming to help the Rangers. She squinted.

Jonathan. He certainly wasn't coming to help. What did he want? She frowned "Sam, you run along and take a basket and find *Pia* some berries. Can you do that?"

"Yeah, making a pie?"

"Uh-hmm," she mumbled, keeping an eye on the rider. Excited to help, Sam grabbed a basket off the porch chair and took off for the woods.

Jonathan stopped directly in front of her and trailed his eyes over her thick braid hanging over her shoulder. His gaze skimmed over her cotton shirt and man's pants. She didn't miss his slight sneer when his eyes rested on her moccasin covered feet.

Gracefully, he dismounted and took off his hat. Spreading his lips into a charming grin, his low, soft voice said, "Clare Rose."

"Jonathan."

He stepped to his saddlebag, and while pulling out a rolled document, he asked, "Can we talk?" His attractive smile lit up his face, but his insolent gaze continued to probe hers.

She turned and entered the cabin with him following. With a gesture, she indicated a chair by the table. Clare took a seat and waited. When he scanned her one room house, a slight sneer on his lips told her what he thought.

"How the hell can you live in this?" His hand flipped out to indicate his surroundings.

His insolent tone stifled the air around her.

He turned and gazed into her eyes, lifted an arrogant brow, dropped onto the chair, and mumbled, "Forget it. That's not why I came. I brought documents to dissolve our marriage." He unrolled the papers, took out a pen from his breast coat pocket and slapped it down on the table.

"Look, Clare, I hope you understand, but I need to…to not be married to you. I mean, you can understand, can't you. People talk. Hell, there's enough talk as it is. I want to move on with my life."

"I understand." She picked up the pen and started to sign, and then hesitated, looking up into his face. "Do I sign Clare Rose Montgomery or use the name of my Comanche husband?"

She wanted to laugh at his noticeably shocked expression, and, for some reason, she enjoyed watching his face turn bright red.

He stammered for a second, and finally mumbled, "Montgomery. Use my name, Montgomery."

She quickly signed the paper, shoved it back toward him, and stood.

With a wicked look, he scooted the chair back and rose to his full height while rolling the document. Not taking his gaze from her, he shoved it into his coat pocket, and lifted the corner of his lips. "Clare Rose, I never thought things could come to this."

"Jonathan, none of this was your fault, so please leave. Go back to your life." Clare moved around the table and stepped toward the door. "If people ask, just tell them we were only married a week which really doesn't constitute a marriage in such a short length of time."

"Oh, but I thought we had a wonderful thing going, Clare Rose." He stepped next to her, reached out, and to her surprised touched her cheek. "Look at you, after all you've been through, you're still the prettiest woman I've ever laid eyes on."

When she took a step back, Jonathan stepped closer, gathered her braid in his hand and invaded her breathing space. His smooth, feminine-like finger rubbed her lips.

Her eyes widened in disbelief.

"Your flaming red hair must have a lot to do with your high-spirited lust for life."

Clare's breath hitched. She backed away. A hungry, mawkish pitch in his tone specified his intentions.

"When I look into those green eyes, Clare Rose, I fantasize about you and what they did to you, my little Indian princess."

"What?"

"Ah…" his hand released her braid to rub the palm of his hand up and down her arm while letting his gaze slither over her body. "You know."

Hairs on her neck prickled. "No, I don't know."

"Did the savages take you with force or did you enjoy feeling them inside of you—the way you did me?"

Clare's breath quickened at the accusation. Her heated blood seared through her body so fast, she had to push the words from her grounded teeth, "You despicable, disgusting person, get the hell out before—"

He slammed his lips on her mouth, trapping her words.

She pushed her mouth aside, demanding, "Get out."

Clare found herself ensnared in Jonathan's arms. She tried to shove her hands against his chest to force him away, only to have him tighten his hold on her, restricting her movements.

She couldn't breathe. His smashing lips pushed hard against her teeth and when he tried to probe his tongue into her mouth, she bit down.

"Ow, you goddamn Indian witch." He growled, gritting his teeth, he grabbed her wrists with one hand, squeezed them together and covered her mouth with the other, smothering any chance of her taking a breath. Towering over her, he shoved her up against the wall, pressed his tall, lanky body hard into hers, and then pulled back just enough to take in her frightened look.

Clare looked up into his nasty grin and her heartbeat sped up, pounding an alarm in her brain. She jerked her arms, trying to break free, but his fingers grasped her wrists so tightly her hands tingled from lack of blood flow.

He grinned. "You can't go anywhere, not 'til I'm done with you. You'll like it." He slammed his mouth over hers, freeing his hand to slither underneath her shirt. When his fingers touched her skin, he sucked in a quick breath, pressing his bulge against her.

Clare tried to scream but his mouth clamped over hers, hard and wet. His kneading fingers covering her breast shot pain through her chest. Wide-eyed, Clare's mind swirled. She tried to bring a leg up, but he pressed harder against her. The more she tried to wiggle free the more excited he became, rubbing his engorged appendage over her abdomen and thighs.

His hand squeezed her breast hard and then covered her mouth. He looked straight into her eyes. "So you like it rough, don't you?" His foul mouth hovered over hers, blowing his hot breath into her. "What did those Redskins teach you? I can do whatever those savages did to you and more. You'll like it. No one needs to know. There's nothing wrong with having a little on the side. Once you've had it, you want more, don't you?"

Her eyes widened. She couldn't breathe. She had to do something. God help her. With all she'd been through no one had ever defiled her in this way. She squinted. There's no way…

Clare stopped struggling against his weight. Her body went limp, her eyes drooped, and she didn't move. To solidify her position with him, she slowly looked up into his disgusting face.

He relaxed his hold, rubbed his hard form against her abdomen and snorted. "Well now, that's more like it. You won't regret it. I'll take care of you if you'll just let me…"

In one sudden move, Clare slumped down enough to push from the wall and free her hands, knocking him aside.

He grinned and stepped to her.

She raised a hand and slapped him surprisingly hard enough her red handprint materialized on his cheek. "You disgusting, despicable white man. I've met Indians better than you."

His distorted, heated face stared at her. In a fit of rage, he lifted his hand and struck her so fast she didn't see it coming, slamming her against the wall.

Clare pushed herself up, touched her backhand to her lip and looked up at the man she had once thought to be a wonderful husband. He took a step toward her. From the look in his eyes, he intended on striking again.

A hand grabbed Jonathan's shoulder, spun him around and pounded him to the floor.

Clare took in a relieved breath when Drury pounded another fist into Jonathan's jaw. And then another, another, and another. Her body shook with every fisted punch striking Jonathan's face.

"Drury," Clare's warning voice sliced into the heated room.

Drury's fist stopped in midair. He pulled the man to his feet, dragged him from the cabin, and boosted him over his horse. With a hard slap on the horse's rump, the animal took off with the man hanging on for dear life.

Clare stood in the doorway. When Drury swung his gaze to her, she tried to force a smile, but crinkled up her face. She shuddered with disgust. Tears burned her vision.

Blinking, she raised her hand and touched her split lips. She pulled her gaze from Drury to her blood smeared fingers. Her shaky breath sputtered out a whimper with the thought of Jonathan touching her breast. Never, had he touched her in such a way, not even during their short marriage. He'd only mounted her and done his business, but now, she felt dirty. Clare stepped from the porch and took off running down the path to the stream.

Reaching the edge of the water, she fell to the ground and scooped up a handful to splash over her arms and face. The hot tears flowed.

"Clare." Drury squatted next to her, reached out and touched her.

"No. Don't." Clare screamed and shoved his hand away.

"Clare, he's gone. He won't be back, I'll make sure."

She turned and read his concern for her in his worried look. This man she could trust. He'd always been truthful with her, never asked her for anything. She believed him.

Pieces of bitterness faded to replace the need of empathy from another being. "He...he..." The tears refused to stay and when they gushed, a moan pushed from her throat.

Drury gathered her into his arms. The grief and agony of the past months spilled shaking her body. She wadded a fistful of his shirt in her hand and released the tears at will.

Leaning her forehead against Drury's chest, she took control of her trembling body and slowly sucked in a deep breath. Soaking in his strength and controlled temperament, he made her feel safe, safe in the arms of a man nourishing a deep hatred for Indians.

Before looking him in the eyes, she released his shirt from her fist, bent over and splashed cold water over her face. With slumped shoulders, she sat up, and stared out across the water, rippling its way down stream.

Slowly, she turned her head to Drury and gazed into his kind eyes, eyes suddenly expressing anger.

"Clare, what the hell happened? Did the son-of-bitch touch you?" Drury asked showing complete loathing for the man.

Clare nodded and sucked in a lung full of air and held it for a second before releasing a long slow exhale.

"It seems I'm now a free woman from Jonathan Montgomery. He brought documents for me to sign. Afterward, he thought he'd persuade me…to…to agree to have some kind of secret relations with him and in turn he'd take care of me."

Clare looked up into Drury's angry face. She dropped her head onto her hand and rubbed her fingers over her forehead. "You know the kind of *relations* all you men want from a woman. Pleasure."

Drury glanced down at the cloth in his hand he'd grabbed before following her. He leaned forward and dipped it into the cold running stream. Wringing it out, he stood, pulled her to her feet, and placed the wet rag on her mouth.

She chuckled, took the rag and held it against her split lip. "It appears, Captain Burchett you have once again come to my rescue."

He was close. Clare swayed toward him. Anger in his eyes melted into passion. Her gaze slid to his lips.

He leaned in and gently laid his warm soft lips slightly against her swollen ones. A shocking, raw nerve prickled goose bumps on her skin.

He lifted his head, turned, and took a step. "I…I best get back to helping McCoy before he comes looking."

Clare blinked. Silently, she walked along next to the man who, once again, bewildered her. She glanced at him. He smiled. She loved his smile. "You…you must think I'm terrible."

"Why? None of this is your cause. You didn't start any of this. Men can be evil, no matter the kind."

Clare gazed up into his eyes, tilted her head, completely perplexed. "Why, Captain Burchett, are you learning to be more insightful?"

He chuckled. "It's Drury, remember? Sensitive, probably not, but maybe slightly more tolerant of people and that's because of you mostly."

"Me?"

He stopped and cast his eyes on her. His keen study bore into her. She glanced down at the rag in her hand, reached up, and pressed it against her lips. Shifting her gaze up, she was taken aback from the smoldering desire he expressed in his crystal blue eyes. Her blood pumped faster, her free hand flew up to cover the vein in her neck. No man had ever looked at her with such a…what…a…yearning, craving.

Clare cleared her throat. Common, logical sense instructed her brain not to give in to emotional feelings over this man for it was not a healthy idea. He more than likely wanted the same thing as Jonathan, except in a more gentle way, maybe. She knew from experience, warm fuzzy feelings didn't last.

"Ah…ah, I best get around back or McCoy will reckon I took off."

"*Pia*, I found the berries. Is this enough?"

Grateful for the distraction, Clare reached for the basket Sam handed her and gave him a huge smile. "This will be plenty for a pie. You did good."

When she looked around for Drury, he had hurried out of sight.

Chapter Eighteen

By suppertime, Clare, with Sam's helping hands, had prepared a meal for the men. "Come on, Sam, the Rangers will want to eat before heading back to town. All the food's outside on the table."

Sam ran out, climbed onto a chair, and grabbed a biscuit out of the basket.

"Hey there little cowboy, you must be mighty hungry." McCoy walked up and patted the top of Sam's head. He stood holding his white Stetson in his hand, swirling the brim.

"I ain't no cowboy. I'm a Comanche."

McCoy grinned, glanced at the captain and patted Sam's head again. "I reckon you are, but can't you be a cowboy too?"

Sam frowned and thought about it for a moment. "I guess. I can ride a horse."

McCoy laughed.

Clare let herself relax and enjoy the moment. McCoy had an easy way about him, putting others at ease. She wished Drury could be at ease with her son like McCoy. "Well, Mr. McCoy, take a seat and dig in."

Drury walked up, pulled out a chair, and sat next to Sam, but she noticed he paid no mind to her son, nor did he gaze upon him.

"Ma'am, be mighty nice of you if you could see fit to let us sleep out here tonight and get a good early start, so we can finish by midmorning."

Clare's eyes widened. "Well, sure, fine with me and Sam. But, there's no hurry. I'm sure you have other responsibilities you need to tend to more than to put a roof on an old cabin."

McCoy shoved a biscuit into his mouth and wiped at the dripping butter running down his chin. With a mouthful, he mumbled, "We'd soon stay and get it done. Might rain before we can finish, who knows."

By the time Clare cleaned up the supper dishes and put Sam to bed, the night curtain had opened up to a sky of sparkling stars. The Rangers had built a small fire near their sleeping blankets.

Clare carried two steamy cups of coffee to the men where they had settled.

When McCoy turned his head and noticed her approach, he pushed to his feet. Drury glanced up, but didn't stand, nor did he take his eyes off her.

"I thought you might like a cup of hot coffee before retiring."

McCoy reached for the cups, turned and bent to give Drury one. He straightened and turned back to Clare, shifting from one foot to the other with a worried expression. "Ma'am, I'm sorry about…about, look I know I can't make amends for what the Rangers done—"

"Mr. McCoy," Clare touched his arm and said, "Please, there is no need to speak of what was done, it's all in the past now, don't you think?"

"No, ma'am, not by a long shot. If you don't mind me saying so, you…you have a half-breed son and Betsy, well, Betsy ain't all there. Her mind can't move past the horrid things them savages did to her."

"Maybe you're right. In a way, I try to think ahead, especially with my son. None is his doing, so hopefully he'll be a better person than those holding him accountable, even though he's innocent."

Clare couldn't help but throw an angry glare toward Drury. His gaze didn't sway from hers, nor did he deny what she said. She quickly shifted her attention away from Drury, and asked, "Are you taking care of Betsy, Mr. McCoy?"

McCoy nodded. "I have a small ranch outside of town heading east," his head jerked toward Drury, "not far from Cap's."

"There's days Betsy seems normal and happy. Other days she won't let me come near. If I mention a trip to town, she clambers up into a shell and won't speak for hours."

"I'm sorry. Does she ever ask about me?"

"No. I told her we rescued you and she stared at me with her incessant blank expression. I'm not sure she even remembers you."

Clare glanced down at her hands. "I left her behind when I escaped. She probably hates me. I thought I could find help and return for her, but then the Comanche band grabbed me and…and the rest you know."

"Yeah, four years of living with the Comanches," he shook his head. "The Cap said they were good to you, how come?"

She nodded and glanced at Drury.

"If they were good to you, then if you don't mind me asking, why the kid?"

Clare released a long despairing breath. "You're telling me folks around here think I have a son because I was violated?"

McCoy shifted on one foot then the other, clearly embarrassed. "I'm sorry, I should never have asked."

"No. I don't mind. Mr. McCoy, the Comanches were never abusive, violent, or hurtful in any way toward me. I married the chief of the band. It was a good life. I was happy there."

The Ranger's eyebrow lifted. "But not so happy with the white men. I see it's been tough for you coming back."

She nodded and glanced at Drury.

"Well, if you'll excuse me, I should check on Sam and go to bed. I'll have breakfast waiting for you before you head back tomorrow." Clare smiled at McCoy, shot Drury a quick glance and turned toward the cabin.

McCoy squatted near the fire, took a gulp from the coffee cup and stared into the flames. "She's nice. So's the kid."

Drury grunted, acknowledging his comrade's words.

McCoy took another large gulp and threw out the rest. He stood, strolled over to his blanket, and stretched out, laying his head on his saddle. "She'll have a hell of a hard time making ends meet, especially with the way folks around here treat her—especially her parents."

Drury glared into the fire. "Your mighty talkative tonight, McCoy."

He shrugged. "Just wondering. I like her. She's hell of a strong woman to endure what she's been through and not come out bitter. Or insane."

McCoy's troubled tone drifted to Drury's ears. He shot a quick glance at him, then covered his arms, closed his eyes, and never said another word.

Drury tugged his Stetson low on his brow, folded his arms across his chest, and stared into the flames. Yeah, she was a hell of a strong woman. One he wanted. Now, more than ever. He should have never kissed her in the first place, and then he did it again. What the hell was wrong with him?

Drury reached over, grabbed a log, and tossed it into the pit. Shit, he knew. These sensations mixing up his emotions and needs hadn't struck him since his wife. Must mean love. Mary Lou minced no words, she'd tell him so. Could Clare Rose Coulson love him? No. Not happening, even if she didn't have a half-breed kid, well, maybe…ah shit, hell.

He stretched his legs, plopped his booted ankle over the other, pulled the blanket to his shoulders, and stared up into the brilliant night sky. A blissful sigh escaped his lips when an image of a beautiful, redheaded woman with large, green eyes drifted before him. Her gaze melted every bone in his supposedly tough Ranger body. Hell.

* * * *

Sam came running through the door. "*Pia*, Drury is coming to eat."

Clare placed hot biscuits on the table and turned to Sam. "What about Mr. McCoy?"

"He took off," answered a deep, pleasant voice.

Clare's gaze swung up to the smiling eyes of the Ranger who immediately caused a twitter to trip her heartbeat. He stood in the doorway with his dingy, black Stetson in his hand. His light hair was wet and finger-combed back from his wash-up in the creek. She noticed he seemed to brighten the room.

"He's worried he's been gone too long. Said Betsy gets nervous."

"Please join us." She turned to her son helping himself to a spoon full of eggs. "Sam, wait for our guest to be seated."

Sam glanced around at Drury and grinned. "He ain't no guest, he's our friend."

Drury's eyebrow lifted and looked at Sam. He strolled to the table, took a seat and picked up a fork while Clare dished him some scrambled eggs. He didn't move when she reached over and filled his cup with coffee. He swallowed.

"Want a biscuit, Drury?" Sam asked grabbing one and handing it to him.

"Sam. Drury can help himself and stop calling him Drury. You call him Captain Burchett."

Sam frowned. "But, Drury...Captain Burchett told me to call him Drury. Didn't you?"

Drury took a bite of jelly biscuit and nodded. "That I did." He glanced at Clare. "The boy has a right to call me Drury. We're friends."

Clare frowned and clamped her mouth shut.

Drury ate in silence while he listened to the boy chatter. He was a smart kid for his age. Good thing too. McCoy was right. The boy had a rough road ahead.

"*Pia*, I'm done. Can I go feed the horse?" he asked pushing at his plate.

"Yes, you can. Just one bucket of grain, remember."

Drury watched the boy run out the door before turning his gaze to Clare. She stared back with a quizzical expression. His gaze slipped to her lips when they parted as if to ask him about something. Being alone with her wasn't a good idea. He didn't trust himself to not kiss her again. Not giving her a chance to speak, he scooted his chair back, took the last sip of coffee, and stood. "I best be going too." He strolled to the door, stopped, and looked at her. He couldn't stop his lips from spreading. Certainly seemed he's been smiling a lot lately. "I'll say goodbye to the boy on my way out."

"Captain Burchett, his name is Sam."

Her perturbed tone spread his lips a little wider. He yanked his hat firmly on his head and said, "Sam." He winked at her and stepped through the door.

Clare's mouth dropped. She strolled to the door keeping her eyes on the man who truly puzzled her. She watched the scene before her in awe.

Sam ran over and hugged Drury's leg. And then Drury did something out of the ordinary—he gave Sam a pat on the head.

Clare unpacked a box containing blue and yellow materials to be rolled onto a board for display in the store. She rubbed her hand over the soft, silk fabric and, for a moment, imagined herself dressed like once before in her first life. She hadn't touched fine silk against her body in a long time. Her head dropped to take in the garb she wore.

She looked huge in the oversize pants, but that's all she had to wear, except her deerskin Indian dress.

Her lips spread slightly into a thin line. Maybe one day, she could afford to buy some and make herself a dress, at least one dress. Then again, for what?

Clare shivered from a cool breeze flowing through the storage room. Thinking she'd closed the back door, she took a step and stopped.

Betsy stood in the opened doorway, staring at her. Her long, brown hair appeared tangled and matted. "Betsy. Oh Betsy." Clare move toward her with her hand out. "Betsy, please, please, come in."

Betsy stepped back and silently shut the door.

Clare rushed forward and pulled the door open. Betsy stood not four feet from her. Clare bit down on her bottom lip. Poor Betsy. No matter how hard it was for her and Sam, their problems would never amount to those Betsy endured.

"Clare Rose."

"Yes, you remember me. Betsy…" Clare couldn't stop running to her. Without a thought she flung her arms around her shoulder and hugged her close. "Betsy. I'm so, so sorry."

"For what?"

Clare moved back and gazed into her friend's eyes. Remembering McCoy's warnings of her unpredictable outbreaks, she wasn't sure if she should mention any part of the past.

"I haven't taken time to come see you."

Betsy moved past her and entered, her nervous gaze shifting around the room. She strolled to the counter. Clare watched her stare at the bolt of silk fabric spread out on the table. Betsy rubbed a dirty hand over the material.

Clare glanced toward the door leading into the store. If Pa found Betsy touching the blue material with such dirty hands, there's no telling what he'd do.

She reached out and put her arm around Betsy's tiny waist, and said, "Come sit and let's talk."

Clare led her over to the stools. Betsy's large, brown eyes stared at her.

"McCoy said you were with child." Her gaze dropped to Clare's abdomen.

"I was…but not anymore. She didn't live."

Betsy nodded. "Good."

Clare pressed her lips together and decided not to pursue the subject further. "Betsy, I can't tell you how sorry I am about…about…"

"Why should you be sorry?" She cocked her head and a blank expression stared back. "Those savages were mean to you too. I hope the Rangers kill 'em all. If I ever see one I'll kill 'em myself."

A chill scurried over Clare's skin while staring into Betsy's eyes, insane eyes filled with hatred.

"*Pia.*"

Sam's sleepy voice drew her attention. He crawled out from underneath the shelf where he'd gotten into the habit of napping. Clare grinned.

"Sam, come meet my friend." She held out her arms for him.

He glanced up at Betsy and yawned. He rubbed an eye and slowly strolled to his mother. Clare picked him up to sit on her lap. She gave him a kiss on the cheek and turned to Betsy. She frowned.

Betsy's dark, odium expression sent a shock wave through her body. Protective instincts made Clare tighten her arms around her son.

"Betsy…Betsy, this…this is my son, Sam."

"He's Indian."

"Half."

Her loathing gaze traveled over Sam's entire face. "He's brown. Black hair. Nothing white."

Her vile tone and dark, threatening eyes struck Clare like an arrow.

"Why do you have him," she demanded between clenched teeth, jumping to her feet so fast the stool went flying backward. "You should have killed him."

"Betsy…no…I couldn't…I…I love him. He's my son." Clare squeezed his small body to hers. She stood and stepped back when her insane friend moved closer.

Betsy took a step, drilling her eyes into Sam, evil eyes wanting to kill an innocent child.

Clare hugged his head against her chest so he could no longer see the woman.

"Leave, I need you to leave."

Without a word, Betsy glared at Sam, turned and ran out of the building.

Trembling, Clare hurried to lock the door. She hugged Sam close. Her hand shook. Her body quivered so hard, she was afraid to hold him any longer. She hurried and put him down, grabbed an apple and handed it to him.

He didn't appear to be frightened, though she knew he had taken it all in. Something deep inside told her Sam wasn't safe around Betsy.

"What in God's name was that lunatic woman doing in here?"

Clare swirled to the demanding voice. Her eyes widened. There in the store doorway stood her mother with an angry frown wrinkling up her face.

Clare's gaze swung to the rifle in her hands, the very rifle her pa had used to shoot the Apaches.

"Ma, what are you doing with a gun?"

Alyson glanced down at the rifle pointing in the direction of the back door. She lifted a shoulder and lowered the weapon. Her gaze turned back to Clare. "That woman's mad. After what those savages done to her, she's insane. No telling what harm she'll cause you and the boy."

"His name's Sam."

"What?" she asked, frowning.

"My son's name is Sam." Clare glared at her mother and waited for her response. When there was none, she shook her head, grabbed the coats off the hook, and mumbled, "Besides, she only wanted to talk."

"Well, you best stay clear of her. I saw the way she looked at the boy."

"Sam. Mother. Sam. Can't you even say his name? Sam." Clare glanced at her son busy munching on his apple and drawing on a brown wrapping paper she'd given him earlier. His little ears probably didn't miss anything even though he seemed to be concentrating on his doodling. "Come, Sam, time we leave for home."

"Clare Rose, do you have a gun?"

Clare shrugged. "I have a knife, and a bow and arrow."

"Good heavens—here." Alyson shoved the gun into Clare's hands. "You best keep this close."

Her mother's gaze ran down her clothing, and after a quick glance toward Sam, she headed back into the store, slamming the door behind her.

Clare stared at the closed door. Those were the most words her mother had spoken to her since her return. She gripped the cold rifle.

"Come on, dear, it's getting late, we have a long ride ahead and we need to get home before dark." Taking his hand in hers, she led him out the door and down the alley toward the stables.

Mr. Hops had her horse all saddled and waiting for her. "Afternoon, Miss Coulson."

She smiled. "Afternoon, Mr. Hops. Thank you so much for taking care of me. I do appreciate it. And, please call me Clare."

He bowed his head and said, "Miss Clare."

Sam giggled.

A deep vibrant voice said, "Clare."

No denying the person belonging to the sexy, slow drawl. Clare swallowed down a twitter of excitement and turned in the direction of the man strolling through the double barn doors. "Captain Burchett."

An eyebrow lifted at her formality. He stopped within inches of her without releasing her gaze. She stepped back.

"How's the roof holding up? You need help moving some furniture into your new room?"

"We'll manage. How can we thank you for what you've done for us?" Clare dropped her head to the side and asked before thinking, "How about supper on Saturday for you and Mr. McCoy."

"Yeah," hollered Sam, sitting high on the horse. Mr. Hops had lifted him up and handed him the reins.

Drury chuckled. "Sure, I'll let you know. If you don't mind, I'll ride out a ways with you."

She nodded.

Once they left the town behind, Drury slowed his horse and waited for Clare to halt her horse next to his.

"Clare." He angled his wide rim hat above his forehead letting the late afternoon sun shine on his face.

Her gaze traced the scar along his cheek, something she rarely ever noticed anymore. His curly, dark blond hair was clipped to the nape of his neck. She shifted her gaze to his eyes appearing deep, sky blue in the setting sun.

"Clare."

She blinked, sat up straight and cleared her throat. "Yes."

"I have to leave your company here, my trail leads down the road." He jutted his chin toward the road forking off toward the opposite direction. "I'll be gone for a few days—governor's sending us out to scout a tribe that's been raiding up north."

"Indians?"

"Yeah, seems a band is on the warpath. They burned and killed several settlers."

Clare but couldn't think of a thing to say.

"We'll still have supper, once we return, if you're still willing to have us. I'll stop by on the way through."

"By all means. Let me know when you're home."

Drury tugged his hat low, reined his horse in the opposite direction and galloped off toward a job she knew he looked forward to, especially if it meant killing Indians.

Clare bit down on her lip, frowned, and swung her gaze away from the Ranger and down at her son's long, black hair and brown skin.

Chapter Nineteen

A gust of wind blew through the open door. Clare glanced back at Sam. The roaring fireplace had warmed the room and he slept cuddled beneath the hide on the floor near the fire. She slipped out and quietly closed the door.

Her garden had a few vegetables she needed to pick before the storm blew in. Late fall was so unpredictable and if she didn't heed the cold weather signs, the vegetables might freeze before she gathered them.

Hurrying around the corner of the cabin, Clare took a quick scan of her garden she'd planted soon after they'd moved in. Thank the Great Spirit, the garden had served them well and filled her son's belly. Eyeing a few late developing squash and corn, she hurried to gather what was left. With care, she placed all she could find on a large tablecloth, then folded the corners together and tied the ends.

Standing, she swayed from a gust of strong, cold wind, sending a shiver down her back. Grey clouds hovered above threatening its storm on the earth below. Holding her coat with one hand, she picked up the bundle of vegetables and hurried toward the cabin.

"*Keshini.*"

Clare sucked in a shallow breath and stopped dead in her tracks. "*Chakotay.*"

Her eyes widened. Her heart quickened. He sat tall and proud on his pinto like a Comanche warrior of years ago. His body was covered with a heavy buffalo hide to protect him from the cold wind, yet, she still read the signs of worry in his face.

Instantly, she swung her eyes toward the road and searched the area. When her head swung back at *Chakotay*, she waved for him to follow her inside the cabin.

Again she glanced back at the road. "Hurry, come in." No sooner had he stepped inside, than his eyes rested on Sam sleeping soundly near the fireplace.

"He's grown." His words were barely above a whisper.

Clare nodded.

She placed all the vegetables on the table, turned and gazed at the Comanche chief. "*Chakotay*, what are you doing here? It isn't safe…there….there's Rangers all around these parts. You shouldn't have come."

He shifted his gaze from the boy to her, taking in the garb she wore and her belly. "Papoose?" His gaze searched around the room and returned to her with a frown.

Clare's hand covered her stomach. She shook her head. "She died before she entered this world."

"Girl."

"Yes, I named her *Kiche.*"

"Spirit in the sky."

Clare bit her lower lip to keep it from trembling. She didn't trust her voice to reply while tears burned her eyes.

He nodded slowly, and again turned his vision onto his son.

She swallowed hard.

"The boy you helped returned to tell us of your life. Thank you for saving him from the town."

"Please sit. I'll fix you some food and then you must leave, leave before someone finds you here. Where did you tie your horse?"

"In the woods. Both are out of sight."

Clare's brow lifted. "Is someone with you?"

"No. I brought Big Black. He belongs to you and you'll need him." His chin jutted toward the boy. "You'll need a horse for *Samarjit.*"

Chakotay sat at the table, but his gaze strayed back to his son. A son he hadn't seen in almost a year.

Clare place a platter of bread on the table, a jar of her strawberry jam Sam had helped her make. She strolled over to the fireplace, and with a bowl in her hand she scooped stew from a pot hanging near the fire.

Chakotay ate in silence, but his eyes kept returning to his son, sleeping peacefully. The fireplace filled the cabin with its loud pops and crackles while the blaze consumed the logs. When he finished, he handed her the plate.

She looked into his sad, troubled eyes. "How's the band doing? Are there many left? Have you found a good place for the winter? Why have you come? Don't you know you're in danger coming here?" Clare pressed her lips, realizing her flood of questions wasn't giving him a chance to answer her.

He placed the coffee cup on the table and then wiped his mouth on the back of his buckskin sleeve. "There's sickness in village."

"No. Not again. How bad?"

"Three died, but many are sick. Can you help?"

Clare glanced at Sam. He rolled over and opened one eye. Both eyes flew open, staring at the Indian sitting next to his *pia*. He didn't move, just laid there taking in the sight of the Comanche.

"I'll have to gather some herbs, but first I'll see if the doctor in town can give me some quinine. The white man uses it to heal fevers. It has a bitter taste, but can help unless the sickness has taken over and their bodies have weakened."

Clare smiled at Sam and held out her hand and said, "Come, your *ahp* is here."

Sam slowly sat up, not taking his eyes off the Indian. He pushed to his feet and hurried to his mother. Clare gathered him into her arms and sat him on her lap. "Sweetheart, this is *Chakotay*, your *ahp*."

Suddenly, Sam grinned, crawled down from his mother's lap and ran to *Chakotay*.

"You remember me?" *Chakotay* asked, pulling him to his lap.

"*Ahp*."

Tears burned her eyes again. Clare hadn't considered her son missing his father or any of the Comanche family in a long time. Father and son made a precious picture before her and she never wanted to forget it, but it couldn't last. She wiped her eyes and took a controlled breath.

"*Chakotay*, give me a day to gather supplies and I'll come to the village. How do I find it?"

With Sam in his arms, he stood. "Give Big Black the lead, he'll bring you to us, not more than a day and half journey, but it's rough territory."

Quickly bending, he place his son on the floor and gave him a slight squeeze. "Now I leave. Wait here *Samarjit* while your *pia* comes with me to get Big Black. Do you remember Big Black?"

"*Pia*'s horse," he proudly stated and pointed to Clare.

"That's right."

Clare filled the bowl with stew and placed it on the table. "Eat your supper while I tie up Big Black with our other horse."

She turned to leave, but hesitated when she noticed *Chakotay* studying Sam in a heartrending way.

Sam crawled upon a chair, picked up a spoon, looked around at his Comanche father and waved his hand.

Pressing her lips together, she grabbed her coat and stepped out the door with *Chakotay* close behind. He stepped in front of her to lead her into the woods where he'd left the horses.

By late the next day, Clare returned from town and her quick visit with the doc, and with the precious quinine he had willingly given her. He'd helped her through her troubled time with the baby and she knew he was an honorable man. He'd not inform anyone of her desires to help the Comanches.

Once home, she gathered all the herbs she was able to acquire from the surrounding woods. She packed the many dried healing herbs she and Sam had collected during the summer months. Before starting her journey, she packed warm clothing and food for the trail. With hard traveling ahead, she prayed to the Great Spirit that *Chakotay* was right and Big Black knew his way to the village. Did *Chakotay* ride Big Black to her place several times in order for the animal to find its way home? If so, then he'd been watching over her and she hadn't even been aware.

Minutes before sunrise, Clare woke Sam, dressed, packed the horse with all their items and settled on Big Black, ready for a long journey. Once she rode to the spot where *Chakotay* had tied the horses, she released the reins and gave Big Black the lead. She and Sam sat back, relaxed and moved with the horse's smooth gait.

She took a deep breath of cold air, glanced up at the dawning sky, and looked forward to the bright sun shining on them throughout the day. Thankful to the Great Spirit the weather had returned to it slightly warmer state and hopefully not turn to freezing until she and Sam returned to their cabin.

* * * *

Drury pulled back on the reins. He leaned forward, rested his forearm on the saddle horn, and pushed his hat rim back on his head to study every move made by the woman he was so enthralled with. He'd been on the road since late last night, on his way back to Silver Sage Creek when he intentionally swung by the cabin. He knew it was early, but she rose early to either head for town or work in the garden.

He frowned. Something was amiss.

Clare stood by the mare packed with bags, and she had Big Black. Where the hell did she get him? His brows pulled together. She had a heavy deerskin over her shoulders and moccasins, ready for travel.

He didn't move.

She entered the cabin.

He waited.

He didn't have to wait long before she came out with Sam by her side. Where was she going? His gaze swung to the chimney where a small swirl of grey smoke drifted upward, snuffed out.

She mounted behind the boy and headed out toward the woods. Both were dressed for cold weather. She was going somewhere for a long time, or for good.

Drury took a deep breath of chilly morning air, and without thinking it through, he kicked his horse in the flanks and followed.

He stayed far enough behind her so she would not detect him, but near enough to not lose her tracks.

Around midday, even with the sun high, the breeze hit his skin and sent a shiver through his body. Damn weather.

Hours later, well after the sun begin dropping in the west, she finally stopped. He stopped. Swinging his leg over the horse, he dismounted and took advantage of stretching his legs. He leaned against a tree and listened.

She was singing. Pretty. He couldn't understand the words, but the melody and soothing tone imprinted in his brain. She certainly was a beautiful woman. He frowned, she was singing in the Comanche language. She was headed back to them. He'd be able to find their hidden village if he continued to track her.

Chaotic emotions stirred within him. She'd hate him. He was a Ranger. It was his duty to report any Indian camps' whereabouts. He frowned. Damn her.

Drury tied his stallion and silently made his way to a secluded area where he could keep an eye on her. Like an alert fox, he lay on his belly and peeked through the brushes.

She built a small fire and fed the boy. He could smell the warmth of the blaze she had built. His stomach growled when the boy took a bite of stew. He rested his head on his arms.

What the hell was he doing? Why didn't he march right up to her and asked where she was going. Maybe he didn't want to know. Maybe she decided to return to the Comanche way of life. Why else was she suddenly in possession of Big Black? She met someone, who? Her Comanche husband? What did she call him, *Chakotay*. He wasn't easy to forget.

Well, if she decided to return to the Indians, he'd just shadow her every move and find out where their village was located. The Rangers certainly wanted to know. They'd been trying to follow trail after trail to expose villages throughout the area. Most times they returned empty handed. Not him. She'd lead him straight to them.

Drury opened his eyelids. He must have fallen asleep. Dawn hovered over the forest. The rustling sound of Clare moving around must have woken him. She had packed the mare and was mounting Big Black.

He quickly and silently made his way back to his mount and waited for her to ride ahead several yards before kicking his horse in the flanks.

Damn her. He should never have kissed her.

Chapter Twenty

Clare hugged Sam close, relaxed and gave Big Black the lead. A worried sigh escaped her lips. She knew he was trailing close.

The shadowy day filled the air with moisture. Her cold fingers pulled the hide snugly around her and Sam to protect them from the ever-increasing wind. She glanced up at the dark, heavy clouds gathering. Snow was coming but hopefully not before they arrived at their destination.

Clare pressed her cold lips together. She hoped he brought warm clothing. Why was he following her? For his own safety, maybe she should just stop and tell him to leave, to go back. No. She had learned how stubborn he was from what little she knew about him. Besides, it was too late now.

Big Black's gait stepped up a notch. She assumed the village was near. Her main concern was the band. They needed her help. How was she going to prevent any confrontation between the two men? Not surprisingly, the snowflakes drifted from the sky the moment Big Black rode into a mountain crevice hidden within a thick forest of trees. The wind carried the wet flakes at a slant rushing into her face. She glanced at her child all bundled up and sound asleep. He was warm against her body. She grinned. He was her life.

Big Black stopped. She swung her gaze down into a secluded valley. Smoke curled up from fire pits. Only a few women were scurrying about. Most were inside their teepees to keep warm.

She sat still for a few minutes and listened. He still followed. Now he knew the location of the Comanche's camp. How could she ever convince him they were good people?

Clare pressed her thighs against Big Black's belly allowing his pace to quicken. She didn't dare glance back. She knew the Ranger's eyes followed her from somewhere out of her sight, and she didn't want to give him away until she had a chance to talk to *Chakotay.*

She pulled on the reins to slow Big Black's entry into the village. A woman with her head covered stepped from a teepee and when she heard the approaching horses she stopped short and looked at the rider. A large grin spread over her face and she ran back into the teepee. Within seconds the entire camp surrounded Clare by the time she dismounted. They all spoke at once with excitement in their voices while touching her and her son to welcome them home.

"*Pia*, look." Clare's gaze turned at a child his age running toward them. She reached up and helped Sam down. "You can go play until *Pia* gets settled." She didn't have to tell him twice, he took off to meet the young friend the moment his feet touched the ground.

"*Keshini*, you came. Welcome back."

Clare swung her gaze to the sound of their Comanche Chief, *Chakotay*. "Of course I came."

"Come, it's warmer inside the teepee."

She followed him and suddenly frowned. Did he think she had returned to him as his wife? She couldn't. Not now. She no longer wanted to be his wife, nor could she live here with them again. She really didn't belong here. But they needed her help.

"*Chakotay*, I have supplies on the horse."

He strolled to the opening and spoke, ordering one of the Indians to bring in the bags. He returned to her side and took a seat near the fire, motioning for her to sit next to him. She did so.

Clare took a deep breath and looked into *Chakotay's* gentle eyes. She smiled. "I think…no, I know I was followed."

His eyes widened, and before she could finish telling him, he jumped to his feet and ran from the teepee. She stood at the opening and gnawed her lower lip.

He was already discreetly speaking while strolling in the opposite direction of where she had come. She knew he'd circle around and find the Ranger.

Clare glanced up into the wooded mountainside where she suspected he lay observing the village. Or, maybe he left, since now he knew the village location. Oh dear God, he'd tell the Rangers. What had she done? Killed her Indian family? Oh God, they needed to leave and leave now before he had a chance to ride back and tell the others.

A gunshot echoed, thundering through the village, ricocheting off one side of the mountain to the other. No. Clare covered her mouth to keep from screaming. Had Drury turned Captain Burchett, the Ranger, shooting the Indians he hated?

Suddenly the village came alive with braves, squaws and children rushing from teepees with frightened faces and glancing all about, not sure where the gunfire sounded. Clare whirled, taking in all the old and young running with their families to hide from the danger lurking. First and foremost on their minds were the Rangers coming to kill all in sight.

Clare wrung her hands, until no longer able to stand still, she ran toward the sound of the shot. There had only been one shot. She stopped.

Clare whipped around to the rushing horses. Their Comanche chief led the riders back into the village with Drury being dragged by a rope. He appeared dead.

Her pounding heart seemed to stop, a mournful scream tried to push from her throat, but nothing escaped her lips.

Chakotay halted directly in front of her and dismounted. He jutted his chin toward a pole in the middle of the village, ordering the braves to tie their captive. His grim, narrowed eyes leaped at her.

Clare bit down on her lip to keep from tearing. He lived. She shifted her gaze toward Drury, and then back to the chief. "*Chakotay*, please, don't kill him." Clare grabbed his arm. "Please, don't."

He shook her hand off.

"Please…" her voice broke. She couldn't keep a choking sound from escaping her lips when she appraised the situation. Stepping back, she hurried to the Ranger, dropped to her knees and touched his shoulder.

Drury lifted his head. His angry eyes kept her from speaking. She didn't care. He was alive. For now.

Angry squeezing fingers circled her arm and jerked her to her feet. Clare stumbled alongside *Chakotay* who practically dragged her into the teepee, tossing her down on the buffalo hide bedding.

"Why did you allow him to follow?" His tone affirmed his rigid body stance. She knew he was disappointed in her.

She sucked in a deep breath, pushed from the bedding and stood, staring into his livid, black eyes. "I didn't know until I had traveled far from the cabin. *Chakotay*, please he's a good man, he won't tell. I promise. Please don't kill him." Clare backed off when he began to pace.

"We need to move camp."

"You can't, please. You said yourself your people are too sick and frail to travel. I'm sure no one else followed us. Just him. I promise, he won't tell a soul. I beg you please, don't kill him."

Chakotay stopped and stared at her. "Why? What is this man…this Ranger to you?"

"*Pia. Pia.*" Sam flew into the teepee and threw his arms around Clare's legs. "*Pia*, the Ranger's tied up. Why? He's my friend."

Clare hugged his head against her and stared up at the Comanche chief.

His long, supple stride quickly carried him out of the teepee without another glance at them.

Clare sat down near the fire and held out her arms to Sam. "Come, you're cold, sit by the fire."

His look demanded an explanation. Clare cleared her throat and ran her hand down the back of his long black hair. "Your *ahp* doesn't know the Ranger the way we do. He's afraid he'll tell the other Rangers where the village is located. Your *ahp* has to make sure he won't lead other white men to this place."

"Drury won't. I'll tell him."

Before Clare could grab his arm, he took off. By the time she stepped through the teepee opening, he was kneeling by Drury with his hand on his arm. She couldn't hear what he was saying, but his little lips were moving fast. In the short time it took her to reach them, Sam had tears streaming down his face.

Clare reached down and placed her hand on her son's shoulders. She gazed into Drury's eyes. For a split second, she thought she recognized a flash of compassion before his blank gaze shot up to hers. He was good at covering his feelings. Clare took Sam by the hand and led his droopy, sad little body back to the teepee.

Once she fed him and put him down for the night, Clare grabbed a heavy buffalo hide and hurried out. Drury was slumped over with his head hung low. At first she thought he was out cold, but when she approached he raised his head and straightened.

Without speaking, she shoved the heavy buffalo hide between the pole and his back to wrap his shoulders tightly for protection throughout the frigid night. She was so close to his face, Clare tried to avoid his eyes, but she couldn't.

Her blood went all warm from just connecting with his gaze, heating her skin until the cold breeze touched her arm sending a chill down her spine.

"*Keshini,*" hollered *Chakotay* from a teepee.

Clare glanced around to find the Comanche chief motioning with his hand for her to come. She turned back. "Many are sick, I must go."

Drury's brows crinkled into a scowl. "That's why you came?"

She nodded. "They need my help."

"Him too?" Drury tilted his head toward the Comanche motioning Clare to come.

"Yes. You remember Sam's father?"

Drury whipped his gaze from the Indian to her, but he didn't reply.

"I must go help them."

Clare looked deep into his blue eyes reflecting worry and confusion. Then she stood, pulled the blanket firmly around his shoulders, backed away, turned, and strolled toward *Chakotay.*

****

Drury opened his eyes and peered through slits against the cold wind. He couldn't wait for the sunrise over the eastern mountain to touch him. If Clare hadn't given him the heavy buffalo hide, he'd have frozen to death. The long night proved the coldest he could remember. Guess he should be grateful the snow didn't fall like it threatened. His arms ached from the tied position and he certainly could use a hot cup of coffee.

He sucked in a long breath and glanced around. Several squaws went running past him to a teepee further down the end of the village. One of the squaws stopped to peek inside an opening. Many others emerged rushing toward the one. After many disappeared inside while a few waited near the opening with worried faces. He frowned. What was going on?

He turned his head eastward. His creased brow smoothed into contentment when the sunrays touched his skin. Warmth. Ahh…now his bones could thaw. If only he could move to a different position to allow blood to circulate through his sore muscles.

A horrid scream filled the air. Drury jumped.

His gaze skipped toward the teepee where the squaws had gathered. Another anguished cry sent a chill through his cold body. He stared at the teepee until he lost count of crying screams flowing out into the air. Then she stepped out.

Clare stood silently covering her mouth. He could tell there were tears rolling down her cheeks. Her face read of pain and grief. She squeezed her eyes shut and dropped to her knees, reminding him of the night her baby died. Sobs shook her shoulders.

By the time the sun drifted downward, a bare-chested Indian painted with yellow and green on his upper body rode up to the teepee on a black and white horse with a yellow-painted face.

A large Comanche exited from inside the teepee. He straightened when he stepped out, carrying in his arms a small form wrapped in a light tan deerskin and wound with a rope. The Comanche handed over the body to the painted warrior sitting high on the painted-face horse. He waited until twenty or so women, men and children gathered behind him, and then slowly, the horse moseyed up the canyon.

The entire procession moved with slumped shoulders and silent tears. His gaze searched out Clare and Sam within the group, until they disappeared within the foliage of the mountainous terrain.

He took a deep breath and leaned his back hard into the pole, and then swung his head around looking for something, anything to get free. How the hell was he going to get away? He glanced around the ground—not even a sharp rock close by, nothing. Even if he did manage to loosen the rope, could he leave? What about Clare? He puffed out a frustrated breath. When he whipped his head around, his gaze landed on an old Comanche woman approaching him.

Her stooped shoulders were covered with a long, brightly colored blanket and her feet slowly shuffled along the dusty ground toward him. She carried a small wooden bowl and a cup. Deep lines marked her dark brown skin surrounding large, sunken, black eyes. She didn't stop until her feet touched against him. Without speaking, she squatted inches from his face and tilted her head.

Drury fixed his eyes on hers. She looked to be a hundred years old. A glimmer in her probing eyes seemed to read his thoughts, making him uneasy. She didn't say a word, just held the cup to his lips.

He took a sip. Hmm, water. He sipped again.

No sooner had he swallowed, she placed the cup on the ground, and then shoved something solid into his mouth. His eyes widened. He almost gagged, except the flavor of the meat was pleasing and he was hungry. He'd need his strength if he found a way to escape. Meat gives strength, even if fed like a baby and with Indian hands. When the bowl was empty, she sat back on her haunches, tilted her head, and with impassive eyes studied him.

Drury watched her gaze trail down the scar on his left cheek and back to his eyes. He had a feeling the old Indian squaw was wise from her years of hardships and struggles. As much grief and pain he'd lived with losing his wife and child, he couldn't imagine the suffering she surely had endured during her lifetime.

With a great effort, she pushed her old bones to her feet, turned, and shuffled her way back to wherever she came from. With a full stomach and the warmth of the sun, he closed his eyes.

Lifting his heavy eyelids, Drury heard the band returning from the burial site. He shook his head to clear the fog from his brain.

The last thing he remembered was the ancient squaw feeding him. He must have fallen asleep. His searching gaze found Clare. She strolled to a pit and threw several logs into the fire, sparking the flames to life. Several squaws helped until the flames grew larger. Then, all the women sat around the pit. Drury wanted to holler at Clare, but she seemed to have forgotten him, so had the boy.

Sam sat solemn faced next to his mother. His small lips moved, chanting with the others. Drury recognized the man and woman approaching them. Many other braves gathered near the group and softly joined in the chant. He had no idea what they were chanting, but the rhythm and Comanche words were pleasing to his ears. The one he assumed was the child's mother had trouble chanting, choking back tears. She raised her arms and shrieked out words he didn't understand.

Drury couldn't stop his lips from quivering or the burning tears in his eyes. He shook his head. Why was he getting so emotional over these Indians? His moist eyes widened when the mother took a knife and cut her arm. The man did the same. Then they both lifted their arms to the sky and yelled heart-wrenching words.

Their words were gibberish to him, but he understood. He knew. Why God? Why my child? Why? That's what he had asked.

The squaw threw a blanket and several items into the fire and cried out. The father held up what looked like a doll toward the sky, spoke grieving words, and then, he gently placed the doll into the fire. The group continued to chant.

It seemed like hours before the man and woman stood and strolled to their empty teepee. Once they entered and closed the flap, the group continued to chant for another fifteen minutes or so, and then they too silently stood and moved off in the directions of their teepees.

Clare carried Sam in her arms and disappeared into a teepee.

Drury waited, but she didn't come out.

Chapter Twenty-One

Hours before the breaking dawn of a new morning, Clare leaned near Drury's face. Again she touched his shoulder, and said, "Drury."

He didn't move.

She pressed her ear near his mouth. His breathing was raspy. She touched his scarred cheek. He had the sickness. God help him, she had used up all the quinine.

She glanced around. There stood a lone Comanche standing guard over the horses. She waved for him to come near. With a knife from her belt, she cut Drury from the pole sending his body slumping to the ground.

Ignoring the disapproving scowl on the Indian's face, her strong tone instructed him to carry the white man's body. He looked around as if wanting permission from someone.

"Now," she ordered again, "In the teepee."

The Indian carried Drury into the teepee and dropped his body onto the bedding. When he didn't move, Clare ordered, "Go. Leave." Without wasting time, she blended an herb concoction, poured it into the water and placed the bowl on the fire to brew.

Clare hurried and tugged Drury's leather coat, black vest, and shirt from his body. She yanked several times to pull his leather holster from his waist, then realized she had to untie the leather string from around his right thigh. His six-gun was missing, evidently confiscated when captured. She struggled to strip the black high-top boots from his feet, and then the worn leather chaps from his legs.

Clare straightened and wiped her brow. Worn-out from just undressing the Ranger, she took several quick breaths and let her gaze skim over his upper body. His chest intrigued her with all its rippling muscles. In comparison to Jonathan, he had a small amount of chest hair and a tiny line of hair leading down to his pant waist and beyond, she was sure. She couldn't stop touching his chest with her eyes.

Clare dragged her gaze away to make sure the brewed herbs had finished. She spooned out the leaves and blew into the liquid to cool it down so Drury could drink the only medicine able to help him.

"Drury."

He moaned.

"Drury drink this. Drury, you need to drink this medicine." Clare shook his shoulder, raised his head, and when he parted his lips, she poured the medicine into his mouth. He swallowed, coughed. After three sips, she allowed him to lay back and sleep. His entire body shook. The fever inflamed his body. She whispered a quick prayer to the Great Spirit. If he could get through this stage of the sickness, he'd live. Hurrying to the corner of the teepee, she grabbed several hides, turned back and found *Chakotay* standing in the opening.

His contemptuous, black disks drilled into the man shivering on the pile of hides. Then, his wry gaze swung to hers. His brows tightened, wrinkling his forehead.

"He's sick with fever," she mumbled, and threw several hides and a blanket over his body. She straightened, turned and fixed her determined gaze at the chief.

He didn't say a word, just stepped back and disappeared, leaving the teepee flap swaying in the cold wind.

Clare hurried to close up the opening to keep all the warmth inside. She glanced across the room. Sam was still sleeping. Her gaze lifted. Please, Great Spirit, guard Sam from the sickness.

Drury's body shook violently and Clare did the only thing she could do, she crawled into the bed, scooted up against his body, and put her arm over his chest to hug him close. She had done the same for *Chakotay*. Not so very long ago, and yet, a lifetime away.

Drury's arm circled her waist and pulled her closer. She glanced up at his face. He mumbled something, a name, but it was incoherent. She only speculated his dreams centered on the family he'd lost.

Hours later, Clare slipped out of bed and prepared more of the herbal medicine. When it was ready, she roused Drury enough to get him to swallow a mouthful. He seemed to have settled down somewhat. His eyelids were closed and his breathing didn't sound raspy like it had earlier.

Daringly, she reached out and lightly touched his jaw. Her finger rubbed the ridge running along his left cheek. His scar was soft. For some reason she had expected it to be coarse. Maybe it was his slight growth of beard giving her the impression of softness. How did this happen? Did he try to save his family from the raiding savages attacking them, or did he fight off Indians while in one of his own Rangers' killing sprees? She knew the wound went deeper than a mere surface scar.

Clare caressed his forehead. Hopefully, by morning, the fever would leave his weak body. She released a tired sigh, stepped to the opposite side of the teepee, and crawled into bed with her son. Closing her eyes, she drifted off.

A moan woke her.

Clare peeked over the covers in Drury's direction. He moaned again. Quietly crawling from beneath the covers, she tossed a log on the fire and hurried to his side. Slipping under the covers, she lay next to the Ranger and touched her body up against his. He was only warm; the chills had subsided. The fever was gone.

Clare bit down on her lower lip. She rolled over to escape from beneath the blankets, but he caught hold of her. She heard him breathe in a deep breath and mumble. Again the name was inaudible to her and yet it sounded something like a woman's name. His arm held her snug around her middle. She swallowed hard and tried to center her thoughts on the burning flames in the fire pit.

He moaned.

His body moved up against hers, cuddling her in a position she'd never been privy to and it was disturbingly pleasant. She'd had two husbands, slept with both, but never experienced this kind of pleasure.

His hand rested up against the bottom of her breast. His restful breathing pressed alongside her when his muscled chest filled with

air, and his stomach muscles pushed up against her bottom–no not
his stomach muscle...it was...it was...oh, my God, she really
needed to get out of this bed, out of his arms, and away from his
body touching her.

She didn't move. Could hardly breathe. Her heart pounded,
pumping blood to all parts of her body. She laid still, closed her
eyes, and when she took a deep breath, he snuggled closer. She
listened to his sinuous breathing rhythm and relaxed against him.

Clare smiled. All the times she'd slept with *Chakotay* and the
short married week with Jonathan, she'd never snuggled warm,
comfortable, and safely against them, not like now. She didn't
want to leave. Why?

What was she to do? She couldn't let *Chakotay* kill him. There
had to be some way to convince the Comanche's council to believe
Drury was an honorable man. First, she'd have to persuade Drury
not to tell the Rangers their location. Close to an impossible task.
He hated Indians. Even her own son he only tolerated and she
wasn't sure why.

Clare squeezed her eyes shut. How was she ever going to talk
everyone into a civil compromise? She relaxed. She was so tired.

Clare's eyes flew opened. Oh my, she'd fallen to sleep.
Sounds outside the teepee told her the morning dawn had sent the
dark night westward. Drury's quiet breathing feathered over her
neck. Slowly she eased her body to the edge of the bedding and
slipped out of the blankets to the floor. Her gaze swung back at
him. He slept peacefully.

She quietly crawled to the other side of the teepee and stood.
By the time she gathered a couple of logs and placed them on the
fire, she heard Sam yawn. He stretched and yawned again.

Her eyes, sparkling with a loving gleam, crinkled. Stepping to
his side, she squatted and touched his face. "Good morning little
one." His lazy eyelids slowly opened, he yawned again, and then
grinned.

"*Pia.*" He jumped up and hugged her.

"Let's get dressed and go out to see what's going on."

The sound of the flap drew their head around to find *Chakotay*
entering with a bowl of stew. After a quick glance toward the

sleeping white man, he strolled to the bedding and squatted in front of them.

"Time to eat and come with me."

"Where are you going?" Clare couldn't stop the concern in her voice or her brows pulling together.

"Riding."

He didn't look at her, only at Sam. "You need to learn to ride better, so we spend the day hunting. We'll be back before sun goes down."

"Yea."

Clare giggled at Sam's excitement. How could she keep him from spending the day with his *ahp*? She nodded. "Promise me you'll stay warm and not get sick."

He jumped into her arms. Clare laughed out loud and hugged him close. Her gaze swung across the room and found the Ranger watching.

Chakotay's head swung around to suspiciously eye the Ranger.

"You're awake." Sam's jovial voice shouted. Crawling off the bedding, he hurried to Drury's side. He stopped short, tilted his head and with a concern tone, asked, "Do you feel better?"

Clare glanced at *Chakotay*. She couldn't read his expression, but his eyes were fixed on the man.

Drury pushed up on his elbow and his studying gaze stared at Clare and then back at Sam. "I reckon. Don't know what happened."

"You won't die like my friend, will you?" Sam asked, expecting an honest answer.

"No. Not today." Drury mumbled and turn his questioning gaze on the Comanche chief.

Clare hurried to intervene. "Sam, eat so you can go with *ahp*." She grabbed the herbs from the basket and started crushing the leaves in the small bowl. "Captain needs to take more medicine and rest in order to get well."

Sam stepped back, took the bowl from his *ahp,* squatted near the fire and shoved a big spoonful into his mouth. He glanced at his father to make sure he wasn't leaving. Once the last drop of stew disappeared, he rushed to his *ahp*'s side and hollered, "Bye *Pia*. Love you."

Clare giggled. "You be careful and listen to your father."

"I will." He stepped toward the opening, turn and waved at Drury.

Drury lifted his hand at the boy and dropped back on the bed. He closed his eyes. Clare waited until father and son departed before turning to her patient. "You're weak. You must take more tea and rest."

"I don't remember. When did I get sick?"

"Last night. I went out to put another blanket on you and I could tell you had the fever. We brought you in and I gave you medicine throughout the night."

Clare picked up the herbs and poured water into the bowl and placed it on the fire. She glanced at Drury. His eyes were closed and his arm rested over his forehead. After several minutes, she retrieved the bowl, stepped to him and knelt. "Please drink this."

He slowly opened his eyelids, aiming his blues straight into hers. Dropping his arm, he pulled up on his elbow and when she touched the bowl to his lips, he took a sip and another one, all the while not taking his gaze off her. He swallowed the bitter tea.

"The Indian with your son is your husband. He must be pretty mad at you for bringing me into your home."

Clare nodded, stood, picked up her basket of herbs and headed for the opening. "Yes, he is somewhat angry. You must understand it's difficult for him to reason why he has to allow you to live again. He's watching you closely. I'll try to convince him you're not a threat."

Clare looked intently into his eyes, but couldn't read whether or not he'd actually be a threat to the Comanches. "Rest, I'll be back after I help the others."

Now, he'd sleep for several hours. The herbal medicine helped, and the small amount of peyote in the tea didn't hurt.

By mid-afternoon, Clare made her way back to her teepee to make sure Drury was resting. She carefully carried the stew the other squaws had given her for the evening meal. Quietly stepping in, she found him sitting with one hand on a boot, trying to shove it on his foot. Her eyes widened.

"What do you think you're doing?" She dropped the basket, placed the pot of stew on the fire log, shoved the blanket from her shoulders and hurried toward him. She grabbed the boot from his foot and threw it in the corner.

"You're not going anywhere. You're weak, and besides, you'd never make it past the Indian guarding the horses." She turned, sucked in an exasperating breath and commenced to filling a bowl with strew. "Here, eat." She shoved it at him with a scowl. Huh, she sounded like she was scolding a small child.

He reached up and took the bowl. Their eyes connected. The vein in her neck pulsated from the mysterious twinkle in his eyes. He seemed to be seeking an answer...to what, she didn't know.

He finally pulled his gaze from her to the bowl in his hand. "I really should leave before your husband returns. You could help me."

Clare dropped onto a hide pallet next to the fire pit. She mumbled, "Eat."

He took a bite.

"First of all, *Chakotay* is the band's chief and he'll make sure a warrior keeps an eye on you constantly. And, he's no longer my husband."

"Since when?" Drury asked between bites.

"After he returned from the time you tried to kill him in the forest. He realized I'll never live with the band again, so he met with the council and they dissolved our marriage."

Drury's brow lifted. "That easy? He just gets permission from a council and it's granted without your presence."

She nodded. "Comanches keep things simple. They're a simple people, like I told you. He and his new wife have their own teepee at the other end of the village."

Drury's eyes squinted at her. "How do you feel about that?"

Clare lifted a shoulder, shook her head, and pursed her lips, thinking. After sitting silently for several minutes looking into the fire, mesmerized by its flames, her pensive tone revealed her thoughts, more to herself than to him. "He made the right choice. She's with child. He needed another son since I took his away."

Swinging her gaze to Drury, she straightened her shoulders, and with a demanding tone, asked, "Now, I really need to know what your intentions are toward my people."

"Your people."

"Well, yes, they are, were, my family for over four years. I love them. Drury, if I can talk *Chakotay* and the others into allowing you to return to Silver Sage Creek with me, you have to promise not to tell the Rangers this location."

Clare recognized the conflict filtering across his face.

"Why should I, Indians are the murderers who took my wife and child from me. They deserve to die."

"Please. This band of Comanche is a peaceful people. They don't go around raiding, raping, and murdering others. They only want to live in peace and be left alone to live their lives the way their ancestors did. They're only hunters and gatherers."

Jumping to her feet, she aimed her words directly at him. Her voice, edged with concern and above a whisper said, "Drury, if white men raped and murdered your family, would you want to kill all white men?"

He frowned, rubbed his scar, and then stood so fast he swayed toward the fire. Clare reached him seconds before he staggered into the pit. The momentum of her force knocked him backward. He grabbed her arms, pulling her with him flat onto the bedding.

Clare found herself bouncing onto his chest with his arms circling around her in a protective manner. She pushed up only to find her face inches from his. A thrill surged through her body when his gaze softened, searching her face, her hair, and then her eyes. She read something in his expression she'd never seen in a man before. He looked at her with the same longing she sensed within her own being.

Drury's hands slithered up her back to her neck. His fingers curled into her hair. He groaned as if soaking in its softness. His large, rough hands gently pressed the sides of her head and drew her to him. When his lips touched hers, his mustache tickled her lips. A thrilling sensation splattered over her stomach and down between her thighs—a pleasant sensation, a heightened awareness, tempting her to explore more.

Clare pulled away slightly, he didn't release her, but the gentle hold told her he wanted more. She did too. She frowned and stared into the bluest, craving need of any man she ever looked upon. Her gaze drifted down to his lips. Just one more couldn't hurt, could it?

Leaning in, she placed her lips on his. She tasted his firm mouth and…and the moment his hands left her head, they circled her body, rolling her over onto the bedding. He pressed his form against her and demanded more from her mouth than she'd known she could give. When his tongue touched hers, her body's unexpected reaction took over, shooting a lightning bolt through her like an arrow connecting with its target.

His hand combed through her strands of hair while his body pressed into hers. His hard form beneath his pants indicated a desire she recognized, but, this was different, she was different. She couldn't stop her legs from slightly spreading. He pushed firmly against her until her hips rose to meet him.

Her hands spread over his bare back, savoring in his taut muscles, clinging, wanting to feel more. She began to squirm beneath every stroke his hips rubbed against her, finding a crucial point striking a shocking thrill between her legs traveling up her body to a quavering mass.

Breathlessly, she clung to him in mouth-watering pleasure. Not even two husbands had performed in such a way. This outlaw of a Ranger's desires made her feel deeply satisfied and wanting him. She hugged him close.

He shuddered and buried his face in her neck, breathing heavily.

Clare closed her eyes. He made her complete. She didn't know why, but he did. Hmm, the thought of her naked body against his, tantalized, stimulated, and startled her excited imagination. Never did she want to forget the feel of him or the sensation they had just shared.

Several seconds later, he took a deep, disturbed breath and rolled to her side.

Taking control of her wanting desires for the man lying beside her, she sat up. "Drury, I…this shouldn't have happened, but…but, I'm glad it did."

"Why," his rough voice forced from his mouth, sitting up next to her. "Now, you think I've exposed my feelings for you enough to promise I'll not divulge this location if I manage to escape."

"No, Drury, I kissed you because I wanted to, not to seduce you to get my way. I don't trick people in order to get what I want. Don't you know me by now?"

He took a deep breath through his nose, rubbed his hand over his face, hesitating on the scar. After a hard stroke down the half-moon scar, he turned his body to the side and faced her. "You're right. I'm sorry." He reached over and took her hand in his. "You can, you know."

She frown, glanced down at her hands he gently held. "What?"

"Tell me to keep my mouth shut and never reveal what I've learned here these past days."

Her eyes widened. Her brows lifted. "What have you learned?"

"Comanches are people. I've watched and listened to the grief throughout the village, especially when a child died. I witnessed your funeral services. Feelings are the same whether white or redskin. I listened to your son's father talking to him this morning. He could not harm a child the way the raiding Indians did my daughter and at the same time love his own son, or show such respect for you."

Drury shifted, scooted his legs up, rested his elbows on his knees, and stared into the flames burning in the fire pit. "You know something, Clare, even the old, wrinkled woman, the one with a long, grey braid and the very dark skin and wrinkled face—she has to be a hundred. Anyway, she gave me water and fed me with her hand when you took off for the baby's burial. Not sure why she did, but she showed compassion for me, something you don't see much of in the white man's world. Especially for you."

Clare studied his piercing eyes staring into the fire. "You mean my parents and the way they treat me?"

"That has to hurt."

She nodded and glanced down at her hand. She lifted a shoulder and looked up. "I can't make any one person understand and accept me in spite of what happened to me in my past or the actions I take now. I live according to my beliefs without judging others."

Galloping horses rode past the teepee. Her eyes widened and swirled toward the teepee flap. Turning back, she could tell he knew *Chakotay* had returned from the hunt. She stood. "I better see how Sam did on his ride with his father. Stay, rest, you'll need it.

Clare hurried out to make her way to the end of the camp where the hunters and her son were dismounting. "Sam, how was your ride?" she hollered waiting for his father to help him from the horse.

"*Pia*," he yelled, flashing the biggest grin he could display on his rosy, red face.

"I can tell you had fun." Clare held out her arms and gave him a squeeze. "I missed you." She glanced up at *Chakotay*. "Was the hunt good?" Her question reminded her of years past when he'd return from other hunts.

He nodded. "Have many more fallen to the fever?"

She shook her head. "No. Most are getting better. Only *Jaquan* died early this morning."

His expression saddened. He mumbled, "She was old, but a good Comanche."

Clare agreed. The oldest Comanche in the band, and she had seen much in her lifetime. Clare was sure *Jaquan* had been the old woman Drury had mentioned who had fed him with her hands. She probably wasn't aware of being sick until later. She had been a tough, old squaw.

"Sam, you run along and see to the Ranger. I need to talk to your *ahp*." She glanced at *Chakotay* and followed his long strides carrying him toward his teepee. "Please, we need to talk."

"Later, I need to see my squaw."

Clare stopped and watched him hurry to his teepee and disappear inside. She knew why he needed to see his squaw—she'd been there before. After every hunt, he came back needing to bed her—sometimes things stayed the same.

She turned and strolled toward her son, who was talking to a small friend about his day. She smiled. At least something wonderful came from being bedded.

"*Pia*, Drury better?" he asked running toward her.

"Yes, little one. He's better."

He grabbed her hand. "Let's go see." He pulled her, trying to hurry her steps toward their teepee. Clare slowed when she set eyes on the sentry standing at the opening. *Chakotay* hadn't wasted time in making sure Drury didn't escape now, since he lived through the sickness. She followed Sam inside.

"Drury, you awake?" Sam asked quietly, kneeling near the form on the bed.

Drury opened an eye aimed at Sam.

Sam giggled. "Open both eyes."

Drury did and rolled to his side.

"I killed a buffalo today."

"Wow. By yourself?"

Sam lowered his head and mumbled, "Well, no, *ahp*'s arrow hit him first."

"But, your arrow shot him too, right?"

The black-haired head nodded in agreement.

"Well see, you helped with the kill."

He grinned. "I did."

Chapter Twenty-Two

Slowly Drury raised his eyelids. He'd fallen into another deep sleep. If he didn't know better, he suspected Clare kept putting something into the tea she'd been giving him. He glanced around. The teepee was dark except for a small flame from the pit. The shadows danced on the walls. On the opposite side of the room he recognized the boy sleeping underneath the covers. Where did Clare go?

Suddenly, drums from outside wafted through the teepee. A slow rhythmic beat—what did it mean? Then silence. Again, the hollow beat of drums echoed. A slow chant began lifting above the beat matching the rhythm of the drum.

What was going on?

He sat up, waited until his dizzy head settled, and then swung his legs to the side. A quick glance into the corner found his boots and clothing in a pile. He whipped his sight toward the opening.

He had to know what was going on. Pushing to his feet, he slowly moved to the corner and picked up his shirt and shoved his arms into the sleeves, and then his vest. He grabbed his hat and placed it square on his head. Dropping to the floor, he pulled his boots on, stood and stepped toward the entrance. He searched around, his gun and rifle was nowhere to be found, not even his holster. Cautiously, he circled the fire pit, looking for anything to use for a weapon. Not even a bow or arrow was left inside the teepee.

The drums stopped.

The chanting stopped.

Drury stood still and listened.

He stepped near the opening. He could hear talking…no, more like squabbling over something. With a finger, he parted the flap and peeked out. No guard. His stepped out into the cold night air. They probably thought he was out for the night.

His gaze swung to the far end of the village. A large powwow was taking place around the campfire. He stepped closer. Their chief was making a point about some heated issue—sounded important. He wished he understood Comanche language.

He stopped in his tracks.

Clare stood. The tone in her voice sounded pleading and then demanding. Drury thought he detected a hint of panic in her words. The only beseeching word he understood was 'Ranger' which meant this powwow was all about him. He'd either leave riding his horse out or die trying to convince them he wasn't their enemy. He boldly walked up behind Clare and took in the circle of Comanche Indian braves.

The entire powwow band eyed him without saying a word. Silence permeated the area with only the crackling fire eating away the wood.

Clare turned, blinked in surprise. "You shouldn't be here," she whispered.

"Why?" He jerked his head toward the group. "This powwow council is about me, isn't it?"

She nodded.

"What did you tell them?"

"You're an honorable man and will not reveal this location, but I don't think they believe me. They want to understand why I trust you."

He took his time and studied each Comanche setting around the fire. He wasn't sure which one was in charge, but he had the feeling it was the chief. He boldly stepped beside Clare and took a seat within the circle of Indians.

The oldest looking *Parabio* in the circle waved her away. Clare stepped back.

Drury didn't look her way when she stepped further back, fading into the shadows. He knew she no longer had a say within the council. He figured *Chakotay* knew enough English to translate for him.

"Here's the way it is now. Clare, *Keshini* has helped me see the ways of your people. You don't deserve what the white men have done to you. You're a great nation and should be treated with respect…" Drury hesitated and glanced around. *Chakotay* spoke his words.

"I am a Ranger."

His word sparked a grumbling clamor between the old and young Comanches. It appeared some disagreement wavered with what they wanted to do with this Ranger.

Drury spoke above their voices. "I know what the Rangers have done. I can no longer be a Ranger. Not now. Not after spending time in your village and watching the way you live. I couldn't understand why *Keshini* had so much love and respect for you, but now I do."

He pushed to his feet, raised his hand to the Texas Ranger Badge, ripped it from his black vest and tossed it into the fire.

****

"*Pia.*" Obviously frightened, Sam ran through the backdoor of the mercantile to his ma, looking back.

Sam's panicked tone whipped Clare's head around to find her son running as fast as his legs could carry him. Clare frowned and reached out to gather him into her arms. "What's the matter?" He sucked in a choppy breath and pointed. Clare shifted her gaze toward the door and caught her breath.

Blazing, angry eyes bored into hers. Betsy didn't speak, but stood in the opened door and turned an enraged stare at Sam. "Betsy, what—"

Before Clare could say another word, Betsy did an about face and smashed head on into Ruby. With intended force, she shoved Ruby against the doorframe and dashed into the alleyway.

Ruby near missed dropping a package in her hand, swung around to watch the wild woman run out of sight. "What the hell was that all about?"

Clare held Sam close and hurried to glance out just in time to catch Betsy's long, tangled brown hair flying in the wind.

She turned her gaze to Ruby, and then to Sam. "Are you okay?" His arms tightened around her neck choking her. "Sam, what happened?" When she tried to pull back, he squeezed harder.

"I reckon the crazy woman scared the hell out of him," Ruby mumbled watching the boy cling to his mother.

Clare frowned at Ruby, turned and carried Sam to a stool and sat him down on her lap and waited until his arms dropped from her neck. Clare kissed him on the forehead. "Now tell *Pia* what happened. Did Betsy scare you?"

He nodded.

Clare hugged him close and assured him, "She's scary, but she just a sick woman, she won't hurt you."

"Clare, you're wrong. The woman's mad and I wouldn't put it past her to cause harm to any person, especially an Indian boy."

"Ruby. Sam's frightened enough without you adding to his big imagination."

Ruby's large brown eyes studied Sam. She pressed her lips together and wrinkled up her nose. "I suppose you're right. Just stay clear of her—no account what she'd be up to if she means harm."

Clare smiled at Sam. "Want an apple?"

He nodded.

Clare touched his feet to the floor and stood. She strolled over to the barrel and picked out a large red apple and handed it to him.

Ruby was right; she shouldn't trust Betsy. The look in her eyes spoke volumes of hatred when she looked at her son.

"What do you think she wanted?" Clare inquired, settling back on the stool. She eyed her son chomping away on his apple while stroking an old, grey cat he'd befriended since their arrival.

Ruby shrugged. "Who knows what particulates cram her brain. Can't be nothing good, I tell you."

"Well, maybe you're right. I'll keep Sam clear of her."

Then out of the blue, Ruby said, "Captain tells me he's quitting the Rangers."

Clare looked into her questioning eyes. "So he says." She strolled to the large table loaded with fabrics and slowly rolled a wide, gingham material over a board for displaying in the store.

"You have anything to do with his decision?"

Clare lifted a shoulder. "Maybe."

"Well, I'll be damned, girl. I guess it took a hell of a lot more woman than me to make him leave the Rangers. I tried for years, but he didn't see to it."

Clare's brows formed a ridge between them. "Why did you want him to leave the Rangers?"

"The kind of hatred he has for them Indians will surely eat him up or get him killed. I might not be educated like some of you, but I know hating so deep into the soul can only eat away at your innards until there's nothing left."

Clare listened to Ruby talk about Drury. Her eyes sparkled and her cheeks turned slightly pink. Why she was more than just fond of the captain. "Ruby—"

"I know. I know." She waved her hand in a matter-of-fact gesture, and then pressed it against her breast. "I do love the man."

"You…you've known him for a long time, haven't you?" Clare leaned against the table and cupped the palms of her hands together.

Ruby's red lips spread wide. "Yeah, might near eight years now. Back when we were young, my cousin and I took off. Found ourselves in Silver Sage Creek without a penny to our names. Old man Appleton hired us to work in the Silver Sage Saloon, first saloon in town." She giggled. "The only one in town."

Ruby smiled thinking of the past. "The old coot up and died. Left me the business. Said I had a head for making it good."

"You do, Ruby. So, what happened to your cousin?"

Ruby's contrite gaze studied Clare before she answered. Her voice softened. "MaryLou, she married Drury."

Wide-eyed, Clare couldn't stop the quick intake of breath.

"He never mentioned MaryLou to you?"

Clare shook her head. "He spoke only a few words about her and his daughter being killed by the Indians. He never mentioned her name." Though, she knew it was the name he mumbled when he had the fever.

"Well, he did love MaryLou, and his daughter lit his face up like the brightest point on a candle blaze."

"Did he get the scar fighting Indians?"

Ruby nodded. "He became a Ranger to make extra money for the ranch he bought. His goal was to work long enough to pay off the acreage and make a good life for his family."

"But the Indians changed his destiny? Ruby do you believe in destiny?"

Ruby's head tilted, her thoughtful gaze studied Clare again. "I believe one's destiny changes according to one's circumstances in each stage of one's life. The destinies laid out before us can strike off into a different directions because of others forcing their destiny onto us." She shrugged.

Clare thought of Ruby's words. "My dear friend, you are much wiser than you give yourself credit." She turned to complete her task of folding store-bought material onto a board to be measured out for customers to buy.

"Did Drury tell you why he was leaving the Rangers? He's changed and I surmise you're the reason."

Clare shook her head. "It wasn't me. He…what he witnessed made him realize Indians were humans too."

Ruby frowned. "How? When?"

Clare bit her bottom lip and studied Ruby for a moment. "If I share something with you, you have to promise not to tell a soul."

Ruby's head jerked back. "My Lord, girl, you know me by now, you can tell me anything."

"Ruby, I went to my Comanche village and…well…Drury followed me."

"That's where you were?"

Clare's questioning expression prompted her to continue.

"When you didn't come in to work and Drury was nowhere in sight, I rode out to see if you were sick, but the cabin was all dark and cold. I reckoned you had gone back to the Comanches."

"I did. They needed my help."

"Why?"

"Many were sick with the fever. The Comanches captured Drury."

"Damn it woman, what happened?"

Clare's gaze shifted from the material to her friend. "Before I reached the village, I suspected Drury was following me, but I hoped he'd come to his senses and turn back."

"Course not, not Captain Burchett. So, he went and got himself captured." Ruby shook her head and whispered, "Sometimes men have no common sense."

Clare nodded. "Comanches are always on the alert and keep a constant outlook for Rangers."

"I didn't think any Indian tribes were close to Silver Sage."

Clare shook her head. "Not far, it's more than a good day and a half ride south of here toward Squaw Mountain. They're good at setting up their villages in hidden locations." Her gaze locked onto Ruby's. "You can never tell anyone where the village is located. Promise."

"Promise, Clare? I confess, all Indians scare me, but after what you did to help the Indian boy here while back, you know…saving his life and all those words you said about not all Indians are bad. God knows I've known some bad white men in my time and they can be just as bad, if not worse, than some Indians."

Clare reached over for a large bundle of fabric to wind around another board. "Look isn't this beautiful?" Her hand rubbed over the cotton floral print material.

"Oh, for heaven sakes, I all but forgot about this." With a mischievous glint in her eyes, Ruby handed Clare the package she'd been holding in her hands the entire time.

Clare grinned and stared at the brown wrapping. "Ruby, what's this?"

"Just something for my friend." She shrugged and proudly stated, "Open it."

With raised brows, she couldn't remember the last time she'd been given a present. "What in the world…Ruby, I—"

"Shush. Just open it."

Tears gathered, blurring her vision of the brown paper package in her hand. "No one's given me a present in a very long time…not since—"

"Clare, don't stand there blubbering, open it."

Excited, Clare ripped the paper away. Her eyes widened. "It's…oh my, Ruby." Clare bit her bottom lip while a tear slipped from her eye. She quickly wiped it away and glanced up at her friend.

Ruby returned her gaze with a pleased expression. Clare
glanced back at the green material folded inside the paper. She
gently touched the gift. Years had passed since she'd received
anything so beautiful.

"Oh for heaven's sake," Ruby shoved her hands aside and
gathered up the dress to shake it out. The green dress unfolded
before Clare's eyes, causing more tears to flow.

"Well, do you like it? If the color's wrong, I can exchange it,
but I thought green goes with your coloring, what with your red
hair and those...ah...listen to me blubbering, but..."

"No, Ruby, I love it, I haven't seen anything so beautiful
since...since...I can't remember when."

Clare threw her arms around Ruby. "You're the best friend a
person could ever have."

"Suspect I'm interrupting something."

Clare swirled to the deep familiar voice with a hint of teasing
to the lift of his tone. She stepped back and gazed into Drury's
eyes. With a quick backhand sweep she wiped away the tears and
grinned. "Ruby bought me a dress."

She turned back to Ruby. "I love it, Ruby, it's the prettiest
dress I've ever had."

"Well, then, go...go try it on."

"Now?"

"Yes, of course. It's time you quit working in men's clothing
and start being a woman again. I'm sure Captain Burchett agrees
with me."

Clare slowly glanced up at Drury. His brow lifted as he
slothfully nodded. "Ruby means business, she doesn't take no for
an answer often. Best do as she asked."

Unable to resist, Clare hugged the dress to her bosom and
hurried to an obscured area behind the shelves. She quickly
dropped the trousers and the long, oversized shirt she'd become
use to wearing every day. She picked up the simple, basic green
dress and slipped it over her head. The fabric skimmed down her
skin until the hem touched the floor. The sleeves were long with a
single button at the wrist.

A smile settled on her lips when her fingers slowly buttoned up the front, all the way to the high neckline. Clare smoothed the palms of her hands over the full skirt. She felt pretty, like a lady.

"We're waiting." Ruby's soft voice hinted her impatience.

Taking a hesitant step, Clare peeked around the shelves and met Ruby's expectant gaze.

"Well, girl, get out here. Did it fit?"

"It did." Her tone expressed her appreciation as she strolled out in view of her only two friends. "It's a perfect fit."

She grinned at Ruby and shifted her gaze to Drury. The look he held sent a satisfied thrill up her spine to her heated face.

Ruby reached for her arm and made her twirl around to inspect the back. "Yup, the dress is perfect for you. Not fancy, but a good, everyday, working dress."

"Now," Ruby stated matter-of-factly, "it's time you started thinking about how you look, missy. You're a beautiful woman and you need to dress like a lady from here on out. You hear?"

Clare threw her arms around Ruby and whispered, "Thank you."

"Oh, my good gracious alive, you're my friend. I love you girl, and I want you to look your best." She stepped back and waved her hand to dismiss any more emotional display.

Clare glanced up into her mother's unexpected hard glare taking in Clare's dress. Without a word, she whipped around and slammed the door shut.

Ruby glanced at Drury, who hadn't said a word. She cleared her throat and said, "Goodness, I've been rambling on, sorry. I best get back to my place."

"*Pia.*"

Clare shot her head around to find Sam running toward her with the same panicked expression he had earlier. He grabbed her dress and pointed a finger toward the backdoor.

Drury's long stride carried him to the door. After a quick search up and down the back alley, he turned to her and shrugged. "Nothing out there."

Sam trembled against her leg. "What is it, Sam?"

"That woman."

"Woman?" She swung her gaze to Ruby.

Ruby frowned, and turned to Drury. When their gaze met, Drury lifted a brow. Ruby clarified in a disturbing tone, "That 'woman' Sam's afraid of is Betsy, she's been nosing around here for no good reason."

"Clare," Drury's low voice drew her attention. "That woman's mad. Unpredictable."

"He's right. I know she once was your best friend, but she's not the same person."

Clare took Sam's hand, gave his a protective squeeze, and stepped toward Ruby. "You two know I'm not the same person either. We've both changed, but I'm sure Betsy needs a friend." When her lip spread to assure them, she knew, in reality, she was anything but certain.

"I'm telling you, keep an eye open for her…she means trouble. Drury knows it too."

Clare glanced at Drury. He didn't say a word, but the troubled concern she read in his eyes ramped up her heartbeat with uneasiness. Wanting to drop the subject, she grinned at Ruby.

Ruby's head drew back. "What are you smiling about?"

"Thank you, Ruby, for being my friend. Without you to talk to, I think I might have become crazy like Betsy."

"No, not you…you're strong, not like her. Besides she harbors hate inside her heart, you don't, not even for people who speak ill of you."

Clare thought of her parents. They didn't speak ill of her, they didn't even speak about her, nor have much to do with her besides giving her a job. She shook her head. "Thanks anyway, Ruby. I've grown to love you dearly."

"That goes both ways." Ruby suddenly threw her arms around both Clare and Sam gave them a hurried hug, and then quickly headed out the door after a swift glance in Drury's direction.

He tipped his hat toward his friend and then turned to Clare.

Clare glanced at Sam who seemed to have settled down and no longer trembled in her arms. "Let's go home. What do you say?"

"Yeah."

Sam pointed to Drury, "Coming home with us?"

"No, 'fraid not. I stopped by to tell you I have to ride out for a couple of days. Raiding up north of here."

"Oh no, again, were many killed?"

"Not this time, seems to be warnings."

"But you're no longer a Ranger."

"I'm not going as a Ranger, Clare. They need me to show them the trail to the mining town I went to last month. I'm the only one able to lead the way. I'll return once the Rangers reinforce the area."

He took in her full stance, covered in a feminine dress, with a smoldering gaze, and in a sensuous tone said, "You look mighty tasty." With a sparkle in his eyes, he turned to leave, and then stopped at the sound of Sam's voice.

"Bye, Drury."

A slight grin hovered beneath his thick mustache. After a quick saluted he took his leave.

Chapter Twenty-Three

Clare threw another log on the fire and stepped back. It was only mid-afternoon and already the sky had turned dark and the wind howled around the corner of the cabin. Winter days threatened severe storms for weeks now and she wasn't looking forward to the long, cold, dark days. Sam needed a coat and warmer shoes. More importantly, he was getting old enough for schooling and she didn't know what to do about it.

Ruby suggested ordering books from the mercantile and schooling him on weekends, which might be the course she'd have to take. But, books weren't cheap. Maybe she'd talk to the schoolmarm in town. She might give her some ideas.

One thing was for sure, the last thing Clare wanted to do was to expose her son to the white man's school and chance getting him hurt. Children could be cruel, especially those in eardrop of their parents' callous words against all Indians. Yet, she couldn't protect him forever.

A loud knock echoed over the howling wind. Clare stared at the door. Slowly, she stepped to the window, parted the curtain, and peeked out. What the hell? She dropped the curtain and stepped back.

Sam ran to the door and reached to lift the lath from the hook.

"Sam, wait."

He turned and stepped back, waiting.

Another impatient knock pounded the wooden door.

She glanced at Sam and hurried forward. "It's okay. Your grandmother is here."

She lifted the latch, glanced at Sam's frowning expression and opened the door.

"Ma," her flat tone stated, connecting eyes with the woman having nothing to do with her since her arrival.

"Clare Rose."

The woman stood there with her gloved hands clasped in front of her, waiting. "Well, daughter, are you inviting me in or are you going to let me freeze to death out here?"

Clare glanced behind her mother's shoulders at the horse and buggy. "You rode all the way out here by yourself?"

She nodded and stepped through to stroll near the fireplace.

"That was dangerous, don't you think?"

She shrugged. "You live out here by yourself, isn't that dangerous too?"

"I can take care of myself and Sam. I'm used to it."

"I suppose you've had to…what with living with the Indians so long."

Clare strolled to the coffee pot and reached up for two cups on the shelf. "Coffee?"

"Sounds good if it's hot."

Clare poured a steamy cup and handed it to her ma. She turned to Sam, who hadn't moved from the door since she'd walked in. "Come," she held out her hand and motioned for him to step forward. "Say hi to your grandmother."

Sam slowly stepped forward with wide eyes boring into the woman. He stopped beside his mother and said, "Hello."

"My, you're tall for your age, aren't you? How old are you now?" Alyson eyed him while sipping her coffee."

"Almost five." His strong little voice spoke up, short and to the point, while holding up four fingers.

"*Pia.*" His low voice drew Clare's gaze.

"Yes, dear."

"Can I feed Big Black now?"

"Yes, you can." Clare turned back to the counter and scooped up a large bowl of grain. "Here you go."

Sam hurried to put a blanket over his shoulders, took the bowl with both hands, and waited for his mother to open the door.

"Hurry back, the wind's getting colder."

Clare turned from the door and directed her attention to her mother. "Why don't you sit, Mother?"

Alyson glanced down at the chair near the table and said, "Well, I suppose." She pulled out the chair, placed the cup on the table, slipped out of her long wool coat, and settled on the chair.

Picking up her cup, she asked, "You let him go out alone, without protection?"

"He'll be fine."

"Well, you never know. I thought I saw a wolf at the forest edge when I rode in. I think the noise of the buggy scared him off."

"A wolf." Clare repeated, busying herself with preparations for a meal. She smiled. "You probably did. We've had a large grey wolf watching over us for many years now."

"A wolf? I swear, Clare Rose, I'll never understand you."

Clare swirled around to face her mother. "Yes, I'm sure you never will, but he's been our companion since we saved his life. No worries. Sam will be fine." Just as the last words flowed from her mouth, the door opened whipping in a strong wind along with Sam. His bright smile flashed at them.

"He ate it all."

"Good, now go wash your hands and we'll have supper."

Obeying his mother, he ran to the wash basin. After a quick dip with both hands, he grabbed the towel and quickly stepped toward the table. He stopped and stared at Alyson. "Are you my *huutsi*?"

Her head jerked back, she blinked, sat the cup down and looked at Clare.

Clare's tight lip smile didn't reach her eyes. "*Huutsi* means grandmother."

Alyson aimed her squint toward Sam. "I…I suppose I am."

After setting the table with three plates, Clare walked to the fireplace, picked up several pieces of cloth and reached in to lift out the pot with boiled meat and potatoes while listening to Sam.

"I had a *huutsi*, she was nice. I liked it when she told me stories. She was nicer than you. The Rangers killed her."

Clare's gaze swung to her son. Sam had never mentioned the attacked the day they were captured. Many a time, she had wondered if he had suppressed the traumatic incident. She sat the pot in the middle of the table and looked into her son's blank expression. "Sam, sweetie, why don't you get us some forks."

He took off to the counter and reached inside a large tin can full of utensils. He took out the forks and turned back. "I have three forks because my *huutsi* is eating with us," he stated while placing the forks at each plate.

Once he crawled upon his chair, he watched his mother fill his plate with meat. His gaze swung to Alyson. "*Huutsi* means grandmother. You don't want to be my *huutsi* because I'm Comanche."

"Sam."

"No…no, Clare, he's right. I haven't been nice to either one of you since you returned. That's why I made the trip out today." She glanced down at her plate. "The meal looks good."

Clare didn't know what to say. She quickly stood and hurried to the cupboard to pull out a loaf of freshly baked bread.

"Wow, how did you learn to cook this meat so tender?"

Clare raised her brow and stared at her mother talking with her mouth full. She giggled.

Sam giggled, reached for a sliced of bread and mumbled, "Grandmother, you're not supposed to talk with your mouth full."

Alyson shot a surprised look at her grandson and put her fork down. Swallowing, she made a big gulping sound and chuckled. "You are so right, young man."

Sam laughed out loud and before they knew it they were all three laughing, blowing the tension out of the cabin to join the wind.

A loud pounding shocked their laugher into silence. Clare stared at her mother.

"Where's your gun, Clare Rose?"

"In the bedroom." She frowned, pushed back the chair and headed for the door.

"Don't open the door, Clare Rose," her ma warned and took off for the bedroom.

The urgent knock came again, vibrating the heavy door.

Clare pulled back the door to stare into Drury's face, drawn with concerned and eyes revealing dread. "Drury…what…what's wrong?"

"Captain Burchett, you about got yourself killed, what with pounding like that." Alyson lowered the rifle.

Sam jumped from his chair and ran to hug Drury's legs.

The Ranger absently patted the boy's head without taking his gaze off Clare. "I need to talk to you."

"Sam, go finish eating with your grandmother." She quickly glanced at her ma and then eyed Drury with a guarded frown. "Something's wrong. What is it…just tell me Drury. What's happened?"

"The Rangers…they're riding out to round up your village for the reservations."

A large snapping breath sucked into Clare's lungs. Gripping her hands together, she held them against her chest. "How did they know where…"

He shook his head.

Her mind filled with images of the Rangers attacking her people. "I have to go." Clare spun around, confused and scared with the possibilities what was happening.

"You can't, Clare," Drury grabbed her arm and halted her movement. "Look at me. There's nothing you can do. They'll be there long before you can get warning to them, and besides, there's nothing stopping them from rounding everyone up."

Clare froze and stared into his tense blue expression. Her low, contemptuous voice flung straight at him while at the same time blinking back the tears. "You know very well they won't round them up. They'll kill all of them—even the children."

Clare heard her mother's sharp intake of breath. With that, she snapped her arm free from Drury's grip and ran toward the bedroom.

Halting briefly at the door, she ordered Drury, "Saddle Big Black for me."

His chest lifted in defeat, and then he backed out and disappeared.

Clare was glad she'd dressed in her old trousers and flannel shirt instead of the dress Ruby had given her. She quickly threw more warm clothes into the bag, an extra blanket, tied her leather knife holder around her leg, and hurried back into the room.

"Mother, I need you to watch your grandson."

"Me?"

Clare paused, turned her worried glare onto her ma's green eyes. "Yes, Mother. You can at least take care of him for me. Can't you?"

Alyson nodded.

"No, *Pia*, I want to go," Sam screamed, running to his mother.

Clare squatted and circled her arms around him. "It will be too dangerous. You need to say with your *huutsi*, your grandmother." She looked him in the eyes and watched the tears stream down his cheeks. "You have to stay, please, for *Pia*. This will give you a chance to get to know your *huntsi*. Deep down, she's really a nice person."

"*Pia*," he sobbed, flooding more tears.

"Sam, sweetheart, I need you to be safe. If anything were to happen to you, well, *Pia* couldn't live without you. Promise, stay with your grandmother."

He puckered his lips and sorrowfully nodded while wiping away the tears. Clare quickly kissed his wet cheeks and stepped from the cabin. Drury had saddled Big Black and was waiting for her.

She kicked Big Black in the flanks and took off. How the hell did the Rangers find out about her village's location? She frowned aiming a hurried glance at Drury. Did he tell them? He had promised. No one else knew, except Ruby. There was no reason for her to tell. She bit down on her lip and stared straight ahead.

Clare rode Big Black hard. Gritting her teeth, she kicked the horse in his flanks and pushed him harder. Tears burned her eyes, slipping out the corners to catch the cold breeze slapping against her face. Please Great Spirit, don't let them murder my Comanche family. Please.

After stopping several times throughout the night to give the horses a breather, Drury reached over and pulled Big Black to a halt to rest one more time before reaching the village. After dismounting, he pulled Clare from the horse. She didn't say a word when he covered her with a blanket, led her to a tree and with his arms circled around her, sat her down. She cuddled up against him and let him hold her close until she slept from exhaustion and worry.

After the short rest, and without saying a word, they rode quickly and furiously. The closer they came to the village, the worse her heart pounded with anticipation of what was ahead. Her mind kept conjuring up all kind of images.

In the faint light of dawn, nearing the edge of the village, Big Black's gait slowed sensing Clare's hopelessness and distress. There was no need to hurry now. Clare had a horrible gut feeling she was too late.

Her slumped shoulders could no longer force the horse to hurry. She let him step forward until smoke from burning teepees in the distance ahead filled their nostrils. No gunfire sounded. It was over.

Unable to stop her tears, Clare released their flow in a steady stream. Her jaws tightened, tears swelled to blur the vision before her. Big Black halted the moment she dropped the reins. The only sounds in the village were soft cries and murmurings from Comanche squaws and many of the elderly being herded together by Rangers. Bodies were strewn over the ground. Her breath caught in her throat until a mournful sound pushed it's way through.

Clare's tight fist rose to her forehead, pounding the back of her hand against her head. Why? Why? She didn't even see McCoy ride up until he stopped beside her.

Her gaze swung to his.

"Why?"

His sad face pulled from hers to Drury. "Cap, I tried to keep the Rangers from firing, but they panicked when an old Injun shot an arrow into one of our Rangers."

Clare slid from her horse and slowly walked down the center of the village staring at dead bodies sprawled out on the dusty earth. Her gaze landed on a tiny form. She knelt to look into the lifeless eyes of a baby not more than six month old.

"Nooooo," she screamed, "No. Why? Why? Why?" Breathless, Clare cried until she couldn't see anything except the infant before her.

Drury curled his hand around her upper arm and pulled her to her feet. "Clare, we should leave."

"No. Never. Not with you."

She shook her head and turned wet, accusing eyes upon Drury. "You, you did this. You…you told them where to come. You promised. You son-of-a-bitch."

Clare jerked her arm from his grip. "Don't touch me…ever…ever again." Whimpering, she bent down and gathered the baby up into her arms and stood. Raising her gaze, she looked into McCoy's eyes and in a raspy mocking tone, said, "The big, bad Rangers were afraid of a tiny, tiny baby."

Despaired emotions consumed her, dropping her head, she stared down at the infant and hugged the small bundle up against her chest. Dragging her feet, she moved past McCoy, and stepped near the Indians the Rangers had rounded up and were guarding. Her tear-stained face lifted to link with familiar faces. Her red eyes connected with *Taabe*, *Chakotay's* wife.

When *Taabe* screamed and lifted up her arms, Clare knew the baby belonged to her. *Taabe* desperately tried to run to Clare, but a Ranger jerked her arm and held her back.

Clare glared. In a low controlled tone expressed her loathing for the man, emphasizing each word she stated, "Let…her…go."

He turned and stared at her. At first he seemed confused, and then his gaze dropped to the dead baby in her arms. His lip lifted into a sneer.

"You despicable white man, you're the monster, the savage, not these people."

His dark eyes shot back at her with angry flames.

"If you don't release her, I swear I'll kill you, maybe not now, but I'll hunt you down and kill you. Do you understand?"

"You can damn will try, Indian lover."

Clare's squinted glare drilled into the man's eyes. An ugly grin formed on her lips. "You forget I lived four years with them. I know how to silently sneak upon a prey and slit his throat in the dark of the night. The animals I've killed never knew I was near. You're worse than an animal. You'll never hear me. Now let her go."

The nervous man shifted from one foot to the other studying her expression.

"Best do as she says," ordered McCoy, as he stepped forward. "And get the rest ready to go, we're moving out."

The mother ran to Clare the moment the angry man released her. She gently took her daughter into her arms and dropped to the ground. While she wept over her loss, Clare moved slowly toward Drury.

She hoped her gaze punctured his heart the way he had hers, but she couldn't read his expression staring back.

"Clare, listen, you've got to believe me—"

"Nothing you say will make a difference. Now, I need to know where they're taking them." She jutted her chin toward the small crowd moving out on foot, following the Rangers.

Drury turned his gaze on the cluster of Comanches. "The reservation in Oklahoma."

"Oklahoma." Clare took in a deep breath and hopelessness pushed out in its released. "A reservation. So, you can civilize them, educate them to be what? Civilized. Like the Rangers?"

She turned her back on him and walked away.

"Clare—"

Her hand flew up to dismiss him. "Don't, not a word. For all I know you'll come for my half-breed son."

She turned her head just enough to set eyes on him, and said, "I never want to see you again."

Chapter Twenty-Four

Clare helped *Taabe* upon Big Black's back behind her, and then she rode off, leaving Drury standing with a worried, puckered brow. *Taabe* hung onto her with one hand while her other hand clung to her dead papoose. Her horse ran at a full gallop. Clare wanted to ride faster than the wind in order to leave the devastation of a soon-to-be extinct nation behind. Returning to her own child was now foremost on her mind. First she had to help bury the baby.

Taabe called her baby girl, *Almika,* meaning *she of the son.* After wrapping her in a blanket and placing her tiny body in a hidden cave, Clare persuaded *Taabe* to come with her to the cabin for she had nowhere else to go, no family left, only other place left for her was the reservation. They rode most of the night, only stopping to rest the horse a few times. Clare wanted to get back home in a hurry. She knew Big Black was strong and sensed her urgency.

At the break of dawn, Clare finally slowed the horse for a breather, giving her a chance to dare ask, "*Taabe* did the Rangers kill *Chakotay*? I didn't see him among the ones they rounded up."

Taabe's eyes filled with tears. She shook her head. "He and four braves went out to hunt two days ago."

Clare heaved a heavy sigh, relieved to know Sam's father was still living. Although, once he returned to the village, she was sure he wouldn't be a peaceful hunter now but a furious warrior.

The second the sunrise peeked and yellow light shined over the light grey sky, Big Black stepped up his pace, sensing his home near and grain waiting. When the cabin drifted in view, Clare's gaze swung around the area, but nothing seemed out of the ordinary. Apprehension weighed heavily on her mind and until she set eyes on her son, she couldn't find peace.

The moment Big Black halted in front of the porch, she slid off his back and rushed up the steps. Quietly opening the door Clare stood shocked at the scene before her. Stunned, she couldn't move from the doorway. Her son sat on her father's lap, laughing. Her mother and father were both displaying jubilant smiles and laughter. Pa looked up at her, but like her, he didn't say a word. Clare swallowed hard and stepped inside.

Her pa's gaze traveled beyond her to the Indian squaw stepping in behind her. Both stared as if they had never seen a Comanche woman before.

Sam squealed, jumped from his grandfather's knee and ran to the woman in a long, tan, deerskin dress and moccasins. "*Taabe*," he hollered.

Her open arms gathered him up into a big bear hug. Squatting, she held him arms length away, but the words she spoke were Comanche.

Her parents both watched with frowns. Clare interpreted her Comanche words. "She's saying how much he's grown."

Their gaze returned to Sam when he asked, "Where's papoose?"

The squaw covered her face with both hands, letting tears of sorrow spill from her eyes.

Clare knelt and held out her arms toward her son. "Sam, don't I get a hug?"

"*Pia*, I missed you." She hugged him close. "*Pia*, where's *Taabe's* baby?"

"Sweetheart, her little one's gone to be with the Great Spirit."

His little head hung low and then he stepped back into *Taabe's* arms and hugged her tightly.

Taabe stood and held out her hand. "Sam, come with me down near the river and sing a song to *Almika*?" He nodded and took her hand and led her out the door.

Clare straightened and watched the two leave, and then she turned her attention back. Her parent's eyes widened when they heard *Taabe* speak English. From their puckered brows and questioning expressions, she knew they wanted to know how things went. They deserved an answer. After all, they were both here taking care of their grandchild.

Clare strolled to the washbasin and washed her hands and face before taking a seat at the table. "Sam loves *Taabe* and knew she was with child. Her husband helped her learn English."

Alyson poured Clare a cup of coffee and handed it to her daughter. "You look very tired. Was it rough?"

Taking several sips, Clare swallowed the strong coffee and nodded at her mother. "When the Rangers attacked the village, they killed her baby."

Alyson dropped to the chair and shook her head. Clare was taken aback by her display of sincere sadness.

"She was six months old." Clare took a deep breath. She didn't realize how exhausted and emotionally drained the entire ordeal had left her. After taking another sip, she stared into her father's eyes. "Now, tell me, why are you here?"

"Clare Rose—"

"Ma, don't interrupt. We've made amends, but you don't answer for Pa."

Her mother's head slowly pulled her gaze from her daughter to her husband. "Please Henry, she's your daughter and he...he's your grandson."

Henry's wrinkled brows bore into his wife's a quick second, and then he slowly pushed out of the chair and stood, shuffling his way to the fireplace. He stood staring down into the flames before slowly facing his daughter. "I'm sorry. I'm ashamed of the way I've treated you. You are my daughter and Sam is my grandson."

"Why, Pa, why have you not welcomed me home?"

"Guilt."

"Guilt? Why do you feel guilty?"

"I couldn't protect you and keep the Apaches from taking you. I should have been able to stop them."

"No, Pa, it wasn't you're fault. Beside that's all behind us now."

Before another word was spoken, Sam ran in hollering, "*Pia, Taabe* sick." He held up his hand showing off little fingers covered with blood.

Clare jumped to her feet and flew out the door with her pa following. Near the river's edge, she found *Taabe* on the ground hugging her arms around her chest.

Clare knelt and gently lifted her head. "*Taabe*, what..." Her gaze rested on the blood seeping through the deerskin dress.

Quickly, she laid her head down, pulled her dress up over her thigh and sucked in a sharp breath when she examined her side. A tiny bullet hole oozed fresh blood over dried blood. "Oh my God, *Taabe*, why didn't you tell me you'd been shot?"

Henry pushed Clare aside, gathered the squaw up into his arms and headed for the cabin. Clare ran ahead to get the herbs she kept for infections and to soak the dried leaves in water. Pa gently carried *Taabe* to the bedding and covered her.

"We need to get the bullet out," Clare mumbled.

"What can we do, Clare?" Pa asked.

Surprised by his willingness to help, she said, "I need a knife, hold it over the fire and make sure it's hot before you give it to me. Ma, I need a bowl of water from the table over there." She nodded.

Taabe's hand touched her. She gazed into the eyes of the woman knowing all she had lost. "*Keshini*, I need to go to my baby."

"No."

"Shush," she whispered. "I do. Tell *Chakotay* we wait for him."

The door slammed open alarming her parents. Sam ran for his grandpa's arms before setting eyes on the intruder. Clare's head swung around to stare into the obsidian eyes of the Comanche chief.

Chakotay stood looking around. His enraged gaze bore into Henry's, and then fell on Clare, before shifting to the still form lying on the bed. A breeze from the opened door whipped his long straight black hair over his shoulders. Clare didn't fail to take in the grief filling his ominous eyes before a shrouded expression replaced it with firm jaws and a blank stare. His silent moccasins carried him to his wife's side. He knelt and touched her cheek.

Taabe opened her eyes to the sight of *Chakotay* bending over her. Her lips thinned out in a slight smiled.

"*Chakotay*. Our baby…we…we wait." She closed her eyes and took her last breath.

Tears streamed down Clare's face, touching his shoulder, she leaned her forehead onto his shoulder and whispered, "*Chakotay* …"

"*Ahp.*" Sam placed his hand on his father's arm and said, "She gone to the Great Spirit?"

He slowly turned, pulled Sam into his arms and buried his face in his neck. Clare lowered her head, hugged his broad shoulders, and cried with her Indian family.

After several minutes, she took a deep trembling breath, wiped her wet face, and remembered her parents. Facing them, she found her pa standing next to the bedroom door, white knuckles gripping the rifle while his eyes took in every movement the Comanche made while holding his grandson.

Clare slowly stood, and quietly made her way to him. Without saying a word, she reached out and took the rifle from him, placed it in the corner, and led him and her mother to the table chairs.

Returning to *Chakotay's* side, she waited until he controlled his emotions and released Sam.

A pistol cocking sound swirled everyone's attention toward the door. Clare sucked in a quick breath. Drury stood in the opening, pointing his pistol at *Chakotay*.

Slowly the Comanche chief stood and pushed Sam out of harm's way. Both men drilled their gaze into each other, waiting for the other to act. Neither moved, frozen in time.

"Drury," Clare's tone pleaded just above a whisper.

Drury dragged his gaze from *Chakotay* to Clare, but kept his pistol pointed at the chief. "Is she the baby's mother?" he asked in such a low voice it took Clare a moment to register his words.

She nodded. "Drury, she's *Chakotay's* wife and the infant was…his…his daughter."

He stared at *Chakotay,* and then shifted his gaze to the body on the bed.

"Drury, you *know* how deeply his grief goes."

"Is…is she dead?"

"Yes."

For several more seconds, Drury and *Chakotay* didn't release their fixed gazes on each other.

She glanced from *Chakotay* to Drury, unsure of any action she should take or what to say to either man, both of whom had lost a family.

"Clare, tell him to pick her up. We need to leave. The Rangers are not far behind me. He needs to go. Tell him…tell him, I didn't cause this…"

Clare looked deep into his serious blue eyes and knew he was telling the truth. She turned to *Chakotay* and started to speak when suddenly he raised his hand and said, "I understand."

Chakotay nodded his head at Drury. Drury lowered his pistol and glanced at Clare.

"She has to be buried with her baby."

Drury nodded. "We'll have to circle around another way to stay out of sight just in case the Rangers are headed back to Silver Sage. "Where did you bury the baby?"

Clare stepped to *Chakotay*. "I'll take you."

"No." Drury's sharp tone quickly drew her attention. "If the Rangers stop here they might ask about the woman. They'll expect you to be here. You stay."

Clare's determined look shot toward her parents. "Pa, tell the Rangers *Taabe* died and I went to bury her. That's all you need to say."

Henry nodded. "We'll watch over Sam."

"*Pia*, I want to go." His heartbreaking voice begged.

She squatted and held out her arms. Sam ran to her and hugged her neck. "Sweetheart, you have to stay."

Clare glanced at *Chakotay*. He nodded. He was right. There could be danger, especially if the Rangers set eyes on them with the Comanche chief.

Chakotay acknowledged her agreement, turned, gathered up *Taabe's* body with the blanket and stepped toward the door. He paused and turned to Sam. And, in English, he asked Clare with a head jerk toward her parents, "You trust them?"

She swung her gaze to her pa's and for the first time since her return, she trusted him with her son.

Sam ran and hugged his father's leg, crying "*Ahp…Ahp.*"

Chakotay's jaws tightened. He glanced at Henry and ordered, "Keep my son safe."

The anguish in Sam's cry released tears she'd been holding back. Sam knew he'd never see his father, the Comanche chief again, at least not in this lifetime.

She pulled Sam from his hold on *Chakotay's* leg to allow him to carry his wife to the horses.

Squatting, Clare gathered Sam into her arms and kissed his cheek. Their tears mingled in sorrow for the tragic deaths they witnessed and by all the saints in Heaven, should never have come to pass. Picking Sam up, she dragged her feet to the table and stopped in front of her pa.

Sam clung to her neck. His sobbing soaked her skin. She pressed her lips to his head and handed him to her pa. Clare wiped her eyes, took a deep breath, and headed for the door.

"Clare Rose, maybe we should take Sam to the mercantile and our house."

She paused, looked at Sam and thought for a moment before speaking. "Maybe so, keep him close and keep him safe." She glanced up at Henry. He knew what she meant.

"Clare Rose..." Her mother's hesitant voice drew her gaze. "Is...is he Sam's father?"

Emotions clogged her throat. She nodded.

Her ma's gaze swung to the boy in Henry's arms. He leaned against his grandpa's chest and quietly sobbed. "So the baby was his half-sister," she mumbled and rubbed away a tear escaping from her moist eyes.

"I'll return late tomorrow afternoon." After one more glance at Sam, she hurried to close the door, ran to mount Big Black and barely had the strength to speak. "Follow me, we'll go to the site were *Taabe* and I buried your daughter." She turned Big Black toward the forest with Drury following behind *Chakotay*.

****

Alyson swiped at the tears she couldn't stop. She turned to Henry and Sam, took a shaky controlled breath, and asked, "Sam, you want some soup before we ride to town?"

Henry put him down and mumbled, "Alyson, you feed the boy, I'll see to the horses. Sam might want to ride in your buggy to town." He stood and asked, "Want to ride with your grandmother, Sam?"

Sam shook his head and sat silently waiting for his *huutsi* to serve him some soup.

No more than an hour later, the Coulsons rode into town with Sam riding with his grandfather. The exhaustion from an emotional morning had left him spent and he had fallen asleep soon after leaving the cabin. Henry hugged him close and glanced at Alyson sitting relaxed while riding in her buggy.

He hadn't seen her look so content and peaceful since Clare Rose had returned. She glanced at him and smiled. He smiled back. The only thing he regretted was taking so long in welcoming their daughter back and getting to know their grandson.

The town had become alive with the hustle of people flocking into stores and standing about rolling smokes and gossiping over trivial stuff. The mercantile was halfway down the center of town, so Henry pulled back on the reins and slowed the horse. With a satisfied grin displayed on his lips, he lifted his head higher. Bout time he gave the town folks time to gawk at him. Best they get used to seeing Henry Coulson with his grandson.

Sure enough, by the time he'd reached the front of the mercantile and halted the horses, many more folks had come crawling out of buildings to gawk with questioning expressions. Otis, his long time helper, had already unlocked the double doors and opened them for business. Otis was getting along in years, but he'd been the only reliable employee Henry had ever had, except for maybe his own daughter.

Sam awoke with curious eyes, looking around at many of the townspeople staring at them. He yawned and rubbed his hand over his sleepy face. Henry dismounted and took the boy in his arms and stepped up on the boardwalk.

"I'll be damned."

Henry met the incensed brown glare of Jonathan Montgomery strolling from the mercantile.

"What the hell, Henry? You tolerating half-breeds now?"

"Mind your tongue, Montgomery. He's my grandson."

"Good Lord, its one you shouldn't claim by all rights."

Henry stared at Jonathan's ugly grin, standing with his hands shoved into his pockets and acting almighty.

"You know something, Montgomery, by all rights, I should claim this child. I'm claiming my daughter's son, my grandson, *Samarjit* Coulson is his name and I'm proud to have him as a Coulson."

"You're not serious, Henry. Giving your name to a bastard…a white Indian's child is unfitted for the name of a man of your caliber. My hell, you're the son of Silver Sage Creek's founder, your father will roll over in his grave, disowning you for declaring an Indian as your grandson. What about your business?"

Henry held Sam in one arm while his other arm dropped to his side. His hand formed into a hard fist. Thoughts of putting Sam down and jumping the man flashed through his mind.

"Henry," Alyson's soft voice brought him to his wits.

He wasn't young anymore, but he still had a strong voice. Aware of many more fellow townsfolk gathering around to hear what he had to say.

Henry's gaze bore into Jonathan. "You son-of-a-bitch. You stand there like the Almighty himself and profess to be a better person than my daughter. She's done nothing but live through a life, you or anyone else, I dare say, wouldn't have the guts to do."

"But, Henry, you know she's trash now, not your daughter. She no longer existed once being kidnapped at the hands of savages. Better she died then return with a half-breed."

"You arrogant, son-of-a-bitch. My daughter is a better person than you'll ever be. You scum…you rode out and tried to have your way with her."

"That's a damn lie." Jonathan's voice quivered at the accusation.

"You sorry-ass of a man, you thought you could have a whore on the side since she'd lived with Indians, but you were wrong, she's not a whore, and more respectable than many living in this town, including you."

"You liar."

"Well, Montgomery, God and a few of us know the truth. Don't we?" Henry took a step toward the door, met the shocked stare of Jonathan's fiancée, and continued past her to enter.

He slammed the door shut behind Alyson and put Sam down, straightened and took a deep breath.

"Henry."

He looked around at his wife. "I've never in our married life heard you use such language before. And, I've never been prouder of my husband."

He grinned. "Felt pretty damn good to get a few words off my chest."

The door quickly opened and closed. Frowning, Henry gazed into the eyes of Ruby. "We're closed."

"I know, sir, but…"

"Ruby," hollered Sam, running to her.

She smiled, held out her arms and gathered Sam up to give him a tight squeeze.

Alyson touched Henry's arm and smiled at Ruby. "Please come in, Ruby. It's good to see you."

"Thank you, Mrs. Coulson."

"Please call me Alyson."

Ruby stared at the woman like she didn't recognize her, cleared her throat, and said, "Thank you, ah…Alyson. I wanted to know if you've been out to see Clare Rose and if she's all right?"

"Come, Ruby, let's have some tea and we'll talk." Alyson glanced at her husband, smiled, and said, "Henry, why don't you give Sam some of those special sweets you hid for yourself."

Henry couldn't remember the last time he'd spread his lips so wide he showed his teeth like an idiot. Guess that's how it was when one was a grandpa. Intending on spoiling Sam, he took him by the hand, opened the door for business, and then led his grandson toward the counter.

Ruby followed Alyson to the far corner of the store where Otis kept the cast iron stove burning wood for Henry's morning coffee. Alyson poured steaming water from a metal kettle into a fine teapot covered with dainty, pink roses. She waited for the tealeaves to brew for a moment, and then poured the liquid into two China cups. She handed Ruby a cup, turned, and took a seat. She looked up at Ruby and motioned for her to take a seat at the small, round table across from her.

"Ruby, I know I've not been sociable toward you and I'm sorry. My guilt grew even worse when I noticed how you've treated my daughter since her return. Actually, you're the only woman in town who's even given her the light of day, and I appreciate you befriending her." Alyson took a sip of tea and touched her heated face. "My, listen to me. I'm babbling."

Ruby placed the delicate teacup on the table and studied Mrs. Coulson. "Alyson, no need for words. Clare and I are friends and I've grown to love Sam. I'd do anything for her and the child."

Alyson nodded, thinking of the clothes and furniture she had given her when it should have been her and Henry's responsibility. "I know. I'm asking if it's possible for you and me to be friends."

Ruby glanced around the store and the women meandering through the aisles, fiddling with items. Who did they think they were kidding? They weren't thinking about purchasing goods, but more likely curious about what their friend Alyson was conversing over with a saloon owner. She shook her head.

"If you mean you want to be friends with me in the back of your store and not like your daughter's friendship which is anywhere and everywhere, then Mrs. Coulson, I can't belittle myself for such a hypocritical friendship."

Alyson's head jerked back. She bit her bottom lip and frowned. "Oh my, that's…that's the type of being you see me as…ah…a conceited, hollow person."

"I'm sorry. I shouldn't have been so honest with—"

"No—" Alyson stated, "—it's about time I was put in my place. I've been unhappy for a long time now and you've opened my eyes. Please come with me."

Alyson scooted her chair back scraping the floor, drawing gazes from the customers, especially, Mrs. Waterford's inquiring glare.

Alyson stood, took Ruby by the elbow and guided her across the room straight to Mrs. Waterford. "How are you doing this fine morning, Charlotte?" Her smooth tone oozed with the texture of warm yellow butter.

"I'm doing well, thank you, Alyson."

The woman's questioning tone didn't go unnoticed by Alyson watching her gaze swing to Ruby. "I think you know my friend, Ruby, the owner and manager of the Silver Sage Saloon."

"Ah, well, ah, yes…"

"Ruby," Sam's excited voice drew their attention.

Ruby squatted to face Sam on his level. "Grandpa gave me hard sweets. It's gooooood." He grinned at her.

"Sweets are the best."

"Grandpa said *Pia's* coming for me tomorrow. Can I stay with you tonight?"

Ruby glanced up at Alyson, who shot Henry a glance. She gazed into the eyes of Ruby and knew she could trust her with her grandson. She said, "If that's what Sam wants, sure he can stay with you tonight. Sam, why don't you spend the day with Grandpa and help here in the store, and then Ruby can come by and take you to her place this evening."

Sam studied his *huutsi* for a couple of seconds. He swung his gaze to his grandpa. He grinned and nodded.

"Well, Sam, I think it's a plan."

"Thank you, Alyson, I'll be sure to bring him to you when you open the mercantile first thing in the morning."

Alyson turned to find Charlotte Waterford exiting the store without saying another word to her, which was so unlike her. Now, she'd know who her true friends were from here on out since Charlotte Waterford was the lead gossip in Silver Sage Creek.

Chapter Twenty-Five

Clare rode into town on Big Black with Drury riding at her side. They pulled up to the mercantile and halted their horses. She glanced around. Usually, she walked from the livery to the back alley to enter the mercantile, but not today. She glanced at Drury, but his attention was drawn to McCoy riding toward him. She was sure the Ranger had information regarding their search for the Comanche chief, but she didn't want to know.

Before her feet touched the ground on her dismount, she heard heavy running feet rushing from the mercantile. She frowned gazing into the panic faces of her pa, ma and Ruby.

She knew instantly. "Sam. Where's Sam?"

"Oh, Clare Rose. She took him," her mother sobbed.

"I told you the woman was evil." Ruby hollered, wringing her hands together. "Clare, Betsy took Sam."

Clare's blood shot to her brain. She trembled, weakened knees near buckled beneath her. She hung onto Big Black's saddle taking several deep breaths.

Betsy took her son. Betsy with hatred in her eyes when she looked at him. "When, where?" she demanded. In the corner of her eye she knew Drury heard and stepped near with McCoy by his side. Clare swung her gaze to McCoy. "Where did she take Sam?"

He shrugged.

Drury mumbled to his friend, "Think about it for a moment, does she have a special place she might take him?"

Drury pulled his Stetson from his head, combed his fingers through his thick hair, and with puckered brows aimed his glare at Ruby. Calmly stepping up on to the porch, he squared his hat on his head, and took Ruby by her arms, turning her to face him. "Ruby, what happened?"

"I was supposed to meet Sam at the backdoor with his late afternoon snack. I was on my way when I heard him holler. I ran down the alley just in time to find Betsy dragging him away.

Drury, I ran after her, but couldn't stop her from getting on the horse with Sam."

Ruby held out her arm to reveal a long red welt. "When I...I tried to pull Sam from the horse, she whipped me with the reins and took off."

Drury turned back to McCoy.

McCoy shook his head with sadness stretched across his face. "There's only one place I can think of and it's the cliff up above Sage Creek.

Without hesitating, Clare mounted and waited for Drury and McCoy to do the same. She pressed her legs against Big Black's belly and the three rushed out of town with McCoy leading.

Clare couldn't shake the urgency of getting to her son before Betsy's madness harmed him. When McCoy slowed his horse to head up a trail along the mountainside, her heart quickened. They had to make it in time. The only thing mattered in her entire life was Sam.

Suddenly McCoy halted his horse, dismounted and glanced at Clare. He placed a finger on his lips and waited for her and Drury to dismount. They moved through wooded terrain on silent feet until they peeked through a clearing. There just ahead, on the edge of a cliff overlooking a deep ravine, Betsy sat with Sam on her lap.

Clare pushed forward, but Drury's hand grabbed her arm. She frowned. He shook his head and mouthed, *listen.*

Sam was talking. His young, strong voice flowed to Clare's ears and the tears formed. He didn't sound frightened. He asked Betsy why she hated him.

"You're an Indian," she said.

"But I'm white, too."

Clare covered her mouth to trap a whimper. Sam had never, ever mentioned being half white.

"I'm not like the bad Indians." His sweet tone revealed his sincerity.

Betsy looked out over the cliff and took a deep breath. "I know." She looked at Sam. "Sometimes I can't control what I do or feel. I do bad things. I heard your ma talking to Ruby about your people and told the Rangers where to find the village. I wanted them dead. I do unforgivable things and it scares me."

Sam reached up and touched Betsy's cheek. "You can be my friend."

Tears spilled over Clare's eyelids.

McCoy quietly stepped into the opening, and calmly said, "Betsy, dear."

She jerked her head around and jumped to her feet spilling Sam onto the ground. "Wade." Betsy reached down and took Sam's hand.

"Please, let Sam go. He's not a threat to you."

A dull, empty look in Betsy's eyes looked into McCoy's eyes. A slight, forlorn smile tried to spread her lips. "No he isn't."

Clare stepped into the clearing.

Betsy swung her gaze to her. "You have a good boy." She looked down at Sam and said, "Go to your ma."

Sam squeezed her hand and mumbled, "Friends."

"No, we can never be friends, Sam. Maybe the old Betsy, but not this one."

She shoved him toward Clare and looked her straight in the eyes, and calmly said, "Clare Rose. I'm…I'm sorry I took him."

"No, Betsy, I'm the one sorry." She grabbed Sam up into her arms and held him tightly. Giving Betsy all her attention, she took a step toward her.

"Why are you sorry?" Betsy tilted her head and frowned.

"Because I left you with the Apaches all those years ago…"

"I know. You tried. It just wasn't my destiny to endure what you went through. You're a stronger person than me, Clare Rose. You'll always survive no matter what destiny is forced on you."

Clare held out a hand. "Let me help you now, Betsy. No one here is your enemy."

Her lips curled, but no sparkle of life reflected from her eyes when she glanced at McCoy, Drury, and then she inclined her head and fixed her eyes on Sam. "No, you're not my enemy. I'm my own worst enemy."

Betsy faced McCoy. "You are my saint, Wade McCoy. I've loved you dearly from the beginning, but now, you need a life."

Wade held out his hand and took a step toward Betsy. "I love you, Betsy. We can get through this, please come home with me."

She shook her head. "I can't trust me. Please live a good life." She turned, took a step and disappeared over the edge of the cliff.

Clare grabbed Sam's head and buried him against her chest. She wasn't sure how long they stood looking out into the empty space where Betsy had stood. Finally, she looked over at McCoy aware of his silent grief. He stared at the space, where his beloved Betsy stood seconds ago.

Drury gently touched her shoulder and indicated with his head for her to head back to the horses. Then, he stepped to his friend. Clare slowly walked the trail leaving the two.

"*Pia,* she's gone to the Great Spirit."

"Yes, my son."

* * * *

A week later, Clare handed Pa a steaming hot cup of coffee, strolled to the storefront, flipped the open sign over, and unlocked the doors. She heard Sam's feet run up behind her and out the door. He stopped and turned to her. "*Pia,* Drury's here and he's got Big Black."

Clare stepped out onto the porch and, sure enough, Drury rode down the center of town holding Big Black's reins. They waited until he halted in front of them. He fixed his eyes on her.

Clare's heart quickened. He never failed to make her body react in such a desiring way. She knew he could see the welcome in her face. Maybe more. He'd been gone a week, a long week. The last they had seen of him was on the cliff where Betsy took her life.

"Drury," Sam hollered his welcome. Clearly the boy had fond feelings toward Drury, since the day he'd helped save the wolf. Now, she was sure Sam loved him. She did too.

Drury dismounted, placed a foot onto the step, reached up and pulled Sam into his arms.

Clare didn't veil her surprised look at his affections toward her son. He glanced at her and smiled a warm, beautiful smile rarely ever seen.

"Will you take a ride with me, Clare?" He glanced at Sam. "Is it okay if I take your *pia* for a ride? Next time I promise, I'll take you. Agreed?"

Sam wrinkled up his face, thought a moment, and then nodded.

Drury put him down and looked at Clare.

"Where are we going?"

"You'll see."

"Sam, go tell Grandpa I'm taking a ride with Drury. You stay with him until I get back. Can you do that?"

"Sure, *Pia*."

Clare mounted her horse and waved at Sam. He waved back, turned and ran into the store. She glanced at Drury. His blue eyes had a twinkle she'd seen once before.

He headed north out of town. Clare noticed the townspeople didn't seem to stop and gawk at her like they did many moons ago. Mrs. Waterford even waved at her. She giggled. She'd said many moons ago. Well, she couldn't help but think in Comanche terms at times.

Drury didn't talk on their ride outside of town. A good half hour later, her curiosity got the best of her. "Where are we going?"

Without saying a word he headed his horse up a small hill and stopped. She halted Big Black next to his horse. When she turned to him, she noticed his crystal blue eyes were focused on the ranch below.

She too, studied the beautiful homestead. The house needed some repairing and the white siding needed paint, the yard, with its picket fence, was in need of major tending to, but other than that, it was once a beautiful ranch and could be again.

Swinging her gaze back, she found him studying her. "I don't understand. Why are we here?"

"Do you think Sam might want to live here?"

"Sam? What...why?" Her bewildered gaze looked over the valley where the ranch laid. "Of course."

"Will you?"

Man of few words. Clare squinted, shooting him a questioning frown.

He dismounted, walked around the horses, reached up and pulled her from Big Black. He took her hand and strolled over and stared down at the ranch in the valley below. He mumbled, "That's mine."

Her head drew back. "Drury, it's beautiful, but, why—"

Drury circled his arms around her and before she could say another word, his lips touched hers for a brief moment. Then he drew back and stated matter-of-factly, "You know I love you, don't you?"

She grinned. "Is that how you Rangers tell a woman you love her?"

"Ex-ranger. I'm a rancher now. I love you, Clare, and want to be with you."

She threw her arms around his neck and planted her lips on his in a hungry kiss telling him this was a love of a lifetime. Pulling back, she said, "Drury Burchett, I think I've been in love with you since you tried to rescue me. Not once, but several times."

"Took you long enough, huh?" He grinned.

"Oh yeah. So, when did you first know?"

"That day I bumped into you, but you were married to another man."

He turned Clare in his arms with her back against his chest. They stared down at the ranch. After several serene moments, with their gaze scanning the valley below, Clare mumbled, "You have a beautiful ranch."

"Our ranch."

She turned in his arms, frowned, and gazed into his eyes. "What are you saying?"

"I want this to be our ranch…yours, mine and Sam's and any other children we decide to have. Will you marry me, Clare Rose? I want you to marry me before you marry another man. I want to be your third and last husband."

Clare Rose laughed with delight, threw her arms around his neck and said, "Yes, Drury Burchett, I'll marry you and love you until the day I die. Best be sure, you'll be my last husband."

THE END

About the Author

Judy Baker was born and raised in the south, but has lived much of her life in the west.

What scares her the most? She's been parasailing over the ocean, ziplining over a deep canyon, four-wheeling on the edge of a cliff while looking down into the ocean, flew in a tiny plane with balled tires landing in a cornfield in the middle of Mexico, and most recently rode on a Harley 2500 miles, but none scares her as much as writing. Yet, she keeps writing.

 When not writing the stories that fill my head, she loves the outdoors. Her favorite thing to do is read while enjoying the surroundings of her wildflower garden. She's also an avid stargazer with three telescopes.

Sweet Cravings Publishing
www.sweetcravingspublishing.com

Made in the USA
San Bernardino, CA
14 October 2013